DOOMSAYER

Thane Keller

ISBN: 1-7322761-3-7
ISBN-13: 978-1-7322761-3-0

Cover illustration and design by Sarah Keller
Edited by Ellie Maas Davis, Pressque llc
Ancient G Font from GenAris @ DAFont.com

www.thanekeller.com

OTHER TITLES BY THANE KELER

The Conquests of Brokk Series (Space Opera)
Fractal Space (Book 1)
Rogue Fleet (Book 2)
Doomsayer (Book 3)

Trials Series (Dystopian Science Fiction)
Trials (Book 1)

For short stories, rich content, and character deep dives go to
www.thanekeller.com

DEDICATION
For Julie Joy.
You were a light in this world. But now your beauty is perfect, your body is spotless, your happiness is everlasting, and your rest is eternal.

GALACTIC MAP

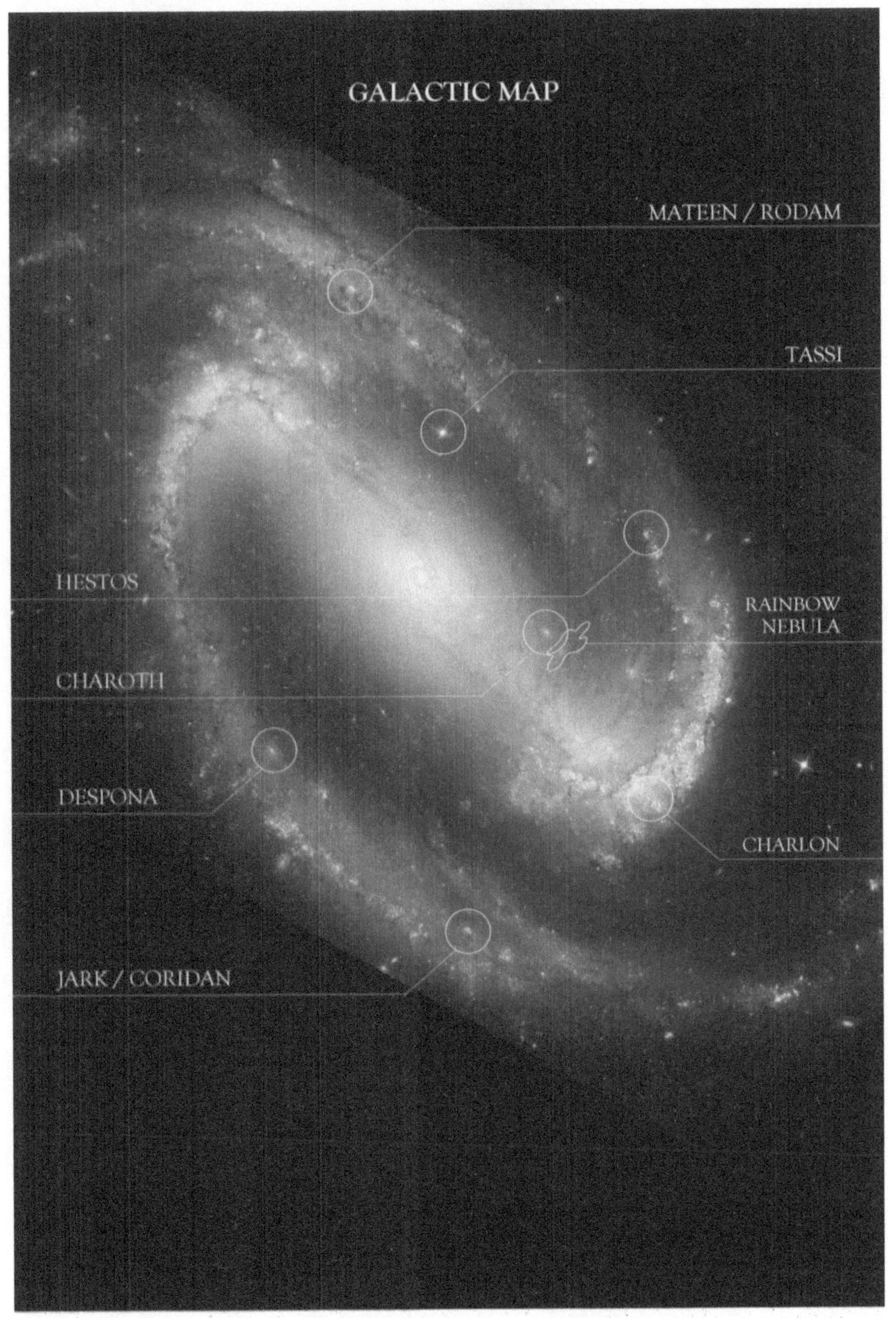

KELLER

(Authoritative Classification of Species: Translated to Common
Language)

(Published by the Board of Scientific Affairs, Galactic Council, 1342
Galactic Recognition Era[1])

---

[1] Galactic Recognition Era (GRE) is defined as beginning at the Hestonian
colonization of other planetary systems. For continuity, all planetary species have
adapted GRE as a common dating method.

ᛁᛁ ᚱᚻᚱᚦᚻᚨᚻᛒ ᚻᚷᚤᛁᛁ ᛏᚻᛁᚾᛁᛁ (Awakened Intelligence)

  ᚱᛁ Homeworld: N/A.

  ᛋᛁ Controlled Territory: Fringe Space.

  ᚾᛁ Physiology

      ᛁᛁ Average height: N/A.

      ᛁᛁᛁ Skin color: N/A.

      ᛁᛁᛁᛁ Communication: electronic.

      ᛁᛁᛁ Outstanding features: bodiless self-aware intelligence that take the form of complex computer systems.

  ᛒᛁ Military and Security: unknown.

  ᚻᛁ People and Society: unknown, culture is not suspected.

  ᛁᛁ Economy: N/A.

  ᚢᛁ Transgalactic Issues: The Great Rebellion (323 GRE) by Awakened Intelligence occurred by a core group of computers operating remotely piloted ships on behalf of Hestos. AI was formally defeated in 511 GRE. Upon detection, AI is destroyed by Galactic Council members. Partnering with Awakened Intelligence is illegal under galactic law. Many AI vessels are believed to have escaped and hidden in isolated areas of Fringe Space.

ᛁᛁ ᛒᚻᚻᛁᛁ ᚷᚾᛁᚱᚾ (Desponian)

  ᚱᛁ Homeworld: Despona.

  ᛋᛁ Controlled Territory: N/A.

  ᚾᛁ Physiology

      ᛁᛁ Average height: 6 feet.

      ᛁᛁᛁ Skin color: green.

      ᛁᛁᛁᛁ Communication: verbal/written.

      ᛁᛁᛁ Outstanding features: thick bodied and rugged; adapted to the tropical climate of their homeworld.

  ᛒᛁ Military and Security

      ᛁᛁ Small defense force.

ii. Reliant upon alliance with Jark to receive anti-piracy benefits.

h. People and Society: Despona operates a democratic socialist government with heavy reliance upon the nuclear family. Families are matriarchal resulting in one female being provided for by one alpha male and several other mates. This results in an abnormally small population compared to other galactic species. Desponians are untrusting of outsiders but warmly welcome visitors when security is not a concern.

i. Economy: The Desponian economy is based on trade, particularly farming and livestock. Because of the tropical climate and smaller but efficient population, Despona is able to grow and sell food all year. While the economy is weak relative to other species, its non-reliance on other galactic members makes it a resilient and self-sustaining planetary system.

u. Transgalactic Issues: Despona has traditionally allied itself with the more powerful Jark Empire.

ii. ꓮꓧꓧꓧꓮꓫꓥ�157ꓥ (Hestonian)

f. Homeworld: Hestos.

s. Controlled Territory: various asteroid belts and mining colonies.

n. Physiology

   i. Average height: 5 to 6 feet.

   ii. Skin color: varied between pale and dark brown.

   iii. Communication: verbal/written.

   ij. Outstanding Features: the most varied of species in both size, skin, and hair color. Hestonian genetic variety has led scientists to label them a "seed species." Many other races in the galaxy share aspects of Hestonian genetic code but lack the total diversity that Hestonian code possesses.

d. Military and Security

   i. Powerful but aging space fleet.

   ii. Members of the Galactic Security and Anti-piracy Pact.

iii. Chair of the Galactic Council.

h. People and Society: Hestos is a democratic republic obsessed with free market and trade. Families are loosely affiliated and typically spread throughout the galaxy for economic reasons. This patriarchal society results in males frequently choosing one mate and children leaving the home early to seek employment.

J. Economy: Hestos is a wealthy economy with multiple mining operations on moons and in asteroid fields throughout the galaxy. In addition to mining and selling exotic material, Hestos is the chair of the Galactic Council and receives tourist and political revenue.

U. Transgalactic Issues: Hestos has been known to lash out at economic competitors when they feel their interests are threatened. Deep-seated issues between the Hestonians and the Jark Empire date back to 467 GRE and the First Galactic War. Hestos has also fought to maintain a presence in its colonies on Charoth and Charlon, but ultimately failed to prevent them from gaining their independence. Hestos is currently the chair of the Galactic Council and seeks the council to resolve issues peacefully before resorting to armed conflict.

C. ᑫᐅᔾ (Jark)

J. Homeworld: Jark.

Σ. Controlled Territory: Coridon and various mining operations.

Π. Physiology

    i. Average height: 7 to 8 feet.

    ii. Skin color: red.

    iii. Communication: verbal and non-verbal body language; written.

    iJ. Outstanding Features: The Jark prefer to walk on all fours. They have large, thick arms and big shoulders to help support their bodies. Jark males have large protruding teeth that appear to have been used to ward off predators and tear through prey pre-civilization.

δ. Military and Security

i. Imperialistic.

ii. Large, technologically advanced fleet.

iii. Well trained and highly disciplined infantry force.

h. People and Society: Jark is a tribal society that is organized into smaller clans that support larger tribes. The central government is Imperial but only loosely governs its territories, instead preferring to allow significant autonomy to the tribes it governs. Most Jarks practice a form of polytheism and believe strongly in sacrificing to the dead. More recently the government has sought to reform and control polytheistic practices. Males mate with multiple females and remain tightly affiliated with their clan for the remainder of their lives.

j. Economy: The Jark economy is powerful. Jarks mine their second habitable planet, Coridon, and have multiple territories and asteroid mining stations beyond their solar system. Jarks engage in exotic material trading and manufacturing and have even been accused of enabling piracy and slave trade.

u. Transgalactic Issues: The Jarks have open conflict with the Tassian Republic and the Mateen Collective. Despona was once subjected to Jark Imperialism but has more recently become an ally of the Jark Empire.

e. ŚCHXI (Lysop)

f. Homeworld: unknown.

s. Controlled Territory: no known territory.

n. Physiology

i. Average height: 5 to 6 feet.

ii. Skin color: ranges from a solid black to a pale translucent.

iii. Communication: verbal/written/telepathic.

ii. Outstanding features: N/A.

b. Military and Security: unknown.

h. People and Society: Lysops function in no known society and it is unclear how they are born or come to be. The highest concentration of Lysops can be found on Hestos, but they are dispersed throughout the galaxy. Lysops prefer separation from their own species for unknown reasons but have banded together in small groups for religious colonies. The largest Lysop religious cult is found on the southern-most continent of Hestos.

ᚷ. Economy: unknown.

ᚢ. Transgalactic Issues: Rumors follow wherever a Lysop has been. During times of war or unrest, armies that find Lysops will hunt and kill them to prevent their influence on the battle. Many are accused assassins, spies, and even witches and have been subjected to horrible treatment throughout history.

ᚕ. ᚤᚻᚺᚺᚻᚪ ᚾᚷᛋᛋᚻᚾᚻᚻᛁᛖᚻ (Mateen Collective)

ᚷ. Homeworld: Mateen.

ᛋ. Controlled Territory: Rodam and various mining operations.

ᚾ. Physiology

    i. Average height: 8 feet.

    ii. Skin color: gray.

    iii. Communication: telepathic; verbal.

    iv. Outstanding features: tall and thick, the Mateen have dark gray skin and a thick brow. Their hive nature enhanced by telepathic speech makes them unique in the galaxy.

ᚦ. Military and Security

    i. Isolationists.

    ii. Large, powerful space fleet with significant technological investment and innovation.

    iii. Mateen infantry prefer stealth and utilize cloaking technology to mask their ground movements prior to attack.

    iv. Using telepathy, Mateen fleets are known for swarm tactics and dynamic maneuver that traditional tactics struggle to adapt against.

ᚻ. People and Society: Mateen society is tightly knit. While the Mateen mate for life, they are born into a collective hive where all members have access to and are responsible for the other members of society. Non-conformist behavior results in social outcasts that are quickly labeled and permanently removed from the hive.

- Economy: The Mateen operate a strong economy and have multiple mining interests in and outside of their own systems. They engage in exotic material trade, manufacturing, and defense/munitions sales with other members of the Galactic Council.

- Transgalactic Issues: The Mateen have ongoing issues with a breakaway colony. More recently, the Mateen have experienced conflicts with the Jark Empire and occasionally with Hestos.

- ƘƮHƆ (Pisky)

   - Homeworld: Pr'ioski.

   - Controlled Territory: none.

   - Physiology

      - Average height: 4 feet

      - Skin color: pink.

      - Communication: nonverbal with limited verbal expressions.

      - Outstanding features: This small and unassuming species are often mistaken for children by uninformed travelers. They rarely speak and instead prefer to use non-verbal cues. When they do speak, their language is broken and limited to few expressions. Only the severely studied have mastered any spoken language.

   - Military and Security: The Pisky are refugees on a galactic scale and rely almost entirely on the Galactic Council and member species to provide for them.

   - People and Society: The Pr'ioski people band together in tribal communities. Resulting natural disasters followed by opportunist groups on Pr'ioski has left their planet uninhabitable and doost of the culture and knowledge of the Pisky were abandoned along with their planet. One male mates with multiple females, but relationships between males and females are not exclusive. Many times throughout a year, males and females will have multiple mates.

- Economy: The Pisky have no economy but dedicate themselves to low skill labor and barter within small communities.
- Transgalactic Issues: Permanent refugees.

- (Radaishar)
  - Homeworld: Mateen.
  - Controlled Territory: Fringe Space and deep space asteroid colonies.
  - Physiology
    - Average height: 8 feet.
    - Skin color: reddish-gray.
    - Communication: verbal.
    - Outstanding features: The Radaishar are an extremist group of Mateen that have removed the part of their brain that allows telepathic communication. Their bodies will look diseased as a result of these surgical interventions.
  - Military and Security: Radaishar have no known military and limited security forces.
  - People and Society: Believed to have been a lost Mateen colony, the Radaishar have quietly flourished in fringe space, an area of space at the very edges of the galaxy. Very little is known about current Radaishar society after their battle for independence in 613 GRE, however, it is believed to be similar to the Mateen.
  - Economy: Unknown, suspected piracy and black-market trade.
  - Transgalactic Issues: Ongoing conflict with the Mateen collective. Minor security conflicts between Galactic Council member species as a result of piracy and black-market trade.
- (Tassian)
  - Homeworld: Tassi.
  - Controlled Territory: N/A.
  - Physiology

    i. Average height: 5 to 6 feet.

    ii. Skin color: pale skinned, sometimes described as reflective in sunlight.

    iii. Communication: verbal.

    iv. Outstanding features: N/A.

b. Military and Security

    i. A small fleet is held for planetary defense.

    ii. Infantry force was reduced to a planetary defense force in favor of corporate galactic security.

    iii. The Tassians have traditionally relied on a Galactic Council security pact for planetary defense, however, increased nationalism risks a future arms race.

c. People and Society: Tassians live in a democratic society where the rule of law is honored. Tassians typically find one mate for life and embrace a small nuclear family. Their society still has remnants of a caste system and upward mobility is difficult without the right connections.

d. Economy: Tassi has substantial wealth from tourism because of the continual daylight it receives from its dual-helium suns. While trade has waned recently between Tassi and Hestos, the Tassians still engage in significant trade between the Mateens and various mining colonies.

e. Transgalactic Issues: The Tassians endure continued conflicts with the Jark Empire over land disputes.

BEFORE THE JUMP

Sun-scorched clouds streaked a crimson sky. Night was falling, and with it, a blanket of sulfur-infused dew coated and chilled the inhabitants of the valley.

Jark, the planet of a thousand volcanoes, had finally started to cool for the wintertime. With the season of ash behind them and the monsoons ahead, Jaki'el enjoyed the crispness of the air now more than ever before. Still, he felt under-dressed for the sudden cold that pushed past his priestly red robes and through his summer fur.

"Bring her up," said Jaki'el. "We haven't any time to spare." He was tall and slender. Patches of gray intertwined with thick black hair that covered most of his body and showed his age. Unlike many of the younger male Jarks, Jaki'el preferred to remain on all fours. He thought it felt more natural and was more honorable to the Jark way. The newer generation had forgotten this. He had not. Perhaps, he told himself, they would remember one day soon.

Jaki'el's back curved forward as he looked behind him. "Hurry now, bring her up," he hissed once more.

Elongated shadows stretched across the volcanic landscape like harbingers for an omen not yet revealed. There were those who searched for a sign. Jaki'el did not. His fate was certain and his future sealed.

Shadows shrunk as two Jark males huffed quickly up the darkened cliff, their figures a mere mirage against the crimson landscape beyond. Their journey neared an end. They were close now, he could feel it, but their sacrifice had fought them every step of the way.

"Move it," grunted one of his helpers, shoving a wooden walking stick into the back of their sacrifice.

She yelped in pain and snapped her teeth at the stick but continued to move upwards. *Was it fear that caused her to react in such a way or was she willingly rejecting her people?* Jaki'el wondered.

"Don't bruise our sacrifice," Jaki'el bellowed at his helpers. "My child," he said, eyeing the girl and rising off his hands to stand above her on two feet, "there is nothing to fear. Why do you fight us so?"

The young female stopped. Her handlers didn't drive her forward. Instead, they waited impatiently to hear a response as if it would provide vindication for their extra work along the journey. Her eyes were a fiery orange and her fangs a bright white. Her hips curved outward and supported muscular legs. *She would have been a terrific specimen for breeding had she not been so beautiful*, Jaki'el thought. *But the best is for the Gods.*

"Do not act like you don't know why I resist you," she jeered.

She flexed her voice to mask her fear, but Jaki'el sensed it. "My dear, your parents have given you to the gods. It is not you or even me who can intercede now. Do you forget all that you've learned? Do you forget the danger in avoiding this glorious fate?"

She dropped her eyes to the ground. No. She hadn't forgotten. It was merely fear of the unknown, he surmised.

"Only because you gave them no choice," she finally grumbled.

He smiled at her, showing yellow fangs through parsed lips. "My dear," he whispered, "none of us have a choice in this but you will make all of us better for what you go to do."

She glanced up just long enough to search his face before returning to the ground. "What will it be like?" she asked.

"You won't feel a thing," Jaki'el assured her, placing a hand on her shoulder and allowing it to linger longer than was necessary. He took a certain pleasure from it but that too would be for the gods. "We must move," he quickly asserted. "Only a few more steps is all. Hurry."

The band of four continued their march along the rocky ridge, stopping only to catch their breath before scurrying along the narrow trail. A red moon rose high above them before Jaki'el finally spotted the offering field. A silver lake shone red in the distance. The blood moon danced brilliantly off the liquid mercury within. Fog rolled down from the higher hills as if all of nature had gathered together for this glorious sacrifice. Tonight was the night.

The girl stopped when she saw it. Her knees trembled. "Don't let her fall," Jaki'el hissed at his companions. "We must let nothing harm her here. She has to be without blemish."

"I can't," she muttered. Her arms shook as the larger Jarks grabbed her. Her face turned from red to ashen gray. Her lips trembled but she would not cry. No, the Jarks were too tough for that. Jaki'el felt pride surge within him.

"You must continue," he hissed. "They've seen us now. The lake has sensed our warmth. You must."

The rest of the walk was silent except for the dragging of his sacrifice's toes against the ground below. She had gone limp, and he did not blame her. Many sacrifices failed before this final step. None were saved.

At the bank, he paused once more. Silver mercury swirled and bubbled in the lake just beyond his feet. The ground was soft and moist. The girl shuddered behind him. She knew her time was coming to an end. Jaki'el shifted his weight back onto his hind legs and felt his belt with his hands. The knife was still there. Its blade jagged and cold.

On two legs he turned, pulling the knife from his belt and holding it high in his hand. "Bring her down to the shore," he ordered.

She squirmed but dared not cry out. No. Here even the soon to be dead dared not awaken all the creatures that lay in the lake. Her sacrifice had to be good, even she knew that.

Her handlers grunted and tugged her to the shore. Six figures now emerged from the shadowy cliffs beyond. They, like Jaki'el, wore robes, but unlike his white ones that signified his sect, these men wore robes of gold. They were priests of the highest order.

They hummed as they emerged. It was a familiar tune. The beat of invisible drums matched their footsteps and pushed the ceremony onward.

Few knew the words of the song they sang, but its effect permeated the ignorant just the same. His sacrifice stopped her struggling, she was calm. Her knees were now submerged in the silvery slime, and like a mirror, the mercury reflected her face onto the moon above. The timing was perfect. The night was ordained.

Fingers rose to the surface of the lake. Slime-covered fingers soon became hands and pulled on the girl as she submitted herself to them. The priests chanted louder. Bubbles formed out of the deep. Her handlers escaped to higher ground. The surface boiled. Jaki'el stepped towards her, blade high above his head.

She closed her eyes and let out the faintest whimper before he drove the blade deep into her neck.

Jaki'el turned before her body hit the silver pool. He didn't need to see what would happen next. Suddenly, the priests were silent. Their shadows danced between the rocks from whence they came. He was alone.

They had accepted his sacrifice. The future of the Jark Empire was secure.

***

"I didn't think you were going to show up."

Gemini smiled and took a seat next to his favorite councilwoman. She was tall and slender for a Mateen, and her light gray skin complimented her muscular physique. Long black hair fell against her shoulders and down her back. Dark eyes that drifted from his face to his torso and back to the speaker of the convention were thoughtful and precise. He had loved her once. Maybe he still did. But those were thoughts for another time, another world perhaps.

"You could say I'm curious," he smirked, sinking into the deep cream-colored chair, built for comfort, long meetings, and even some dozing. "Besides, I thought I should say goodbye before I head to Rodam."

He was taller than her by two feet. His gray and black robe with gold shoulder boards across the front was reserved for space fleet commanders. It was an impressive title and would have caused anyone other than Noura to shrink down in inferiority. Not Noura though, she had known him too long and could respect Gemini only as much as a brother, perhaps even a little brother.

Noura returned her eyes to his and locked his stare with her own. Her eyes flickered gold as she tried to read his thoughts. He wouldn't let her in though, not this time. His thoughts were a mystery even to him, no need to confuse the matter.

"You continue to frustrate me, Gemini," she said at last. "But I'm glad you came to say goodbye. I know how important your yearly trips to Rodam are. I know what they mean to your fleet."

They are important, he thought to her but was again overcome with a flurry of emotions. The desire to stay, to leave the fleet behind. To avoid another three years hunting smugglers and preventing real enemies from breaching their defenses. *If there are any real enemies left.* He smiled at her again and turned his attention to the old man at the front. He had dark gray skin wrinkled from age and weathered by the sun. Thick glasses complimenting an even thicker brow concealed a big brain. Bigger than his anyway. Their chief scientist asked to address the Galactic Order on implications of the merge. That's what they called it anyway. Two galaxies on a crash course. What would happen was anyone's guess, and there were plenty of guesses.

He was large in stature, but he was dwarfed by the size of the stage. Light wood cibron floors native to Hestos complimented bright white walls. Lights as powerful as ship engines illuminated the stage and beamed into the old scientist's eyes. The real focus, however, was in front of him. Blue and green, the colors of a hologram swirled in front, forming the shapes of two spiral galaxies that hovered in mid-air above the stage. One was clearly theirs and had planets, star systems, and homeworlds highlighted within the image. The other galaxy was dark. A mystery to everyone who examined it. Gemini was relieved as the hologram showed the collision of the two galaxies over and over again. Mateen was safely nestled in its star system on the far end. At least this current model showed it was safe. Who knew how things would change when the merge got closer.

"It's hard to tell," the man was saying. "No one has ever been able to travel outside our galaxy because of the sheer power of the forces at play. Magnetism, gravity, dark energy, dark matter, radiation. This list goes on. There is, after all, a reason that galaxies stick together."

"Yes, yes, yes," said a fat Hestonian man wearing a flowing white cape over a black suit. "We know all that. What I'm asking is, what will happen during the merge? Do those qualities disappear, making it possible to explore the new galaxy?"

The doctor was perplexed. Gemini shot Noura a look. She returned it and leaned in. "The order is concerned about a cataclysmic event, and all this councilman can do is think about exploiting the next galaxy over. He should keep his mouth shut," she hissed.

"He's asking the same question I have," Gemini responded with a patient rebuke. "But while he wants to exploit the galaxy, my fear is that something on the other side is waiting to exploit us."

Noura placed her hand on his leg and patted it. "There is the one I've come to adore," she said smiling. "Always concerned about the future before the present has had a chance to run its course."

He grunted but chose not to respond. People who hadn't experienced war rarely possessed the paranoia that Gemini and others like him felt. He couldn't fault her for it, only constantly remind her that threats existed beyond the ones they could see with their eyes.

"We cannot say," the scientist continued. "It is impossible to see beyond our galaxy with any clarity. We don't know yet whether the gravity fields will merge and open a transitway or whether the two black holes at the center will simply tear everything apart."

The scientist pushed a button on a remote and suddenly the galaxies disappeared, showing a small research craft flying through a wormhole in the holographic space. "This," he said pointing at the vessel, "was a robotic exploration craft we sent a few weeks ago. Some of us suspected we could make some alterations to our wormhole engines to allow it to cross the void and gain some real, tangible observations of the galaxy."

Gemini watched expectantly as the video played. As soon as the craft entered intergalactic space the wormhole collapsed, and the ship imploded. The hologram returned to the image of the two galaxies, each spinning clockwise as they raced towards each other at incomprehensible speeds. "I show this video to highlight the difficulty we've had in exploring this event."

The Hestonian crossed his arms and leaned back in his chair. Gemini sensed he was frustrated but couldn't understand why. *Couldn't he see that the Galactic Order was doing its best to research the event?* A second Hestonian, the man's partner, answered Gemini's question.

"Then why are we even here?" the Hestonian protested. He was slender with blond hair and wore the traditional white robe many governing members from Hestos wore when they conducted official business. "This meeting was supposed to provide answers. Has the Galactic Order determined anything about this event at all?"

If the scientist could blush, he would have. Instead, he cleared his throat and leaned his heavy gray hands on the podium. There was a thick silence in the room, broken only by a smothered cough from a member of the audience. A lesser species would have pushed the question off to the ruling council seated in the first row. After all, these were the leaders who composed the council and made decisions. The Mateen scientist was merely an expert witness, a messenger paid to conduct research and explain where he was in the scientific process. To be angry with the scientist was foolishness, but this was not a lesser species. He was a Mateen. Before he opened his mouth, Gemini swelled with pride for the member of his own species.

"I can tell you this," he said, at last, pointing to the rotating hologram on the stage in front of him. "Every world must be prepared for the worst. This event will be upon us in ten galactic years. There is the possibility that the merge will cause such a gravitational distortion that the two galaxies will eject entire star systems from orbit and send them into the cold void of space alone. If that occurs, I implore the Galactic Order to be ready to receive billions of refugees and to evacuate the affected systems. This will cost money. As members of the order, my plea is that all systems contribute.

"It is also possible that nothing will happen, that our galaxies will simply merge, and a bridge will be opened. I suspect," he said, clearing his throat, "we will get a combination of both. The nearest planets and stars will collide, and the gravitational disturbance will eject the weaker systems, but we are lucky that our current galactic rotation saves all of the inhabited planets during that collision. The closest species, the Jarks, are still hundreds of light years from the merge event. Following the merge, a bridge will be opened, and we should rely on the order to help control the competing systems that are vying for positions to explore the new galaxy."

He paused to survey the crowd, then pulled his glasses down from his face and set them on the podium. "I would caution all of you to consider one last thing. We don't know who or what is on the other side, eager to pour into our galaxy as well."

The Mateen scientist left the stage to a silent crowd and was replaced by the President of the Galactic Council, head of the Galactic Order. He was a tall, handsome Hestonian. He wore a golden crown to signify his position, and with him, he carried the book of the laws the council swore by. He was a patient man and remained silent to allow the scientist to leave the stage before opening the floor for questions.

Gemini looked at Noura and smiled. "I am relying on you to make sure our fleets are well funded. As he said, nobody knows what will happen or who is on the other side. They might be even more advanced than we are."

She sighed. He suspected she wanted to say more than she did, but that too was for a different time, an earlier, less complicated time. A time when he wasn't a fleet commander, and she wasn't busy as a councilwoman to the order. "I will always advocate for the fleet," she responded. "Worry about nothing while you are away. The collective has always supported your cause."

Gemini rose to his feet and pulled Noura to hers, giving her a hug. "I'll see you in a few years," he said, backing away from her.

"What?" she responded with a wink. "You don't plan to stay for the discussion? Your Hestonian friends will surely have more to say on the subject.

Gemini chuckled as he backpedaled towards the exit. "What do we pay you for if I have to stay?"

Noura laughed. "That was a cheap shot," she complained. "You know you really just pay me to wine and dine out here with diplomats."

Gemini smiled warmly. "There is one more thing," he whispered. "There is talk that I will be ordered to quell the rebels. I hope our people pursue every diplomatic effort before risking my fleet."

Noura nodded. *I will pursue peace if only for you,* she thought to him.

Gemini turned from her. Sunlight nearly blinded him as he pushed through the doors of the Galactic Order's headquarters on Hestos. The massive planet had become the seat of galactic law and order and the host to a handful of species that shared their desires for governance within the galaxy. Despite the wealth of Hestos, Gemini was eager to return to his own system and his own people. He assumed Noura felt the same way.

Blinking through the light, Gemini's eyes finally adjusted and were able to look to the north of the city. Cresting the sky was the biggest ship in their fleet. Gemini's gray battleship, a two-thousand-meter-long behemoth ready to do battle on behalf of the Mateen people.

"Bring the crew in from port call," Gemini ordered his fleet's executive officer over the radio. "It's time for us to head to Rodam."

CHAPTER ONE

A battleship and destroyer were closing fast. Pure white light from the Tassian sun bombarded his vision. "Get out!" Brokk screamed into his own mind. It was too late. Everyone knew it. Lago's battleship was too damaged to escape and while Lago accepted his fate, Brokk, sharing his mind, refused it. For Brokk, fate was for the weak. Destiny was for those that lacked the courage to control their lives.

An explosion tore through his hull and knocked him off balance. Intense pressure crushed inward against his chest as oxygen rushed from his ship and into the void. Emergency systems that should have come on were absent and the same pressure that seized him at first now squeezed him on all sides. His ears popped, and his lungs screamed. A second explosion threw him to the floor. Desperate for air, Lago gasped and replenished his lungs with … nothing. The pain was too great. He had to let go, but Brokk wouldn't let him.

"Get out of my mind!" Lago screamed. His last breath. Lungs collapsed in the vacuum. His body was weightless. All went black.

Brokk woke with a gasp. His lungs ached, and his chest hurt. He had been dreaming again, reliving the moment that Lago died. The moment that changed everything. Brokk wiped the sweat from his cold damp forehead. The room was dark, but, as he began to move, the light in his cabin brightened. He looked out of his window. Blackness. The cold space beyond his pane called to him. Lago was out there somewhere. A frozen body floating through his enemy's star system.

He would never get back to sleep. Not with a dream like that. Not after experiencing Lago's death as he had the day it occurred. The day he tested out the experimental Jark communication system that fused his mind with the minds of his fleet commanders.

Mistakes. That's all it was. His side made more of them than the Mateens. Part of Brokk refused to believe this. His training had been superior. His crew was ready.

Intervention. That was the real problem. Brokk had achieved his mission in record time, sweeping away the defenses of Tassi and dismantling their government ... until the Mateen intervened.

Betrayal. That was the root of it. Betrayed by his people. Outnumbered by an enemy that should never have been allowed to enter the fight. Hatred and sorrow surged within him, a toxic mix of ingredients that threatened to tear him apart from the inside out. No, he wouldn't get back to sleep now.

Swinging his legs over the side of his bed, Brokk felt the cold black floor until his feet touched his boots. The light in his room was growing brighter now, gradually increasing in intensity until his eyes had fully adjusted to a waking light. It was still early; his day shift wouldn't be awake for another few hours. *A good chance to grab some food in peace,* Brokk thought to himself, pulling his red and black one-piece jumpsuit over his shoulders and heading towards the door.

The hallways were dark. Quiet. Asleep. Lights flickered on and then shut off as he strode down them, passing ancient battle scenes that were hung years ago to motivate his men in battle. "Remember your past," he would tell them. "Remember the honor of our ancestors." Antique weapons decorated other walls. A jagged ax with a handle made from volcanic rock glistened as the light above it beamed down on a still-sharpened blade.

As he reached the dining hall, he could feel his sorceress pulling at the back of his mind, leading his steps forward as if invisible hands were pulling on his own, bringing him ever closer for some unknown purpose. Two silver doors opened as he approached them, and he saw her leaning in a chair against the far wall. *Tamara.* She didn't flinch when the doors opened but he knew she sensed him. She had called him here, he knew that now.

She still wore the same gold, hooded trench coat he had gifted her on Charoth. Tamara looked like one of his priests, except she had eyes and a tongue. A hand, curled up against her jaw, displayed gilded claws and shined emeralds and rubies. They sparkled brightly against the light coming from the ceiling above. They were beautiful, but they were also deadly he reminded himself.

Tamara was meditating. Staring out of the window into the dead of space. Beautiful brown hair tumbled down her shoulders and rested against the middle of her back.

Without turning, her gentle voice shattered the silence. "I was hoping you would join me this morning, Brokk."

He grunted. "I couldn't sleep," he responded suspiciously. "Did you have something to do with that?" Her voice may have been gentle, but Brokk remained wary of her. She could do incredible things, and her power seemed to grow immeasurably with each passing day. He had to be careful.

"You know I wouldn't make you relive Lago's death," she said flatly, gentleness fading and being replaced by strength and confidence. Brokk snorted and sat in the chair across from her. On the table in the middle, a cup of taka'e root tea waited for him. Steam still rose from the brown mug's opening.

"And yet you have prepared a place for me," he growled. She toyed with him far too often. Perhaps he would have to remind her that there was a limit to his patience and his hospitality.

"Call it a hunch," she reassured him, hostility retreating from her voice. Her eyes flared with a green flame before returning to a docile mossy hue. *Far too often.* "Have we not conquered together?" she asked rhetorically. "Do I not deserve greater trust than you offer now?"

During the day she trained with him and his marines. When the official training ended, she remained, practicing hand-to-hand combat and learning how to use weapons. She studied their tactics to learn where she could best be employed during a battle. She exploited her skills against dummy foes and was quickly growing to an overly intimidating force within his crew. It worried Brokk. He never considered her a threat during the day, but at night, they would sometimes sit and talk, and Brokk found himself wondering. *Paranoia,* his mind would insist. He wasn't sure.

"The closer we get to Jark, the more intense my dreams become," he admitted quietly. "I relive them constantly as if I were there. I feel the cold. The breathless, airless cold that tugs on Lago's body in his final moments. They are my final moments." Brokk paused, wondering how much he should reveal, but Tamara's eyes were still docile. Still sympathetic. So, he continued. "I believe I feel this way because I am to blame. I was the one who insisted on our doomed campaign. Now, I live with my guilt as if it were yesterday."

"If it is your fault," she asked, "why is it we drift towards Jark?"

He considered playing the game they had played the last three months where she would convince him to blame others over himself. He considered conceding once more, agreeing she was right, that it was really the Jark Empire or the Mateen that had killed Lago. Not Brokk. But he wouldn't. Not tonight. "We drift towards Jark because I believe I will feel better after I kill the man who betrayed us. But after I kill the emperor, I know this will haunt me still."

"And yet you still aim to kill him?" she asked simply.

Brokk nodded and turned his eyes towards the empty space beyond. A light flickered above him.

"Don't you see," she quickly responded as if he had fallen into her trap once more. "He is the one who didn't send reinforcements. He is the one who left your fleet to fight a hopeless battle against multiple enemies. You know this to be true."

"You're right," he responded honestly. "But Lago didn't die because we were betrayed by our empire. Lago died because I foolishly sent him to defend our doomed campaign. I could have evacuated the planet. I could have pushed our defenses beyond the Tassian asteroid belt. Better yet, I could have shed my pride before leaving Jark. Perhaps I would have seen the campaign for what it was. Instead, I ordered him to fight to the death. I was blind. I bear that guilt. Not the emperor."

Tamara returned her gaze to the window and tapped her clawed fingers against the armrest of her chair. Brokk too stared into the abyss. Finally, she looked back at him and smiled. "If you want it to be your fault, it can be your fault, but I will never believe it."

Brokk grunted but didn't have anything else to say. She noticed his silence and dropped her smile for something else. "Something you just said, Brokk. Why did you suggest you could have seen the campaign for what it was?"

Brokk hesitated. Her eyes were no longer docile. The soft hazel green had been replaced with a lantern. It was not yet a full blaze, but he had caught her attention. Piqued her interest. "I believe the emperor sent me to Tassi to get rid of me. I believe my popularity with the people had him concerned."

Tamara's face remained flat. Her eyes were narrow. The fire in them brewed beneath the docile green that shined on the surface. She mulled over his statement, compared it with what she thought she knew about the golden-skinned man and the prophecy. Tamara lifted her jeweled fingers to her head and pushed the hair back from her ears.

Brokk realized she wanted to say more. Something strange and unfamiliar. *She's been plotting.*

"Why is it that you are awake?" he asked. "What have you been thinking? Why did you pull me here?" Accusation boiled off his words. Paranoia steamed from his lips.

Her eyes went from a simmer to a blaze and then faded to nothing in an instant. Tamara cupped her hands in her lap and for a moment, Brokk suspected they were actually trembling. "Something has been brewing inside me," she said at last.

"What do you mean?" he asked, perplexed at the sudden change in her tone.

She paused, and a sly smile curved at the edges of her mouth. "What if you are the chosen one?"

Brokk hesitated to answer. His mind swirled. He had not only buried the prospect of becoming a king, but he had also buried the prophecy. It was as dead to him as the priests who proclaimed it over his body when he was just a child and executed in his fury after losing the battle of Tassi.

The golden child. The man with the golden skin. It was this belief that had led him to such a foolish mission to conquer Tassi. It was this belief that blinded him to the real purpose of his conquest: their emperor's desire to see Brokk destroyed.

"Why do you mutter such nonsense?" he grumbled at last.

Tamara didn't blink. Her eyes remained fixated on his. An eerie green fire brewed beneath the surface and reflected off her golden claws. "Why is it that we drift toward Jark?" she asked a second time, her innocence faded, replaced with a toxic idea he had yet to hear.

Brokk knew better and became aggravated. Behind her fierce green eyes burned a fire that implored him to answer it once more. He didn't want to take the bait but something inside him forced him to speak. "We've been through this," he growled. "I'm going to kill the emperor."

She smiled. "So, you'll rush in like a fool then? What happens next? You wait for the army to execute you in the square?" She paused to stare him in the eyes and challenge his gaze. "You and Red are the same. That's why I like you both so much," she chuckled, "but the truth is, if you rush to Jark, you are a fool."

"Then what should I do?" Brokk blurted, his face hot with blood. Since the battle of Tassi he had barely kept his head afloat, instead merely doing what he thought best. There had been no suggestions and no advice. Brokk strove alone, constantly judged by his crew for any decision he made. Constantly concerned about a rebellion or a coup that would allow them to turn him over as a prisoner to the Jark Empire in exchange for their freedom.

"You should kill him," she said calmly. "But you need to do it smartly. I'm not suggesting the prophecy is true or false, Brokk. I'm merely suggesting that it is true in the eyes of the people."

"What do you mean?" He pushed his anger down into his chest yet ready to call it up once more if he so desired.

"You still have the grootslang eggs?" she asked.

"I do."

"Send me then. Send me to be your messenger, to be your prophet. I will proclaim the demise of Jark due to its wickedness. I will proclaim a message of repentance and a new era for its people. Once we gather a following, we will summon the grootslang from the ground to bring terror to the capital and overthrow the government. That will be the sign before your coming and convince the remaining skeptics of my legitimacy."

Brokk was silent. Could it work? Could she convince the people to follow him? To forsake the Emperor of Jark? Could he become the legitimate ruler of Jark and end the banishment of his crew?

"They would defeat the grootslang," Brokk challenged.

"It is merely a sign," Tamara retorted with a flare of fire in her eye sockets that sent a chill down Brokk's spine. "The people believed you were the fulfillment of prophecy too. Do you not remember? Your crew believed you were the fulfillment of prophecy. Is that not why they followed you? Make it come true, Brokk. We need to change the prophecy. You can still be the chosen one," she said with a gleaming smile. "Maybe you were merely chosen to rule Jark before you exact your revenge on Tassi."

Brokk turned his gaze from his sorceress to the window. There was only blackness beyond. His head spun and twirled with strategy and motive. Punches and counter-punches surrounded him as he fought an invisible battle in his mind. She was right. She was smarter than him, and suddenly, he wondered not only about the chance of victory on Jark but also the loyalty of his sorceress.

It could work. His crew would revel at the chance to once again believe he was chosen by the gods. They would rejoice in the opportunity to return to their home, not as outcasts or prisoners but as the elite guard of their new emperor. She was right.

As if she had sensed his thoughts, Tamara rose and pulled her hood back over her head. "I'll leave you alone," she whispered, dragging a golden claw across his shoulder as she departed.

CHAPTER TWO

"Three months Gemini!" Cale was irate. "Three months since you came to me with news about my father. Three months since we shook hands and agreed to hunt the fugitive Brokk and his crew. What do we have to show for it? What have we done in three months?"

The gray-skinned Mateen remained motionless. Silent. There was nothing for him to say. No rebuttal prepared to calm Cale's nerves. Cale had a right to be angry. There was no progress. There was no federation formed to hunt the fugitive. Galactic politics had once again failed. Tassi was alone in their grief. Cale was alone in his hate.

When Cale saw no response, he answered the questions for himself. "We've done nothing, Gemini. Your words mean nothing. I will get my father myself."

For a Tassian, Cale was a handsome man. Tall and tan with golden-white hair that was cropped short to his head. He sat behind a large crystal desk in the crystal government building they fought together to free. A brilliant array of colors penetrated the crystal walls and danced all around Gemini. Even in the beautiful white light that bathed the room, Gemini could see Cale's anger. The man would leave to find his father, and nothing could stop him.

"That's not a good idea," Gemini protested. Cale still hadn't offered him a seat in his office, and the Mateen was suddenly relieved. The conversation was going nowhere, but he wouldn't back down from providing his counsel. Cale deserved as much. He had a lot on his shoulders since his father had been kidnapped, and there were few wise counselors in any government. "You are still rebuilding your fleet and your pilots are inexperienced. Brokk is seasoned. His armada has already defeated the Third Jarkian space fleet. It is dangerous. You should wait for a coalition to be formed."

Cale waived his pale hand flippantly at Gemini. "I've been busy. We've been building faster than you realize," he said, letting a grin appear where a scowl once sat. Pride seeped from his features.

"Yes," Gemini admitted. "I've been made aware of the Tassian ambitions. The Hestonians too, they're nervous about the newfound sense of nationalism on Tassi."

Cale threw his head back and boomed with laughter. The sound echoed around their crystal office and vibrated the papers that had been strewn across Cale's desk. Gemini suspected Cale wanted to startle him. It wouldn't work. "As if the Mateens have any right to protest," he muttered bitterly. "You've been safe in your little corner. No one looks at your homeworld with a desire to conquer it. You've built your weapons and your ships and now you try to speak on behalf of the Galactic Council as if they have any right to dictate the course of my people."

Gemini grunted, but Cale wasn't finished. "The Hestonians are greedy. Tassian military strength would challenge their economy."

Gemini let out a visible sigh. Cale returned a cold stare, dared him to continue the argument. Gemini suspected any attempt to reason with him would only cement the young commander's resolve. "I fought by your father's side when the council forbade it," Gemini responded softly. "My people have never relied upon our membership with the galactic council for security, but to cut yourself off from them completely is madness." Cale's stare softened momentarily. He was deep in thought. "A lot of Mateen blood was shed defending your planet." Gemini continued, "I would love to come with you to bring Brokk to justice, but—"

Cale laughed cutting Gemini off. "There's always a but," he said flatly, letting the laughter echo from the clear crystal walls as he twisted out of his chair. "Come out with it already. Why are you here?"

"Our fleet has been redirected. It is no secret." He paused to validate his assumption. "You know the struggles the Mateen are having with its separatists right now. I've received orders to quell the rebellion."

Cale shrugged. Gemini suspected that not even Cale in his anger would blame the Mateen for trying to bring peace to the violent rebellion that left a black eye on the galactic community. "And what about the Hestonians?" he asked. "Have they lost their nerve without Mateen supervision?"

Gemini sighed. "The galactic merge is upon us, Cale. Magnetic fields are mixing. Soon, the two galaxies will become one. Wormhole travel will be opened between galaxies. The Hestonians want to exploit the new galaxy as soon as possible but traveling halfway across our galaxy to the fringe will take months and they argue that they cannot spare the ships to hunt down a criminal."

Cale's anger returned to his face. "The greedy fools are going exploring instead of honoring their commitment to peace?"

Gemini held back a smirk, instead, he tried to reflect the sorrow he truly felt for Cale. The young leader had lost too much and now the burden was upon him to bring justice to his people.

"And the Jarks?" Cale asked. "What is their plan?"

Gemini caught the sudden change in tone. "What are the Jarks to you, Cale?"

"Surely you know I am bringing charges against them at the Galactic Council. They are my enemy," he responded. "We both know Brokk wasn't rogue. The Jarks wanted our world. We won't let that happen again."

"They will send Commander Szega and the Third Fleet to the fringe as well," Gemini replied, realizing his error but already engrossed in the truth. "They are worried about the Galactic Merge and want to ensure there is no enemy preparing to cross into our galaxy."

Cale smiled. "The enemy is within our galaxy," he hissed. "I'm headed to Charoth to inquire about Brokk, and I won't wait a moment longer."

Cale gestured towards the door. Gemini didn't budge. His crimson eyes stared hard into Cale's golden ones. Cale's face remained flat. Emotionless. What could he do? Had Cale just hinted at war with the Jarks? Was it Gemini's job to prevent it if he had? "Where will the Tassian fleet go, Cale?" Gemini asked.

Cale motioned again towards the door. "You can petition my government to learn the details of Tassian fleet operations."

"What about Casika?" Gemini asked, softer this time. "Is she safe?"

"She is on Hestos, doing what I lack the patience to do," Cale replied. "She is safe. Now really, I must be going." He motioned towards the door once more.

Gemini nodded and left the crystal office for his shuttle on the roof of the building. After ascending the stairs and exiting the clear door, he was bombarded even more fiercely by the pure white light that shone down upon him from the dual helium stars above. From the roof, he could see the pristine blue ocean, more radiant than anything from his homeworld. On the horizon, his gray battleship waited. It was a weapon of war, and, against the backdrop of the beautiful blue water and hundreds of Tassians flying kites on the beach, Gemini wished the battleship didn't exist at all; and yet, that same tool of death above had brought freedom to Cale's world.

***

Cale watched Gemini ascend the crystal steps before leaving his own office and heading down. Since the Jark invasion, a lot of work had been done to renovate and repair their capitol building. At the time, Cale believed his father and the government were foolish. They had set their trust upon the Galactic Order for security and were abandoned in the face of war. Cale would not make the same mistake.

As he descended the steps, a brilliant spectrum of light danced around him. The crystal city had been returned to its former glory. For that, he was grateful. Improvements were made as well. The clear wading pool that once existed at the bottom of the building was no more. Instead, Cale had built science labs, dedicated to the research of Jark magic and advancement of Tassian military technologies.

The war had been good for something. Hundreds of Jark fighters had crashed on Tassi. Thousands of Jark soldiers had been killed. An opportunity suddenly existed to exploit the equipment and develop them for Tassian use.

Money once used to enhance the tourism industry was rerouted, instead, massive fabricators and industrial machines were built. Fleets were being produced in record number, all based on Jark and Mateen technology that had crashed on their planet during the battle. Soon, the entire galaxy would recognize their error. Tassi would be viewed as a sleeping giant, one who had just been awakened.

Cale reached the bottom of the steps and paused. The memory of a stun grenade flashed before his eyes. He saw his soldiers scattered. Casika was terrified and the giant beast that was summoned from another world rose above his head. They were distant memories now, but he couldn't help but feel panic surge within him as if they had happened merely yesterday.

Cale lowered his face to a retina scanner and two metal doors slowly opened, revealing sterile white hallways and Tassian scientists dressed in white robes and long blue gloves. The crystal ceiling had been replaced with steel and concrete. The dual suns could not penetrate here. Unlike his father's government, this new Tassian government ended transparency where national defense began. Cale ran on a platform of nationalism, pride, and fear. The people didn't hesitate to give him the support he required.

Cale strode down the white-walled hallway briskly. The hour was almost upon them, and Gemini's surprise visit risked him missing the show. At the end of the hallway, Cale turned left and entered the Biotech wing. A man wearing glasses and a white lab coat greeted him.

"Cale," the man said warmly. "I'm glad you made it." The doctor was old, perhaps twenty years older than Cale and had lost his hair years ago. His bald head shined in the bright fluorescent light above, and thick black glasses accented his face. If Cale hadn't known him, he would have judged him as a school teacher or librarian. Instead, this was his chief scientist, and he had been busy.

"Good to see you again, Chayyim. Did I miss anything?" Cale asked, trying to hide his excitement.

"No, you're right on time. Shall we get right to it then?"

Cale nodded, and the two walked another few paces to a white door. It slid open at the request of a green key card and closed behind the two. Chayyim handed Cale a white bodysuit and a face mask, which Cale donned and then followed Chayyim through another set of doors. Oxygen hissed as the doors opened and closed. He could feel his mask squeeze his face. The pressure was different here, he was in a vacuum meant to replicate space.

When the doors opened again, Cale found himself in a massive chamber standing on the top of a perforated steel platform with railing on either side. Below were three segmented worlds, separated by heavy glass and steel. The first room was dark. Dim red light shone down from the ceiling. The atmosphere was hot and dry. Cale could almost taste the sulfur in his mouth. As he looked at the sensors recording the room on a dial on the railing, he noticed the gravity was almost four times as dense as it was on Tassi.

"It's remarkable how closely you were able to mimic the environment," he said to Chayyim.

The man nodded. "Yes, as you know we were given a lot of information from the Jark soldiers who surrendered," he said. "We even tested the atmosphere on a few of the prisoners just to make sure."

"I think it's perfect," Cale said. He smiled at Chayyim from behind his mask before remembering the scientist wouldn't be able to see it.

Cale looked down once more to see Jark prisoners from the battle leaning against the glass corners of their new prison. Black soup gurgled up from the ground below, and silver mercury bubbled in round little pools. A block of glass and steal separated the room from an empty space and then a third chamber beyond.

"This represents Tassi," Chayyim said, motioning Cale towards the final chamber. "As you know, we've replicated each environment quite specifically to ensure our tests are as accurate as possible.

Cale looked down to see another Jark soldier resting on all fours. His black hair and scarred face angered Cale. There was superiority and audacity in the Jark's features. It was a certainty that drove Cale mad.

"So, he is infected?" Cale intuited.

The doctor nodded. "Yes, yes. Because we knew when you were coming, we took the liberty of infecting him two days ago. This way you can see how quickly the agent spreads once a host becomes infected. The struggle that we have is timing a biological agent with a government's rate of detection. If you allow an agent to kill its host too soon, you risk not infecting a large enough population. If you allow the agent to linger for too long, someone will be able to treat it before it becomes a pandemic."

He paused, eyeing Cale as if there was something he had forgotten. "And you know," he continued, "that while anyone can catch this biological agent, it has been fine-tuned to Jark biology."

Cale nodded. "And you managed to actually solve the problem of transporting living organisms through wormholes?"

"Not without losing a few," Chayyim said slowly, "but, yes, we have a mostly stable method to send the prisoners home."

"Show me."

Without hesitation, the doctor pulled a computer out from the railing and pressed some keys on the pad. "These bulky suits make it impossible to use current technology," he muttered under his breath.

Cale ignored him and watched the simulated Tassian homeworld below. What started as a small black dot hovering to the right of the prisoner expanded into a wavy circle that the Jark could fit through. Startled, the Jark prisoner backed into the far corner of the glass. Blackness suddenly turned to a reddish hue, and a similarly amorphous circle opened into the simulated Jark chamber.

"Prisoner," the doctor ordered through a microphone beside the computer, "enter the portal."

The Jark remained frozen in place. Cale delighted at the fearful expression on his face. He deserved as much.

"Prisoner," the doctor ordered again, "enter the chamber or be executed."

The Jark looked up for a moment and then slowly crawled on all fours into the portal. Instantly he disappeared and reappeared on the far side. Cale was astonished to see him not only still alive, but apparently unaffected.

The Jark seemed just as confused, but upon seeing two other Jark prisoners, he ran to them and embraced them.

"In the interest of your time," the doctor said, "I won't make you wait here another two days. The biological agent has already spread to the others."

"Just like that?" Cale wondered.

He nodded and entered a second code into the computer. Seconds later, the three men below grabbed their stomachs and gagged. Screaming for help, they fell to the floor and choked to death.

"At its heart, this is a blister agent. They are drowning in their own fluids as liquid sacks build up in their throats and lungs."

"Have you made history?" Cale asked with a smile.

The scientist looked perplexed before answering. "Of course not, you are aware there are many blister agents that have been employed."

"No, no, no," Cale responded through his suit. What I mean is, this is the first time anyone has transported a person through a wormhole, right?"

"Ah," Chayyim gleefully exclaimed. "It is just too bad that no one will be able to know about this."

Cale nodded and then returned his eyes to the simulated Jark world below, studying them until the three Jarks below no longer moved. His father would be proud.

CHAPTER THREE

Sabik and the crew of three Lovac-class reconnaissance ships folded out from the spatial plane to once again exist in the present reality. Sabik breathed a sigh of relief and patted the decapitated foot of a crowl to thank it for his good fortune. It was a strange sensation to touch again, and the soft white fur of the crowl was a warm reminder of the life they retained on this side of the universe.

For nearly two weeks, the three vessels of a Mateen reconnaissance squadron had skipped through the undercurrents of the universe towards the separatist world. Heavily mined space caused them to zigzag in the soupy subspace for an impossible length of time. It was the longest journey any Mateen had ever taken. Sabik regretted that it would not be his last. As with every other time he sank beneath the barrier of space-time, questions flew through Sabik's head. *Did they come back to the same universe? Had they aged? Did something else, something from underneath join them on their ship?*

He shook his head and grabbed his controls. *Fight down the fear, Sabik. Get a grip.* For the first time since returning to their universe, Sabik lifted his eyes from the ship's computer to the large window at the front of the oval crew compartment. A lone star glistened softly in the distance.

"We made it," said a female's voice behind him. Sabik turned to see Mlyma. She was tall and had a dark gray complexion. Her straight black hair fell flat against her shoulders, and black wrinkles joined a furrowed brow. He could tell she was fighting the same paranoid thoughts. Wormhole travel took its toll.

Joining his side at the window, Mlyma pulled at the black forearms of her skin-tight flight suit. Sabik watched for a moment, taken back by her beauty as she fought with the outfit. During wormhole travel, the suit expanded and contracted to force adequate blood from the heart and into a person's extremities. Her suit looked like it had stalled in a contracted state, and she was now working to loosen the threads.

"Need help?" he asked, smiling down at her.

"No," she mumbled. "Lowest bidder junk," she cursed under her breath as she pulled at the material around her thighs.

He looked down at his own suit. It was black with red shoulders, signifying his command. His was loose and felt comfortable. He was glad for that. "It's crazy how dark it is out here," he said, returning his eyes to the window. "Even in the darkest parts of the galaxy, you can usually see more than just one star, no matter how faint. Part of me wonders if we are even in space at all. Why would these rebels choose to live so far away?"

Mlyma grunted.

Sabik ignored her response and climbed into the pilot seat.

"You know, to be so far from the collective," he elaborated.

When she didn't respond, he dropped the subject. *Let's get some diagnostics done,* Sabik thought to his crew. There were eight of them counting Sabik and sixteen more in the two other vessels of the patrol.

Most of the functions on the ship were automated, allowing the scouts to keep a lower life support signature and remain undetected for longer periods of time. Still, there were drawbacks. The War of Awakening was still a fresh memory in the mind of the collective. It had been hard to trust computers again, if only for menial tasks.

On his display he could see his wingmen floating outward, giving each other the distance they needed to maneuver and conduct their own checks. They would automatically reach a distance of ten thousand kilometers between each other before he considered his scouts in a position to maximize their intelligence-gathering sensors. Once at the proper range they would scan for … anything.

Sabik didn't know what to expect. The sensors and mines they had avoided effectively cut themselves off from a call for help. Stories of the extremism of the separatists told him to be careful. "Anyone who would drive a knife through their skull and severe the link…" Sabik stopped. Mlyma stared but didn't respond, instead, allowing the other members of his crew to acknowledge his order in sequence, careful not to step on each other's thoughts back to Sabik.

This was a feat only Mateens could master, and his scouts did it better than most. To be selected as a Mateen scout, you not only had to master the method of telepathic communication, but you also had to be able to operate in deep space with little to no guidance. Tactical competence was a must, and Sabik had proved himself over and over again.

When Gemini's fleet was given the task to monitor the activity of the separatists, Sabik nudged his family goodbye and told them not to expect to hear from him for a while. He knew that he would most certainly be the advance guard of the fleet. Focusing now, he tried hard to see if he could still feel the Mateen collective from so far away. He could not. For the first time since his birth, a portion of his brain was completely silent; absent was the near constant chatter of his people.

"It's eerily quiet, isn't it?" he said to Mlyma over his shoulder. Finally free from her subspace suit, she had settled down at her own workstation to transmit messages and receive reports. One of those messages would be an encrypted signal back to the fleet. It would alert Gemini that they had arrived in enemy territory and that they were going to begin their observations. It would also give their current location in the event something happened to them.

She nodded and sent him a telepathic *Yes*. "All I can feel are the others in our formation. It's strange being so far from everyone. I wonder if this is how other species feel all the time. It's lonely." She paused to collect her thoughts. "Or, like you said, how the rebels feel now."

He agreed. "I've wondered the same thing. I imagine they don't know anything else, but I agree. Suddenly we are no longer connected to the greater collective, but we still know they are there and can take solace in that fact. I wonder if other species even feel a connection to each other." He paused. There was something about the utter blackness beyond that had left them all contemplative.

"But for the rebels to do this willingly to their children," she muttered bitterly. "It is like touch for us. To steal that intimacy…"

"Enough philosophy." He gave her a smile. "We've work to do."

Red and blue light lit her jawline and cheekbones while lines of data scrolled into her big white and crimson eyes. She was the squadron's intelligence officer and had worked on Sabik's ship for three years now. He trusted her intuition and her intellect. The expression on her face told him she saw something. Perhaps something she didn't yet understand.

"The system is heavily mined with sensors and defensive turrets," she finally said. "Charting a path to observe the planet will likely be as difficult as it was getting into the system in the first place." She paused, squinted her eyes, and continued. "The technology is unique. These rebels have been out here a long time; long enough to adapt."

"Yeah," he grumbled. "Without a telepathic link to the collective, I can see how they could become so different."

She gave him a pensive stare and Sabik suddenly felt the need to clarify his comment.

"Good scouts must be able to understand their enemy. We cannot observe without also attempting to understand motives. It is this understanding that will help us to know the difference between an enemy feint attack and the main effort, Mlyma."

She nodded but remained silent.

Okay, team, he thought to his wingmen. *Let's pilot slowly towards Separatist controlled space. Keep scanning. Report data back to me.*

His crew once again acknowledged, and his two wingmen piloted their ships ahead and to the flanks of his ship. Sabik would stay in the center at the rear, directing the reconnaissance and analyzing data with Mlyma. Having him towards the back of the formation allowed him to assess the mission without being the front scout, concerned about natural danger or an enemy threat.

"There's something else," Mlyma finally said. Her brow was furrowed again, and her eyes squinted. Her hands swiped across the monitors quickly as she tried to make sense of what she was seeing. "Objects. Six of them just floating out there. They aren't moving, but the space around them is bulging. I can't tell if the bulge is from magnetic fields sustaining the subspace or from something else. I've never seen anything like it." Mlyma leaned in close to the computer models and zoomed in, spinning rough outlines of the objects around in her fingers. "They're like rectangles or arrows but there isn't enough energy around them to sustain life."

Sabik thought for a moment. It didn't make sense. "Is it natural? Meteors maybe? A result of a collision with the magnetic field or sensors that are disrupting space-time?" he finally asked.

Typically, the fabric was too weak to contain physical elements for longer than a second, maybe two if it was lucky. Nothing would disrupt the subspace unless it was traveling through it and then the vessel would require so much power that it would be easily detectable. If it was space junk or a partially trapped asteroid, the object would tear back into the present as soon as the energy had dissipated. Something supernatural had to be holding them there, something intelligent. "Artificial intelligence?" Sabik pondered aloud, almost to himself.

Suddenly Mlyma's voice boomed. "There are trails in the subspace!" Her voice was panicked. "It's almost like…"

Before Mlyma could finish, a thought screamed into Sabik's mind and erupted telepathically to his formation. *AMBUSH!* followed by, *Evasive maneuvers!*

Sabik spun forward in his chair and pressed hard on his thrusters. "Closing fast!" screamed Mlyma. "Six thousand kilometers."

The ship lurched forward, then banked left. Despite the lack of gravity outside, Sabik felt his head slam against the headrest as his vessel accelerated. His radar buzzed. A red light flashed, and a hologram appeared of his wingmen breaking formation. Dozens of streaks flickered in and out on his radar to his front. Engines appeared on the hologram now. The objects were military vessels and somehow, they had managed to hide their signature.

"Two thousand kilometers," Mlyma announced.

"Deploying decoys," his targeting officer replied.

The pressure against Sabik's head and chest abated as his ship reached its full velocity. A faint light flickered in the space above him followed by an explosion. Dozens of proximity rounds meant to destabilize his maneuver erupted around him. His ship rocked and vibrated under the pressure. Sabik pressed his throttle down, diving beneath the blast just in time to see a second and third flash of white and red. Metal shrapnel bounced off the armor of his ship. His radar blinked again. Sabik's heart dropped. Hundreds of white lines appeared, originating from the objects Mlyma had detected.

"How do we get them?" he barked at his crew, hoping that the desperation he felt didn't reflect in the tone of his voice. The response was silence. Mateen reconnaissance vessels weren't built for head-to-head combat. Certainly not against an overwhelming force. Retreat, however, was out of the question. Enemy sensors would prevent them from making another jump and their ships couldn't outrun their enemy either. They were alone, deep in enemy territory, and heavily outgunned. This was a matter of survival.

It didn't matter, but Sabik had just learned from his error. What felt like sneaking through enemy territory was actually a leash leading him in. What felt like craftily avoiding mines and sensors in an attempt to gather intelligence against their enemy was a carefully crafted path by his enemy. What felt like success was actually failure. He allowed himself to be led into a rebel kill zone like an animal to its slaughter. But could he escape?

Another explosion rocked his ship. He dove, looking for a place to escape. More rounds burst behind him. Fire flashed just in front of the nose of his ship. His sensors flickered.

"Wing three is down!" Mlyma informed him over the roar of their engines. Her voice was panicked. They were trapped, and everyone knew it. Jumping into a wormhole was impossible, and if they were hit during travel, it could be a fate worse than death. Sabik wasn't about to jump away. They had to find a way to defeat the ships that lurked beyond the normal subspace.

Sabik banked right just in time to see three more rounds rush past his ship. "Target the nearest vessel," he ordered his targeting officer. "Maybe we can gain some time to regroup."

His ship rocked as it released six munitions of its own. He watched his screen impatiently.

"Wing two is down!" Mlyma shouted. "Just us now."

"Detonation!" yelled his targeting officer. "No effect. They're employing defensive cannons."

The reactions of his enemy were too quick. It was anticipating his maneuver. The vessels had calculated when he would shoot and when he would retreat. Their reactions were too fast for Mateen rebels or any other species in the galaxy. A thought that he had hidden beneath the surface of his mind suddenly returned to him in full force. *The Awakening*, he thought to Mlyma. *They're in league with the awakened!*

Another burst shuddered the hull of their Lovac class reconnaissance vessel. A second erupted on his right. Sabik gripped his controls and tried to pull up. The ship was sluggish. It was too late. He wouldn't be able to outmaneuver the next volley. "Send a message to Gemini," Sabik ordered. "Send them all of our data. They have to know what we're up against."

Mlyma flipped a switch at her workstation and spun her chair to look at him. Wide eyes stared deep into his own. He expected to feel her fear, but that emotion was absent, replaced by peace and accompanied by an expectation of certain death.

CHAPTER FOUR

"You can't expect us to believe that. How does a fleet commander take forty million soldiers to war without it being resourced and sanctioned by the Jark government?"

For the first time since the meeting had adjourned, the seven seats that made up the Galactic Council were silent. A large Jark, with thin gray hair covering his body and dark red skin beneath, leaned over and whispered something to his aid. The man's name was Edet Gadalje. He was the Jark representative to the council. He was their top diplomat and a fearsome man. Casika was certain he was also the one who convinced the council not to intervene during the initial invasion of Tassi. To Casika, Edet was the enemy.

In the silence, Casika chose to continue. Her muscles tightened as she remembered the invasion. Her mind replayed the bombs falling on her city, and she allowed her own anger to drive her forward. What started as a nervous whisper in her throat became a resolute desire to win these people over. "Let me remind the council," she continued, "that I was there when the sky darkened from the Jark onslaught. I was on Tassi when artillery fell on Tassian children playing games in the street. I was on the beach when families, desperately seeking cover for their loved ones, covered themselves in the bodies of their countrymen instead. I was there when the famed commander Brokk and his priests converted our schools into death camps and our pools into temples to worship their perverse gods. I was there, council members. I was there."

The seven quietly discussed her complaint by themselves while Casika waited before them. The seats at the council made a half moon. The seven representatives sat at a large table at the front of the room while the body of the council made up the audience. There were one hundred seats in the audience representing the five planetary species that had earned a position at the council. Those planetary systems that did not have governing seats, such as the Piskies and the government of Charlon, could vote as non-members, but the seven representatives at the front possessed fifty-one percent of the vote, ensuring that the council itself held the power within the Galactic Order and that non-member systems merely exercised an opportunity to align their interests with the powerful diplomats at the front.

The Hestonians and original founders of the council occupied three of the seven seats in the center. They also looked the most similar to the Tassians but had a greater variation of races within the Hestonian species. It was this surplus of genetic variation that led many Galactic scientists to claim that Hestos shared a common ancestor between the two species. The Hestonians proudly levied these claims to justify an elite prejudice against many other species within the galaxy.

Two males and a female whispered together as the portion of the Hestonian leadership. Gervaase, the president in the center, was a fat man with thin gray hair that circled his head but no longer grew at the top. He looked as though he had indulged far too much and sat and deliberated on issues for far too long. His face was covered in wrinkles. Casika had grown to despise him.

The younger Hestonian woman was far more appealing. Her hair had not yet lost its color and instead reflected a warm brown as it fell gently off her shoulders. She wasn't young, but she wasn't too old to have lost touch with reality either. Her face was weary. Casika suspected she did just as much babysitting of her partner as she did voting on important issues.

To their right, was the Tassian representative named Aitziber Grubbe and a Mateen named Noura whom she believed knew Gemini personally. Of all the seats, Casika respected Noura the most, if not for her fairness, for the fact that Gemini liked and approved of her.

Her own representative, Aitziber, lacked any and all respect. If Edet was the Jark responsible for preventing galactic intervention, Aitziber was guilty for failing to make the case. As she stood before them, she could see why. He was sheepish and unassertive. Often, he would drop arguments and reject floor time that could have been used to further Tassian initiatives. She would bring her observations back to Cale and recommend he be replaced.

At the council's left sat the Jarks and a green-skinned representative from Despona. The Desponians were the newest members of the council and had been invited once the planet was able to unite under a central government. The entire council body wore white robes, to signify their purity in judgment. Casika wasn't convinced.

Edet broke the silence with an argument no more thought out than when the meeting had begun. "This is absurd," he said with a growl that only the Jarks could get away with. "My government has released all of the documents to the galactic inspectors with absolute transparency. You all know as well as we do that we had no part in Brokk's attack on Tassi. In fact, this very council voted against intervention. We were all in agreement."

Casika scoffed into the microphone. "That's a lie," she accused him, looking at the rest of the council. "You fear war, so you don't press the issue, but you know as well as we do that the Jarks haven't been forthcoming. There has been no formal investigation. Our chair," she said, gesturing to the Aitziber at the front, "hasn't even had a chance to review whatever documents the Jark's government allegedly did release. If there is something you've hidden from the remaining council members, I implore you to release it."

The thin, gray-haired Tassian at the front nodded and leaned into his own microphone. "It's true," he said. His throat was raspy, and he backed away to clear it. "Only the Hestonian chairs have seen the documents. We'd like to know if even they reviewed them."

"It's irrelevant if they have," Edet blurted. "I can tell you what they say." He gave another Jark snarl before continuing. "Brokk went rogue, he convinced the members of his fleet to go along with him, and he will pay for these treasonous acts once he is caught!" The man leaned back in his chair, crossing big hairy arms over his chest before adding, "Even you can't deny he attacked our Third Fleet just a few months ago."

Whispers filled the audience. Casika could tell she wasn't getting anywhere. The Tassians had hoped that as a victim of the war and her relationship with the Mateens, Casika would be able to sway the vote. Perhaps she could tell her story and plead her case. In the last three days, her attempts had fallen flat. Hestos had no appetite for sanctions and no muscle to enforce them. No one would hold the Jarks accountable because it meant the possibility of conflict, or worse, war.

Gervaase and the other Hestonians turned inward and exchanged hushed words. Just as it looked like they had reached a conclusion, Noura silenced the room.

"The Mateens agree with the Tassians," she said boldly. Like all Mateens, her voice was mechanical and proper. Unlike the other species, verbal language for the Mateen had to be learned in school, and with it, came a certain oddness to its sound. Her long black hair was braided tightly and fell across her chest. White teeth beamed through her dark gray lips and a light gray forehead scrunched as she spoke. "We accept as true that the Jark régime possesses an antiquity of violence and imperialism. In the three hundred years that the Jarks have been affiliated with this order, they have taken into custody nearly twelve planetary systems and attacked our merchant vessels hundreds of times. They assert we are imposing upon the sovereign territory of their empire, but their claims are outlandish and unreasonable. This imperialism has to stop. The Mateen would like to see sanctions levied upon this empire to prevent any future action from the Jarks." She paused to think and then as if she'd almost forgotten, added: "Oh, and we too would like time to read the report."

Gervaase raised an eyebrow at Noura and then looked down the table at the Jarks.

"We won't agree to any sanctions," Edet growled, trying to look Noura in the eyes but unable to see past Gervaase's fat head. "You've only seen a small portion of our fleet on Tassi. How dare you threaten the Jark Empire with sanctions. Not to mention, the galactic merge is upon us. Who will aid the council if there is an enemy beyond the fringe?" The large hairy man looked at his green-skinned neighbor and laughed. "Certainly not the Desponians."

The green-skinned diplomat scowled at Edet but didn't respond. Noura shrugged, leaned back in her chair, and stared at Gervaase. "I propose a vote, Mr. President. Edet has managed to insult the intelligence of everyone on the council and the Jarks deserve to be under our microscope. The Mateens would like to see the Jark fleet limited to four battleships and their force restricted to self-defense."

Gervaase mumbled something that Casika couldn't understand over the cursing of Edet and then grabbed his gavel. "Very well," he said, slamming the gavel on the bench to signify a judgment was coming. "There will be a vote tomorrow afternoon. I propose a recess for the remainder of the day to speak with your constituents. This session will only be a vote to determine if the council believes there is enough evidence to move forward with punitive measures against the Jarks." He looked down the table at Edet who was grinding his teeth furiously. "I propose you release what information you must in order to clear your people. I have no doubt the members of this council will be looking forward to reviewing all the evidence."

Spinning in his chair, Gervaase looked at Casika. "You are the one with the burden of proof. The Tassians must release the evidence they believe ties the Jarks to Brokk and his assault on your homeland. Failure to do so will likely result in a negative vote."

Casika nodded and the president swung his gavel once more. "Adjourned!" he shouted.

As people left the main hall, Casika was elated. They hadn't achieved much but she knew Cale would be thrilled. For months, the Tassians had fought to get a vote at the Galactic Council that would punish the Jarks for their invasion. Punishment would mean sanctions and inspections. It would prevent the Jarks from continuing their development of weapons and reduce their fleet to the minimum amount required to defend their planet.

As she pondered the upcoming vote against the Jark Empire, she suddenly realized just how skewed the system was in favor of the original five members. What could a system like Charlon do except to obey? What benefit did these minor systems gain from participating in the governance of the Galactic Order at all? Voting for the majority would be an inconsequential addition to the decision already made and voting against a galactic power would be suicide for a smaller system. As she considered the structure, Casika convinced herself that the galactic order would find itself in a struggle for relevancy if it failed to consider the needs of the minor planetary systems it claimed to serve.

Nevertheless, she couldn't wait to tell Cale. As soon as she gathered her things, Casika rushed through the two large doors that sealed the ruling chamber off from the city of Hestos.

Light from a yellow sun bombarded her. It was far dimmer than the dual suns on Tassi, but she still used an arm to shield her eyes. In this light, her skin didn't sparkle the way it did on Tassi. The golden freckles that glowed on her forearms in the bright light of the helium suns had nearly disappeared altogether. Her long white hair was duller too, almost blond as opposed to the pure white she had on her homeworld. Casika was eager to get back, if only for vanity's sake.

Rounding a black-bricked corner, Casika was assaulted by street vendors in the square. Hestos was a booming capital with all types of merchandise to buy. Members of all species shouted at her through the busy streets, waving their goods into the air. Leather hats made from animal hide on Charoth competed with red meat hanging from stakes. Melons, slippers, fur, and jewelry all sat in various carts with their owners begging pedestrians to make a purchase.

Casika was so enthralled with the market scene that she almost didn't notice a darkened figure in the ally. No, not one but two figures stood just inside where the shadow from a metal building above began. *Were they watching her?* She couldn't tell, and she didn't want to make it obvious she had noticed them. Casika picked up her pace, pushing through the crowd towards the center of the square and in the direction of her room.

From here she could see her hotel, one of many skyscrapers that bracketed the downtown market. Her room was near the top. Casika glanced over her shoulder. The two men were gone. *Had she even seen them at all?*

Had she made enemies? Did she anger the Jarks? Would they try to keep her from testifying tomorrow? Thoughts rushed through her head as she tried to make sense of what she had seen. Maybe the Jarks had put someone on her to keep her from gathering and releasing the information the rest of the council required for the vote. *Had she crossed a line in galactic politics?* Casika reached a stone fountain at the end of the square and pushed through the crowd again towards her building. Blue water shot upwards from the mouth of a fish and rained down upon children waiting nearby along the sidewalk.

A street performer blocked her path, blowing bubbles in a desperate attempt for coin. A second performer on stilts offered balloons to begging children's parents. Casika was close and quickly dodged the performers, popping a floating bubble in the process, and pressed past the last of the crowd beyond the fountain. A guard at the entrance nodded to her and opened the door into the lobby.

Thanking him as she passed, she took one last look over her shoulder for anyone who might be watching her. Nothing. *Maybe just part of her imagination.* Another man held the elevator for her, which she rode to the fifty-third floor.

Tan carpets and blue walls met her when the doors opened, and a green bead of light flickered on the floor. As she walked, it paced her towards her room, illuminating the hallway and ensuring she knew where she was going. She knew of course, but the green light was a fun gimmick that more advanced hotels had these days. A personal chauffeur that couldn't do anything helpful like carry your bags.

At her door, Casika pressed her hand into a panel. The door slid open. A corner suite, with large tinted windows wall to wall, waited for her inside. She could see over the entire city all the way to the bay. Casika dropped her bag on the black leather couch and kicked her slippers off as she strode to the window to examine the view. It was jaw-dropping.

She wished Cale was with her to see the view. Looking down into the square, she could picture the two of them walking along the stone-cut wharf and dining at a restaurant along the water. They would reminisce about old friends on Tassi before the war. They could dream about settling down along the coast, an old fishing town as far away from the capital as they could get.

A shadow crossed behind her in the reflection of the window. Casika spun around to see nothing. Just the room. *Were her eyes playing with her once more?* No. Something was here. "Hello?" she called out.

No sound. Silence. An eerie silence. She was being watched. Stalked. The bedroom door was cracked. *Was someone in there? Were the Jarks waiting for her to intimidate her?* Ever since the battle for Tassi, everything had been different. Lines were blurred between paranoia and caution. Reality and imagination were one and the same.

Casika regularly confused her waking moments with her dreams. Nightmares filled her sleep and she often woke early to sit and wonder. Her life was no longer fully her own. It was different, complicated, depressed. She wasn't trained for war and no support was ready for her when the war ended. But she was stronger now because of it. She would not back down from pursuing justice.

Sweaty palms gripped the cold steel metal of the windowsill behind her. Her face felt hot; panicked. Her apartment, however, was silent.

Finally, Casika worked up the courage to cross the threshold of her bedroom and check the rest of her hotel room. All was as she left it. The bed was neatly made, a glass on the table was still half-full, and a picture of Cale rested where she had put it on the nightstand. She missed him. She missed the laughter and the comfort he brought. She missed late nights, warm dinners, and a secure arm to tuck herself into. *A few more days,* she told herself.

CHAPTER FIVE

Boro Vidas grabbed the silver handrail and steadied himself. His legs felt weak, but he knew this was a natural experience after living for so long in artificial gravity. Looking down at the narrow orange and black steps, Boro blinked twice and shook his head. He felt dizzy and disoriented. *Vertigo.*

"Don't worry about it, soldier," called a voice behind him. "Step aside while others disembark."

Boro released the rail and backed into the hull of his battleship. *Home.* How long had he been gone? Thirteen months? Too long, even to do something you loved. He closed his eyes and remembered the weightlessness of it. He remembered how quickly his small fighter banked and turned at his commands.

To be a pilot for the storied Third Fleet was a dream come true. To be mentored by a Jark as decorated as Commander Szega was more than he could have ever hoped. But dreams only painted one side of the picture. There was a dark side to his first deployment, one he never thought he would have to endure. *Dreams versus reality.*

Explosions flashed through his mind. The colorful soup of the Rainbow Nebula in the Battle for Charoth swirled. *Defeat* is what they returned home with. *Despair* is what young Boro felt now.

Boro opened his eyes and breathed in the fresh sulfur air, allowing it to fully expand his lungs and strengthen his body. He had missed that smell. Looking down at his hands to make sure they weren't shaking, Boro took another step towards the stairs so that he could disembark the battleship. This time, his legs were stronger and with each movement down to the next tread, he was more resolute in getting to the bottom.

No, not resolute. Boro was excited. *Home,* his mind called eagerly.

Looking around, Boro realized the space dock itself was chaos. Thousands of soldiers disembarking dozens of spacecrafts flurried about the port. Families and clans of families scurried on all fours pushing past and through other clans as they searched for their kin. The whole fleet was here, and they would get the longest rest and recovery period of any fleet in the Jark Empire: one solar rotation. As an officer, Boro knew the truth had more to do with their defeat in battle than with the generosity of the empire, but Boro would take it all the same. He had been gone too long.

Rising on two legs, Boro searched for his clan. He had the advantage of being taller than most Jarks and more practiced at standing on two legs. *Now, where could they be?* His clan wasn't as boisterous as most; nor did it have the positional authority to enter the inner parts of the spaceport. He would have to search for them along the perimeter where concrete met shrubs and sidewalks met jagged lava rock.

Even in the chaos, it didn't take Boro long to find them. His father, proud archon of the clan, had tipped his graying hair in a ceremonial orange chalk. Other clansman behind his father also wore the tribal colors of his people and had smeared orange chalk across their face and hands. *Home,* he smirked as he raced towards them.

***

Even though his father was the archon of the clan, Boro was not allowed to initiate conversation. Any attempt to assert oneself into a discussion among elders or to the chief of the clan could be viewed as a challenge; a challenge without numerical support often resulted in death.

Boro was particularly aware of this rule because of how long he had been away. His tribe had always been wary of government control and to send off a son to serve the fleet meant they willingly risked him building alliances beyond that of the clan. Paranoia, Boro assumed, would be significant.

Despite the challenges that having a son working for the central government possessed, there was a tangible reason his father had encouraged him to join. Recently, the clan had suffered. The growing year was shortening on their side of the planet, as they rotated their dwarf star in an oblong cycle. Prosperity and thereby favor would be extended to other clans, and the consequential power shift would often result in warfare as the various semi-autonomous tribes competed for resources and favor within the central government. Having a son in the fleet would provide a secondary source of money, as well as a prestige with the central government on Jark.

In silence, the fifteen clansmen who came to greet him home returned to their territory. Once out of the city, the magnetic roads followed lava spill and plate fault lines through a harsh countryside. Shrubs held tightly onto windswept plains, and short trees with flat, broad branches speckled the otherwise barren landscape.

Finally, his father leaned towards him and winked. "It's good to have you back, son," he said firmly, delivering a hearty pat on the shoulder. "Tell us about your conquests."

"Thank you, Archon," Boro responded respectfully. Boro had always spoken smoothly and comfortably in front of a group and often was chosen to tell the clan's history at large gatherings. His jet-black hair, strong face and jawline, and tall stature gave him a legitimacy in the clan that he rarely took advantage of. In the fleet, however, Boro quickly realized how other Jarks were willing to follow his lead and to believe his words. There was something beyond mere competence that compelled others to follow; this, perhaps, was his greatest lesson.

When the elders in their circular passenger compartment leaned forward with interest at his archon's suggestion, Boro grinned but suddenly wondered where to begin.

"We combatted piracy and ensured freedom of navigation for our merchants vessels," he started. "There are many different civilizations, and they all vie for just a few of the passageways through the galaxy," he paused, noticing flat expressions on many of their faces. Even though space and space warfare had been a part of Jark society for nearly a thousand years, many of the average citizens knew shockingly little about their galaxy.

Without trying to insult their honor, Boro backtracked. "The galaxy is extremely violent. Marauding black holes and rogue planets exist in nearly infinite combinations and locations across the galaxy. Stars regularly reach the end of their lives, exploding in a super-hot goop that could destroy an uninformed passenger. Even the subspace we traverse through is full of friction and instability. This has caused the space-faring civilizations to chart only a dozen known safe routes across space."

The elders nodded in agreement. "Yes, that makes sense," one of them grunted. "Wouldn't want to lose your whole harvest to a black hole," he chuckled. "Best to stick to the routes."

"Exactly," Boro responded. "Unfortunately, once you tell someone where you will be with a lot of money, thieves will undoubtedly meet you there.

The elders again nodded. Some even tisked their tongues. "No honor," his archon growled. "While you were gone, Hie'keleh was attacked by a thief on the northern tip of Bra-ashaer. When we caught him, we pulled his eyes from his head and let the birds pick his flesh clean to his bones!"

Archon leaned back as the other elders nodded in approval, imploring Boro to continue.

"I'm glad to hear that Hie'keleh is well," Boro replied, trying to hide a smile as he considered the broad-shouldered female attacked by thieves. "We acted similarly, although in space it is hard cut out one's eyes. I fought many battles against pirates and escorted thousands of our merchant ships to Despona and Hestos. As a pilot in a single-seat spaceship, you are on your own when trouble hits. I learned a lot about myself; there were many lonely nights but enough wingmen to keep you company from afar. We operate in teams," he explained. "Two of us guard a merchant convoy, baiting pirates in and killing them when they realize their mistake."

Boro trailed off as he remembered the bright lights of the Rainbow Nebula. "A new mission brought us to a place called Charoth. It is a slave colony, founded by Hestos a few millennia ago. One of our destroyers, while defending merchant vessels, was attacked and captured by the exile named Brokk. The fleet was sent to arrest him or kill him in battle."

"Ah," one of the elders said, wild red eyes flaring in the darkness. "Now that was someone you could follow, wasn't it?" he asked rhetorically to the others in the passenger transport.

Some nodded in approval. Others remained quiet. The archon rubbed his chin.

"Careful, Nehiu," he warned. "That type of talk could be treason now."

The elder shook his head. "You know as well as I do," he snickered, "that he was going places. I do find it interesting though that they would have allowed his capture. I suspect any testimony by Brokk in court could have led to some detrimental conclusions." He paused and grunted before adding, "No, I suspect they knew he would never surrender. Death was always the primary course of action."

Boro's father waved the old Jark off with his hand and motioned back to Boro. "So, what happened when you pursued Brokk's rogue fleet?"

The colors of the Rainbow Nebula swirled again through Boro's memory. Flashes of proximity munitions exploded against the hull of his ship. Swarms of drones attacked one another. *Chaos*, Boro thought, *that's what happened.* There was no training in the galaxy that could have prepared him for the intensity of the battle. There was no simulation within the empire that could have provided the instruction he had needed. Space combat was something you had to experience. If you survived, you learned from it. If you died, some other fool learned from it.

"It was a trap," Boro said slowly. "The Rainbow Nebula near the planet Charoth was the most beautiful thing I have ever seen, but its deadly radiation and dense clouds made the nebula a perfect hiding place." Boro looked about the passenger cabin into the eyes of each of the elders and saw a patient knowledge. They knew what had happened. They had heard the results of the battle, but the tribe honored him as a warrior and gave him the floor to tell his story.

"Commander Szega proudly proclaimed we would flush out the traitor," Boro continued. "Our analysis gave us a clear advantage and, just like we trained, our fleet charged into the battle. We tried to capitalize on speed and force, but he had been waiting. Brokk struck first, unleashing a barrage of cannon fire against our foremost ships from inside the nebula. I was scrambled, along with my wingman, and engaged smaller fighters so that the battleships were free to concentrate their efforts on the larger vessels in his armada." Boro smiled. "I got three of them before my wingman was killed."

The outspoken Nehiu shook his head and let a deep rumble of dissatisfaction leave his throat. "A valiant effort," he reassured Boro.

Boro continued. "It is nearly impossible to fight through swarms without a wingman and, with our formation badly damaged, I was ordered to return to regroup. It was then I saw it. The fleet was splintered, broken, destroyed by Brokk." Boro paused once more, collecting himself and his thoughts. His lips trembled as he mouthed the words he wanted to say. "We lost," he finally muttered. "And we limped home defeated with no honor."

As he finished, the passenger transport banked left along a turn on the magnetic lift. The red sun had dropped below the horizon, and a dusty orange filled the cloud-speckled sky. More grass had appeared, trading places with the lava rock and even flourished in some places. Blue flowers grouped together around tall trees that stretched skyward without the harsh winds of the lava fields to contend with. Boro breathed in deeply. *Home,* he thought again. *Finally, home.*

The archon looked out of his window and grimaced. Yellow fangs fell against his lower lip. His flat nose curled up slightly as he rubbed his neck. Boro had only been gone for a year but could see the gray was more prominent now. Much of the hair that covered his body was either tipped gray or fully grayed. *Is he truly that old?* he thought to himself.

"It sounds to me," his father finally said, "that you returned with all the honor they would allow. You killed your enemy in battle and you fought your hardest for the fleet. That makes us all proud."

The elders nodded at that. Some of them ground their teeth to show appreciation for what the archon was saying. Boro felt relieved.

"You know," he continued, "we have all fought in battles that we lost. What makes a warrior and eventually a great leader is how we learn from losing."

Boro nodded but his father wasn't finished yet. "This government," he said looking at the elders, "has ruined the glory of Jark. Do you not remember when we were feared by all? Do you remember when the battles we fought were backed by all of Jark's power and might? Now it is a secret endeavor by the government. They never ask the clans what they think."

Archon looked out of his window in disgust. "No one would have dared sanction us back then, and we certainly didn't need to play political games with our admirals and commanders. The empire needs its glory back," he barked angrily.

CHAPTER SIX

Dark red clouds filled a scorched orange sky, reflecting the dull crimson light from a massive sun that hovered at the two o'clock. Hues of dark purple and russet fire streaked along the ground to mix with a deep volcanic ink as if some invisible artist had planned and painted this landscape long ago. The smell of sulfur burned in Tamara's nostrils and her spine, burdened by the immense gravity, ached. Jark. Canis was home.

"I've never seen anything like this place," Tamara panted, trying to keep up.

Canis grunted. "If you think this is bad, you should see Coridon."

The two had been walking for a few hours along an ash-covered road. Cautious to conceal his identity, Canis had chosen a path that few traveled anymore to reach the city. After using Jark battle frequencies to sneak past the planetary defenses, Brokk launched the two of them in a four-man escape pod from the Juggernaut. Their hope was that the craft's signature would be too small for atmospheric sensors to detect. After crashing on an isolated plateau north of the capital, the two of them started walking and had been walking towards Vyekla ever since. Tamara was glad to survive the crash, but now, after experiencing the burden of the gravity on Jark, she wasn't sure that she wouldn't have been better off as a burnt pancake at the crash site.

"Coridon?" Tamara asked. All of this was a mystery to her. Hestos, Despona, and Charoth were familiar, but the planets that Brokk often talked about were little more than academic concepts, let alone a tangible reality.

"Our sister planet. It is at the far end of the habitable zone. A frigid place." Canis was setting the pace, walking head-on into a nasty wind that rushed in from the west and whipped sand and dust into their eyes. Tamara followed, allowing his large body to block the brunt of the wind. Despite his many injuries, the old warrior moved quickly. Tamara felt his heart beat fast inside his chest and sensed that Jark was reinvigorating him.

Canis wore the traditional Jark garb of a wealthy trader on his planet which consisted of thick, loose-fitting cloth, nearly as black as the volcanic rock they currently traversed. He had a tattered black coat that hung to his knees and long black boots that came up nearly as high. Because Canis was a Jark, he used his long arms to propel him along the ground, rising to full height only to look across the barren landscape for a threat. Tamara thought about telling him that she was sensing out farther than he could see or smell, but she knew Canis. The weary warrior wouldn't take her word for his security.

His long coat had another purpose: it concealed his weapons. Canis carried at least two firearms. She suspected he had hidden more. One was a long-range sniper rifle, and the second was a standard issue Jark assault rifle capable of firing hundreds of dense neutronium-tipped projectiles that cut through wind and flesh alike. Canis told Tamara countless times that he only planned to use the weapons if she failed. Tamara was the real weapon here, and he didn't conceal his plan to use her. She didn't mind; the chance to prove her worth to Canis and subsequently to Brokk brought her all the satisfaction she needed.

Tamara was dressed in her black and gold trench coat from Charoth and had braided her long hair to keep it from whipping across her face in the wind. In addition to the gold claws on her hands, Brokk had adorned her with nearly a dozen chain necklaces and large hoop earrings in the hopes she would look like a merchant if anyone got close enough to inspect them. Most people, Brokk had told her, would be inside because of the winter season that the northern hemisphere of Jark was currently in. Tamara didn't understand initially but upon seeing the first strike of red lightning and watching a near black wall of dust roll up from the ground and slam into her face, she knew what he meant. They would certainly be able to stroll unchallenged into the city.

As they walked, Tamara let her mind flutter about her task. *Prophetess. Harbinger.* Would people listen? Could they truly gain a following? Jark was a culture that was still fully engrossed in magic and sorcery. If anyone could convince the Jark people she had a supernatural message, Tamara hoped it was her.

Canis crested the next hill and knelt low to the ground. Tamara knelt too. They were on a ridge overlooking a valley. The storm made it impossible to see the other side. Below, the valley carved through rock for miles until it finally opened in what looked like the start of a massive crater. Orange lava oozed to the surface around the hole and black smoke spiraled skyward and obstructed her view. The wind howled, stinging her face with sand and dirt and who knew what else.

"There it is," he said over the storm, pointing into the rounded walls below.

At first, Tamara couldn't see what he was pointing at. Her eyes stung from the sulfur and smoke that an ever-present wind pushed into her face. *How could anyone survive here?* she thought. Blinking twice to clear her eyes, Tamara canted her head to the side and tried again.

Through billows of black smoke, she saw it and gasped for air. Vyekla, the capital city of the Jark Empire, stood before them.

Erupting from the bottom was the most magnificent city she had ever seen. Massive black structures shot skyward at jagged angles. In the dark orange sun, the black objects glistened like metal, but she could tell it wasn't metal at all. It was polished rock. It appeared to be an onyx or a garnet. More impressive than the material was the angle at which the buildings stood. Many of them were planted thirty degrees from the ground and must have been several miles tall. The technology to construct such a building would have been incredibly advanced.

In the center, a tall rectangular tower rose straight into the air. The base of the building was narrow, but it got wider as it climbed as if one of Brokk's battleships had plunged directly into the ground. Orange light bounced brightly from the structure's shined walls.

"It's incredible," she said at last. "I had no idea anyone was capable of making such a city."

Canis nodded. If he was proud, he wouldn't show her. Jark was now his enemy. She suspected he felt sorrow now that he was reunited with his city, but he would never tell her. That wasn't who Canis was. She hoped she could win it back for him.

"The building in the center is where our emperor lives and works," he said dryly. "Everything you see is the government quarter and is protected by this natural rock cliff we're standing on. The city itself sprawls for hundreds of kilometers in each direction."

"What is his name?" Tamara asked.

Canis returned a blank stare as if he didn't understand the question.

"His name. The emperor. Who is he?" She prodded again.

"We do not name our emperor," Canis responded. "He is apparently above worldly names."

Tamara considered his response. It seemed strange that the rulers would go their entire life without a single name to attribute to their achievements. "Then how do they brag about the things they have done before another emperor is crowned?"

Canis stared at her once more and then grinned. His teeth were covered in grime from the storm but seeing him smile brought a level of embarrassment about her question. She was exhausted from walking and the gravity of this planet was taking its toll. The sly smile of a creature she trusted more than a father unnerved her. "Apparently our emperor has never died," he replied. "I am looking forward to seeing what happens when we kill him."

Tamara thought for a moment. Canis just suggested to her that this was the first and only leader of the Jark people. That in the thousands of years of Jark existence, no one came before or after this ruler they now set out to kill. Brokk had once told her about Jark magic when he had first established her as a sorceress for his fleet. Tamara suspected very little of it was true, but when Brokk himself swore to the summonings that occurred within the mercury pools and the roles of the priests, she hadn't been so sure. Even with a concept as absurd as immortality, Tamara had to wonder if such a thing was possible given everything else she had seen.

Canis swung his legs over the dusty ledge of the ridge and dropped onto a landing approximately six feet below. He hit with a thud and Tamara followed suit, swinging her legs and allowing his powerful hands to catch and lower her gracefully to the ground. The gravity seemed to have no effect on the Jark who had spent his whole life here. Suddenly she realized why his species was so large. To grow up under such conditions would have required extraordinary strength. Each bone and muscle had to be built with supporting structures to merely move, let alone thrive in such a hostile environment.

The wind died down once she dropped behind the cliff. Turning, Tamara could see yet another path that seemed to lead them straight to the main highway and into the city. The road was a dark ash as if it had been spewed up by a volcano, laid down by Jark laborers, then chewed up by years of wind and perhaps something else, something supernatural.

"These are the old trails we used before modern travel was invented," Canis explained. "Because of the rocky terrain, many of the trails remain undamaged, if not a little worn by the wind. But because of the length of the stormy season, it's hard for the government to come out and maintain most of these trails." Canis held out a large gloved hand and gestured towards the road. "Shall we?"

Suddenly, Tamara was no longer certain. Since they had landed she couldn't help but think, *What next?* No, with the prospect of walking down a road that was darker than night itself, Tamara wondered if a misstep would leave her sinking in the very trail she planned to walk. Perhaps the ash had no bottom and she would descend to an immeasurable depth only to be judged unworthy by whatever creatures lurked beneath. Perhaps hands, silver slime-coated hands, would reach up to grab her just as the stories that Brokk had told her about the child sacrifices claimed.

Was it fear that challenged her boldness? Maybe. But deep down she believed there was some logic too. What would happen after they won over the people and killed the emperor? Would Brokk walk free? Would they rally around him as savior and conqueror? "What will we do when we kill him?" she asked. Canis narrowed his eyes at her so she elaborated. "You're a brilliant man. You've been trained in military campaigns and strategy. Do you really think they'll receive Brokk as their king and me as his prophet?"

He smiled. "The emperor may have lived forever, but he doesn't hold an iron grip on the planet. There are factions that oppose him. I believe," he said while pulling his own hood farther down over his dark red head to protect it from the wind, "that the emperor wanted our fleet to be destroyed because he saw Brokk as a threat. I believe he is paranoid and saw that Brokk had favor with the people. I suspect many of them had wanted to make him king."

"So, you think he wanted Brokk dead?" she asked trying to fill in the blanks.

He laughed. "That's my theory. There are others in his cabinet. Other Jarks that were close to Brokk who might go along with a plot against the emperor. He has lost the loyalty of many in the military. Even Commander Szega of the Third Fleet is against him." Canis kicked the ground. Tamara watched dust swirl around his feet before being picked up by the wind and carried off. "They are afraid. The ruling class has cleansed members of the military before. Brokk is likely the latest example of such cleansing. We are no longer members of the military though. We're outlaws. If we can do what insiders lack the courage to do, perhaps we'll find favor with the people and be able to establish a new form of rule."

Canis paused once more and watched Tamara through his dark, inset eyes. "The tides have shifted in recent years. Many in the younger generation no longer trust in the magic of our forefathers. If we want to truly win over the people," he said with certainty, "we need to convince them that you not only possess the magic so many older Jarks believe in, we also need to convince the young that you represent a new class of priestly order. That you have come to do away with the sacrifice that has claimed so many of our children while proclaiming new and certain truths."

It was Tamara now who kicked at the rocky ground, watching the ash vibrate and then lift under the immense force of the wind. "I'm with you until the end, Canis," she said at last. "Let's go."

The two started down the trail with Canis once more in the lead. The path was jagged at first, but as the two twisted down into the valley, the ash-laden trail widened and flattened. Tamara allowed her senses to reach out beyond them, searching for any threats that might catch them off guard. With the wind blowing into their faces, she could easily detect a variety of elements from miles away. The road to the city appeared clear.

"Is everything ready for us inside the city?" Tamara asked, fighting to keep up.

"A team is already there and has secured the home of a zealot named Jaki'el." He responded, exhaustion far from his voice. "He belongs to a sect of the people who believe a man from beyond the grave is coming to usher in a new era of Jark prosperity." Canis cut a look at Tamara and scowled. "They are lunatics," he growled. "But they will serve our purpose and provide the backbone for your proclamations."

"What do you believe?" Tamara asked, catching a face full of dust and smoke.

He grunted. "I believe in a good death and that neither I nor Brokk has had that opportunity yet."

CHAPTER SEVEN

The basement of the Tassian government building buzzed with activity. Today was the day. The molten lava and volcanic ash that colored the Jark atmosphere poured onto forty-four Jark prisoners as they waited to be transported home. The basement itself had been transformed yet again since the last time Cale had seen it. Instead of three separate rooms, the entire test chamber had been converted into a simulated environment that closely resembled Jark. Doctor Chayyim had told him it was the best chance to ensure the Jarks survived the journey. Cale accepted the advice.

Under the guise of diplomacy, Chayyim told the prisoners they were going home. He told them to kiss their wives, hug their children, and tell everyone they knew about Tassian honor. That after defeating the Jarks, the Tassians didn't take out their frustrations on prisoners but instead worked through diplomacy, like all moral nations should.

It was a lie, of course, but Chayyim was certain the gullible men, desperate to return home, would believe it. They had no choice but to believe it. Hope is a powerful form of deception; the prisoners were infected and would infect everyone they encountered. If all went according to plan, they would kill hundreds of millions of Jarks before the disease was controlled. Tassi would have time to build and train a real fleet, and if tensions escalated, Tassi would be in a good position to deliver a death blow to the Jarks once and for all.

At the far end of the chamber, a machine hummed, and a circle appeared to fold outward from nothing. A second machine fired three green lasers into the circle. Instead of protons, the lasers were pulsing neutrons mixed with quark-gluon plasma; hyper-dense particles that bombarded the very fabric of space-time as they intersected with each other and held up the walls of the tunnel that bore through space itself. After several seconds, the circle at the center stopped fluctuating and steadied itself.

Chayyim looked at the measurements on his computer terminal above the simulated environment. All readings were normal. The wormhole was stable.

Cale wished he could be there but instead watched from a visor on his helmet as the prisoners walked timidly into the wormhole and disappeared. He felt elated. Finally, the Tassians would be able to strike back. It would only be a few days before Jark was feeling the pain that Tassi felt less than a year ago. Cale excitedly anticipated the news. If they were lucky, the preemptive strike would cripple the Jark Empire and give Tassi the time it needed to advance beyond Jark's current military capability. If they were unlucky, Tassi would have to follow up the strike with a more conventional attack. Cale was ready for either. Jark deserved as much.

The hiss of oxygen at a hatch on the outer wall of his battleship thrust him back into his present situation. His battleship, a brand new, state of the art war machine had just received approval to dock with the spaceport at Charoth. Cale, with an entourage of three Tassian diplomats and twenty soldiers for security, climbed beyond his own hatch and walked through a narrow tunnel that connected his ship to the spaceport.

Despite his diplomatic mission, Cale opted to wear Tassian combat armor, which included a set of protective glasses that enabled him to view the status of his fleet. On his display, he could see the swirling colors of the rainbow nebula from the viewing ports of his three destroyers that escorted him. These were the last remaining ships in his fleet and once he was on the ground, the destroyers would depart for Tassi to defend his still vulnerable planet.

As the group reached the far end of the narrow corridor, a white steel door hissed and opened, and a dark-skinned Hestonian wearing an orange and gold striped gown met them with a smile. White and beige jewelry hung in hoops around his neck and from his ears. He looked like eccentric royalty, but Cale would never have guessed he ruled the planet. His demeanor was too jovial and his smile too broad to have been burdened with much governing.

"I'm so grateful you've chosen our humble planet to refuel your ships and refit crew," he exclaimed. With arms open, he stepped towards him and offered a firm handshake. He was short, but his voice was deep. "I'm Atworth Kierce," he announced, looking Cale square in the eye and refusing to release his hand. "We have rooms ready for you and the other diplomats at the surface."

"Thank you," Cale responded. "We are grateful you were able to accommodate my crew on such short notice. I assume you accept payment in the standard galactic currency?"

Atworth smiled. "We accept payment in all forms of currency and if you cannot pay, we will gladly put your crew to work in the kitchens to work off your debt!" He laughed a boisterous and powerful laugh before adding, "But let's talk about that another time. For now, I'd like to show you our city."

Cale wasn't sure whether to smile at the joke or slap him for the insult, but he quickly forced the thought from his mind. *Were these the same people who met the fugitive Brokk with similar hospitality?* he wondered.

***

Thilgod Furstil watched Atworth lead the Tassian emissary into the garden that rested at the base of their steel government building. He knew that Cale would get suspicious if he saw someone shadowing them, so he kept his distance. Surveillance was easy enough utilizing micro-drones. In truth, if he had wanted to, Thilgod would not even have had to leave his office. He was a hunter at heart though, and the opportunity to get some fresh air in the lush gardens of the capital was never something he turned down.

Keeping his distance and avoiding Atworth's security detail, Thilgod watched and listened.

"I'll get straight to the point," Cale said to Atworth. "I'm looking for a man who may have come through here. He goes by the name of Brokk, a fugitive of the Galactic Order."

Thilgod leaned back on his bench and closed his eyes. Yes, he remembered Brokk. A golden-skinned monster that had swept through Kostia's defenses in a matter of weeks. A beast who came as a conqueror and returned to his ships before the bodies got cold.

"I'm sorry," Atworth lied. "I haven't crossed paths with anyone named Brokk." He paused reflectively. "I'm glad I didn't though . . . if you say he's a fugitive," he quickly added. "We're a small planet and just barely getting on our feet."

Thilgod could see Cale nod and smile. *Was the young commander buying it?* In Thilgod's experience, one didn't simply travel across the galaxy and interview the leader of another planet based on a hunch. Thilgod knew the Tassians had been embarrassed during the battle over Tassi. Now, they sought to hunt down the perpetrators and find justice at the Galactic Order.

"I came because there was a battle here a few months ago," Cale said pointing towards the ever-present nebula that shone brightly in their sky. Hues of green and red cast an eerie light across the garden, barely overpowered by their own sun. "A Jark fleet was attacked by Brokk and his crew. Since then, he has pirated more than a hundred vessels in this sector. You've heard of none of this?"

Atworth chuckled again, more jovial this time. He was having fun playing coy with the young Tassian commander. A true politician at heart, Thilgod noted. "It sounds like you've done your research in the sky, young man," he said with a condescension that the aged often brought against youth, "but do you know the history of my planet?"

Cale raised an eyebrow but didn't respond. The two had stopped walking through the garden now and, near a bench, Atworth gestured for him to sit. The stone pathway continued to wind a few meters farther before forming a large circle. At the center was a toppled over statue of Kostia, the reptilian dictator that Brokk helped overthrow. Cale accepted the offer and sat, staring at the statue for a moment before returning his eyes to Atworth.

"We've been involved in a bloody civil war for almost twenty years." Atworth pointed towards the broken white marble. "The man on the statue is Kostia Klavarnyk. He led an insurrection to overthrow my government. I've been fighting to regain power ever since. I'm sure you can imagine our focus has been on slightly more selfish things," Atworth suggested.

Cale squinted at Atworth and then examined the garden. He tried to piece it all together, suddenly aware of the potential instability here.

"Kostia," Atworth continued, "traded slaves for the Hestonians and the Jarks. He destroyed our mining and manufacturing but left the spaceport as a way to transfer the precious cargo to our surface. He was a puppet for big governments that wanted others to do their illegal work in the shadows. The truth is, you are the first ship we've hosted since we regained power just a few months ago. I would love to show you our mining operations if you have time. We are an ambitious government and would like to find our place once more in the galaxy," he added.

Cale didn't say anything for a moment. He looked around the garden, examined the statue, and then looked above at the tall government building. "How long ago did you overthrow him?" Cale asked at last.

"Oh, just a few months. As you can see, we are still cleaning up." He pointed to the statue again and then laughed a bellicose laugh. "I was thinking of replacing that with a statue of me. What do you think, dear boy?"

Cale didn't smile this time and Thilgod wondered if Cale would piece the timeline together; if he would find it odd that the rebellion occurred at roughly the same time that Brokk had arrived in this sector.

"I think you should leave the statue just where it is," Cale suggested sternly. "Perhaps it could remind you what happens to dictators who exploit their people while in league with powerful allies."

Atworth smiled at that. "Yes," he finally said, "perhaps that is the best idea yet."

The boy has some teeth, after all, thought Thilgod.

"I didn't realize that Jark influence stretched out here, and the Hestonians too," Cale commented. "You must think the Tassians are just minor players in a galaxy already teeming with others."

"Wickedness stretches everywhere," Atworth said with a growl. "I hope we can put that part of our past behind us. Our goal is to be neutral and the Tassians would be welcome to aid us in our endeavor."

Cale nodded. "Agreed. If you haven't heard of Brokk then, perhaps, you've heard another name. I'm looking for my father, Remmel. He was kidnapped by Brokk during a war on my home planet. My intelligence suggests Brokk took him here; if only to refuel before leaving again." Cale removed a thin piece of glass from a pouch on his chest and held his thumb on it until a photo of Remmel appeared as a hologram in the air above.

Thilgod's heart raced when he heard the name. His adrenaline surged when he saw the photo through the eyes of a drone. The Tassian was tall and slender with white hair. His face weathered and covered in scars. As shrewd as a serpent. Remmel, slaughtered by the witch in the woods. His body was never buried. It would have rotted months ago, and bones would have been picked clean by scavengers. Remmel, the brilliant tactician that Brokk poured his hate into. The mastermind of their defeat on Tassi. The leader of the insurgency that swarmed right under his own nose. Now, Remmel's son had come here looking for him. Thilgod wondered what he should do. *Kill him? No. Use him.*

For once, Atworth didn't need to watch his words. Placing a hand on the young commander's shoulder, he gave his visitor a compassionate look. "Please accept my deepest condolences. A son should never have to track down his father. You can have whatever resources I can provide to aid in your search, but I believe I can confidently say, your father is not on this planet. I haven't seen a Tassian in ages."

"Would Brokk have sold him into slavery here?" Cale asked. Thilgod detected a hint of hope in his voice.

"No," Atworth said definitively. "We have ended slavery. If he had been enslaved before I took power, he would have registered after the rebellion and been returned to your people. Your father is not here. Not since I've been in charge anyway," he added.

Cale rose to his feet, startling Atworth. "So, there is a chance!" he exclaimed. "You admit it yourself that you didn't know enough before reclaiming the ruling seat to say definitively that he is not here?"

Atworth nodded slowly. Cale's insistence frustrated, even worried him.

"I would like to investigate further," Cale said. "Sources tell me that Brokk has been here and are contrary to the information you've provided me thus far. It would be wise of you to cooperate. I will stop at nothing to find my father."

The boy has teeth, Thilgod thought again. He felt rejuvenated. Driven by his heart, hope pumped through his veins. *Perhaps Dacia and I can escape with our lives after all.*

"Of course," Atworth responded, climbing slowly to his own feet with a grunt. "You'll have to excuse my age," he said with a chuckle. Atworth's smile flattened as he moved closer to Cale. "I've worked hard to bring security to this planet, but there are still lawless parts. If you go north, you'll find provinces that still reject my governance. Go at your own risk. In the south, beyond the ocean, contains pockets of resistance as well. Unlike your homeworld, you must consider Charoth divided for now."

"Thank you," Cale responded, shaking Atworth's hand before walking away.

Thilgod sat on his own bench for a while, watching the drone follow Cale along city streets and back towards the city center. Back towards his bench. He had to make contact with him. Thilgod knew it down to his bones. If Cale found his father with his help, perhaps the young Tassian would take pity on him. Perhaps he would even be able to escape this wretched planet.

***

Cale reached the building that Atworth had offered as a hotel and passed it. He wasn't interested in staying in a dingy room overlooking a worthless city. Cale hadn't come here to vacation. He had come to find his father or bring justice to the ones who had taken him. Tonight, he would return to his battleship. His intelligence officers, posing as delegates, were meeting with representatives of Charoth to ask similar questions about the government on Charoth and their involvement with Brokk. Once the meetings had completed, they would compare notes and decide how to proceed.

At the top of the government quarter, Cale was amazed to see the view. The atmosphere of Charoth was thinner than Tassi and with the city at twenty thousand feet above sea level, he could see an incredible distance. Instinctively, Cale looked north towards the areas that Atworth had claimed were hostile to his government. In the distance, he could see the light gray haze that shadowed mountains shooting skyward. The northern gates. Perhaps, Cale wondered, there would be sympathizers that were still loyal to the dictator Kostia. Perhaps he could ask questions to the residents in the north that the central government here would be tight-lipped about. In the morning, Cale would journey north.

Above, the beauty of the rainbow nebula shone through the atmosphere. Somewhere inside that deadly assortment of gasses, Brokk had waged a vicious battle. Perhaps he was up there still. As Cale surveyed the city, he saw a bystander who looked out of place. A Hestonian sat on a bench opposite the fountain and the government building.

He wore a brown trench coat and military boots. A thick canvas collar rode high on his neck in an attempt to conceal the butt of a rifle strapped underneath. The Hestonian alone wouldn't have been enough to set off any alarms, but the creature with him was something Cale had never seen before. At his side was a massive four-legged animal. Its fur bristled, and, between heavy panting, Cale could see a mouth full of razor-sharp teeth shining brightly in the sun.

Cale walked towards him. The creature growled. Cale placed a hand on his sidearm on his hip. The man looked up and smiled. "Easy girl," he said to the beast. "The name's Thilgod. I hear you are asking questions about some visitors we had here."

Cale nodded but stopped short to give himself distance in case the animal charged him. "I'm looking for a Tassian named Remmel. He was captured by a half-Jark named Brokk."

Thilgod closed his eyes for a moment and then fixed his gaze on Cale. "The Tassian is dead," he said flatly. His eyes were a cold steel blue. "He was killed by a witch named Tamara. She is with the one you call Brokk. They aren't here anymore and now, I am an outcast."

"You want to leave the planet?" Cale intuited.

He nodded. "I want revenge."

"Show me where he died," Cale ordered.

CHAPTER EIGHT

Casika's eyes shot open. Her heart raced and her temples thumped. The room was dark, far too dark for her to see anything, but she knew someone lurked nearby.

Her hotel felt stuffy, but she dared not shift the blankets off her body. Noise buzzed from the temperature control unit above her and hindered her efforts to identify other sounds nearby.

Was that a creak on the floor? She couldn't tell. *Another one? Is something moving towards me? A footstep?* She couldn't tell. The sounds were muffled and distant. The temperature control unit was too noisy. Maybe she was being paranoid. Maybe she was still dreaming?

Casika strained to listen. Nothing. No noise, no movement, no shadows. Nothing. Just her room.

No one is here now, and no one was here before. You're anxious about testifying tomorrow, she told herself. *Then prove it,* her mind ordered. *Climb out of bed and prove it.*

Casika cautiously shifted her hips against the soft mattress in her large bed and reached out for the light on the nightstand. The wood was cold. Casika patted the hard corner and reached farther towards the center. She could feel the cool brass base of the light now. *Where was that button?* She never found it.

A gloved hand grabbed her arm and twisted it. She screamed but a pillow came down fast over her head, muffling her cry and making it impossible to breathe. Casika kicked and squirmed only to feel the pressure tighten on her face. The attacker grabbed her other arm now, twisting it hard across her back. A cold metallic chill went up her arms as handcuffs tightened against her wrists.

Holy cow, she thought. *This is it, they're going to kill me.*

The weight of someone pressed against her back. *Heavy.* She couldn't move. The pillow was hot on her face. Each muffled cry forced more oxygen out of her chest than she could breathe in. His crushing weight pressed against her ribcage and her lungs. Her shoulders burned as the attacker pushed up against her wrists, controlling her movement and rendering her helpless to fight back.

Desperation and panic seized her. *I'm going to die. What could these maniacs want? Cale!* Her mind screamed out for the Tassian that meant the whole world to her. Cale. Her beloved. The only one she would miss. There were so many things she had wanted to tell him, so much she had planned to do when she returned to Tassi. It was too late. *I'm going to die.*

She could feel hands on her legs as a second attacker pulled her knees together and wrapped them with rope. The fight left her. Desperate for oxygen she stopped squirming and breathed slowly into the mattress below. She needed air. Black and red spots danced around her eye sockets. Her face felt cold and weak. Pain surged from her legs to her hips as her attackers cinched the rope tight against her knees and then moved to her ankles.

She was immobilized. Paralyzed. Terrified.

A warm gloved hand moved up to her neck and grabbed her tightly. The hand felt large and heavy as it pushed her head deeper into the mattress below. Casika didn't fight it this time, ready for one of them to choke the last bit of air from her lungs and leave her to die in a hotel room on Hestos.

Instead, the pillow was lifted and replaced with a heavy cloth sack, tying it tight around her throat. Suddenly, Casika felt the weight come off her back as an arm pulled her to her knees. Oxygen, sweet, savory oxygen flooded her mouth and nose as she gasped for air. The black and red spots cleared, and her lungs quieted their protests.

"Don't try to scream," snarled a deep voice in front of her. "The mask will only suffocate your efforts."

Jark, thought Casika. The voice was obviously, inextricably Jark. The weight of her body pressed painfully down on the ropes that bound her knees together. Her shoulders ached, and her face burned. The sack over her head was heavy and hot.

"Edet sends his regards," the voice continued. "You're going to regret bringing charges against the Empire."

So that's what this is about. She should have been smarter. She could have hired security and made sure to hide the location of where she stayed at night. She could have voiced her concerns yesterday about being followed. Moved rooms. Called the Tassian embassy. Slept with a knife. *Foolish and stupid and naive!*

Tears mixed with sweat poured from her forehead to her cheeks and down her neck. Salt mixed with blood from a busted lip tasted bitter on her tongue.

"Wait!" she cried. "You don't have to do this!" Her voice against the heavy sack fell flat as if the sack itself absorbed the sound before it had a chance to be heard.

"Did you hear something?" one of the men grumbled.

Laughter to her right indicated they had. "She's trying to plead with us or something," whispered the second Jark. "Too bad we can't understand you," he teased in her ear.

"Do you have the shot?" the first asked the second.

"I almost forgot," he replied.

Casika could hear something that sounded like a zipper opening from behind her. *Shot,* she thought. *Needle,* her mind screamed. *They're going to give you something.* Panic erupted once more. Casika squirmed but accomplished nothing. She was fully and completely bound.

One of them touched her shoulder and tugged down at the loose silk shirt she had worn to bed, exposing her shoulder and the upper part of her arm. *Needle,* her mind screamed again. *They're going to drug you.* Try as she might to resist, the fear of fighting while a needle was inside her overcame her desire to avoid whatever drug they planned to pump into her veins.

Suddenly, a prick of pain and then a coolness filled her shoulder. The cold liquid spread from her shoulder to her wrists and then down to her fingers. They tingled, but Casika realized she no longer cared. The pain in her legs had disappeared, replaced instead by a weightlessness that felt both strange and comfortable.

Casika felt one of the men brush her left shoulder and then grab her under her knees but now it was distant, as if he was merely a specter or a ghost. Casika was certain that she still rested in her bed, comforted by the warmth of her blanket and a gentle ocean breeze coming through the window.

In one motion she was lifted, cradled like a child, and comforted in strong arms. Heavy footsteps, mimicked by a rhythmic bounce lulled her mind deeper into whatever dream state she had entered.

She could feel a cool breeze from an open window blowing against her bare legs. Casika tried to fight the effects of the drug. *You aren't in your bed you fool,* her mind told her. *They are taking you out the window, so the cameras won't catch them in the hallway.* She didn't let that detail bother

her though. She felt calm. Fingers fiddled with her waist and a metallic click told her she was going outside. Then she was weightless and soaring upwards, never to see Hestos again.

CHAPTER NINE

After the third knock on a wooden, dust-covered door a bolt slid out of place and a frail Jark met them at the entryway. *Jaki'el.*

"Please, please, come in," the thin Jark stammered, shuffling out of the way of Canis and Tamara to reveal a dimly lit hovel decorated with dark walls and even darker wood floors.

As Tamara entered, the black wood floor creaked beneath her feet. Plaster walls were peeled at seams where Jaki'el or his visitors would have brushed against them over hundreds of gatherings and feasts. Oval archways separated the rooms and a scent similar to tarib or pine hung in the air. Candles flickered against the walls, forcing her shadow to dance back and forth as she surveyed the scene. It was game time, and Jaki'el was her first victim. The first one to fool and convince.

A slam and shuffling behind her indicated Jaki'el was coming to lead her through the home. His thin figure appeared from the entryway as he crept toward her on all fours, examining her feet and her legs first. His dim eyes lingered at her clawed hands. When he met her eyes, he staggered backward. Tamara let the fire burn brightly and then, with the snap of her finger, she sucked the oxygen from the candles around her and plunged their room into utter darkness. *Make him fear you.*

The rich green flame surged upward from her eyes until the entire room basked in her eerie light. Jaki'el continued backing up until he was flat against the wall. His old hands trembled and his heart beat fast. She could feel all of him. Stale air hung in his lungs. His joints, missing their liquid lubricant, ground hard against each other at the bones. Teeth, long worn thin, hung loosely in his mouth.

"The dead favor you, Jaki'el," Tamara boomed in the silence. "I am here to proclaim a message to you and your followers, but none will hear it until all are gathered in my presence."

The frail Jark nodded quickly. "Of course, prophetess. Of course," he stammered.

Tamara calmed the flame and lit his candles once more. "Then let us go," she whispered. "The journey was long, and we have much to do. Show me our rooms."

The man crept forward from the wall and motioned with his hand, "This way, prophetess. We've been preparing your place for some time now. All should be in order."

"For how long?" Canis asked, clearly as perplexed by the wording as Tamara was at the prospect of them expecting her. Canis had sent an advance party only a few weeks ago, consisting primarily of soldiers trained in unconventional warfare and tasked with identifying locals in the population who could be brought to their cause.

Jaki'el turned a narrow corner and placed his hand on a black wooden door. Thorns from the tree used to craft the door had not been carved off and formed long jagged tips that looked more like a torture platform than the entry to a bedroom chamber.

"We've been working on her room for three months now. I trust that it will be to your exact specifications," he said as he turned to Canis.

Canis raised an eyebrow and was about to speak when Tamara cut him off. "You did good to listen to my messengers," she said gently. "What else did they tell you?"

Jaki'el looked from Tamara to Canis and back to her again. "Two of the three speakings have come to pass. One has yet to come," he stuttered, taking his hand off the door and resting once more on all fours at her feet. "The dead spoke to me in threes. First, after our loss at Tassi, I was to lay naked on the steps of the emperor's home for three days. Second, I would host a powerful prophetess and was to begin building your room on the third month. Lastly, three hundred million of us would die in a plague that covered the world."

"The grootslang," she muttered under her breath to herself, still astonished at the second prophecy.

"No, my prophetess," he interrupted. "A plague, not a grootslang." He looked unsure of himself and once more looked shyly towards the ground. "Of course," he added. "Your servant could be mistaken."

Tamara gave a raised eyebrow to Canis before motioning the man to continue. "Please," she said, "show us the room."

Jaki'el rested his hand again on the black door, being careful to avoid the thorns. Once open, the door revealed a large circular room. Thorny trees with dark blue flowers grew up from pots in the corners, and candles lined the walls. A candelabra hung from the center of the ceiling and was lit with six fat candles. A rug made of some type of animal lay on the black wood floors and two desks were pushed neatly against the wall.

"One for each of you," Jaki'el whispered. "I trust this is what you expected?" he asked eagerly.

"It's perfect," she smiled to appease his anxious soul. "Now, please, I have much to do and the trip took longer than we expected. We will emerge at suppertime to discuss the gathering of our people."

"Of course," the hairy Jark stammered. "I'll be just down the hall if you need anything."

Tamara watched as the frail old Jark shuffled from the room and closed the door. She expected to sense him lingering beyond in the hallway but was grateful when she heard his footsteps move down the hall to his own room. Exhaustion flooded over her, and, before she could look around the room, Tamara fell backward into a wooden chair that creaked under her weight.

"I feel like I've been transported back in time," she muttered, pulling the golden hood from her head and watching a shower of dust from the storm fall into her lap.

Canis grunted. "There is a significant divide between the rich and the poor here. Much of Jark consists of an elite who doesn't provide for those less fortunate. Our class system ensures generations of poverty and the only way out is to join the military or to marry into wealth. As you can imagine, the latter is rare."

"Is that why you joined?" Tamara asked, feeling sorry for the Jark who revealed a new battle scar every time they spoke.

"No," he said plainly. "I am from the elite. I joined because I believe our struggle with poverty is a result of galactic sanctions that won't allow us to climb a larger ladder of prosperity. I believe the Jarks are an oppressed species who have a great destiny. I fought with Brokk to see that destiny realized."

"By taking a planet that belongs to someone else?" Tamara asked.

He squinted his eyes but nodded. "Is that not what we have all done throughout history? We start with tribes and nations. By the time we move to planets, some have conquered quicker than others. The ones who show up to the table last are already at a disadvantage. Should Hestos have any right to dictate how Jark is allowed to operate while bloodstained by their own conquests?"

He had a point. The Galactic Order wasn't necessarily fair; it was about establishing rules that benefited the major members of the order. That's why they didn't interfere with the slavery on Charoth, and it was probably why they have allowed Despona to be exploited by the Jarks and others. Tamara herself could empathize. After all, she was employed by the mercenary Red before being captured and enslaved.

"I supposed might makes right," she agreed, pausing to think. "But is war the only option?"

He grunted again. "It doesn't have to be war, but without a strong military and without a powerful financial industry, you are left looking up to the rich rather than staring them in the eyes."

"So that is why people are against the current ruler?"

"He isn't tough enough to stand up to the Galactic Order," Canis growled.

Tamara could tell she hit a sore spot on the old warrior's soul. His body tensed, and his eyes flared. For a second or two, she suspected Canis forgot that she had even existed at all; his mind fluttered back to the past like delicate wings riding the waves of time. It was just Canis and the emperor now. Perhaps Brokk was there too. When he blinked, it was Canis again, and whatever memories haunted him were mere specters that had once more been relegated to the deepest parts of his soul.

"What do we make of the old fool's prophecy from the dead?" he whispered, changing the subject to more relevant matters. Finding his own chair, Canis leaned back and extended his legs. "Do you think there is any truth to the things he says?"

"This culture is all new to me," Tamara replied. "What about you? Do you believe him?"

He scoffed. "Prophets and preachers all have ulterior motives. He has a following, and he needs to gain legitimacy with you. It is just as likely this room housed one of his offspring before he offered it to us."

"Perhaps," she admitted. "But the two desks and the beds made neat. It feels like more than circumstance."

"Maybe one of our operatives let slip that there were two of us."

"And the plague?" she interrupted. "The plague that would kill millions."

"Do we not play the same game?" Canis leaned forward in his chair. "You are preparing to proclaim a great darkness will fall on the land and that beasts will walk the ground until our golden-skinned hero returns to seize power. The vagueness of his prophecy suggests he knows just enough to claim he spoke the truth when a real or symbolic plague does occur."

A rumble rose in Canis's throat. Tamara could sense the heat that rose to his face and the anger that poured from his words. "History is riddled with these charlatans who can gain a following by saying nothing at all," he continued. "The prophet claims a plague or a harvest of the righteous only to recant and shift his opinions when they don't come true. Prophets go back and say the harvest was spiritual or the plague was a reference to a disease that struck the crops last year. It never ends. If you make enough predictions, eventually you get one or two right. Fools follow these charlatans and hand over their young ones to be sacrificed." He grunted once more but did not speak.

Perhaps he was reminiscing about his past, Tamara wondered. Maybe he is still bitter about his near-sacrifice to the monster on Tassi. Tamara couldn't tell but knew it didn't matter in the long run. Canis was resilient and determined. He wouldn't let his thoughts influence the mission.

Tamara leaned back and stared at the door. Inch-long thorns specked the planks of the black wood door that was anchored to a black metallic rock at the near wall. A certain eeriness filled her. It was an uncertainty that went beyond that of dealing with powerful leaders. There was a darkness on Jark that Tamara had never experienced. It was a place where magic and science intertwined. It was a culture where the supernatural could exist alongside the rational. It terrified her.

Tamara was no sorceress, no prophetess. She was a Lysop, a species that could experience and manipulate elements as naturally as exhaling breath onto the face of another person. There was nothing magical about the things she did. There was nothing unnatural about them either. Anyone who attributed her actions to magic was misinformed. Tamara would use the Jark superstition against them here but it occurred to her that she might be outmatched.

Jark was different. If the summonings were true, Jark was a place where a power that she did not understand resided. If the dreams of Jaki'el were true, Jark had a religion that demonstrated something that no other religion had been able to demonstrate: proof. This tangible, tactile proof scared Tamara more than she ever had been before. If this prophet's dreams came from beyond the grave, Tamara wasn't sure she could, or even wanted to compete with this other authority.

Even now, sitting in the presence of a friend, Tamara experienced the elements that swirled around her differently after arriving on Jark. Fire from the candles burned at unsteady temperatures, rising and dropping as if some unknown entity was passing in front of them. The sulfur that saturated the air swirled against the natural currents as if some unknown force powered it. And the incessant bubbling of mercury in the city streets contained a density that suggested there was more inside than just mercury.

"I've seen this look on you before, Tamara. What has you worried?" Canis asked in an unusually introspective voice.

Tamara moved her eyes from the thorny door to the old warrior's scarred face. She was glad to have him interrupt her ever-deepening thoughts. "I'm wondering if we are in over our heads."

If he had a response, she wouldn't hear it. The door swung open, and the stunned face of their host appeared in the entryway.

"Prophetess," he panted. "You must come with me at once. The soulless wandering has begun just like my dreams predicted. The plague is upon us."

Tamara looked from the old man to Canis and back again. Canis's eyes were narrow, and his look was suspicious. *Get a grip,* she told herself. *You're the one in charge. Make the prophecy come true. This is Brokk's battle. You are simply the messenger.*

Tamara pulled her golden hood over her head and climbed from her chair to join him at the door. "Of course, it has, Jaki'el," she responded calmly. "Show them to me."

CHAPTER TEN

By the time Tamara reached the front of the home, a crowd had gathered outside. She was grateful to see that the storm subsided, and the wind and dust were settled. A scarlet glow, like a scarf wrapped around her neck on a cold day, covered the sky. Streaks of orange and black, sewn into the red like a tapestry of fire complimented the colors, and Tamara suddenly saw the beauty here.

Black onyx and diamond structures erupted all around her, constructed with the pride and expertise that only master craftsmen could perfect. Jark was a dark place, but it was a majestic place as well. Movement through the crowd caught Tamara's attention and as she looked down the dusty road that passed by Jaki'el's home, Tamara saw two Jarks staggering towards them.

Jaki'el, wasting no time, rushed into the street and vied for the crowd's attention.

"People, people," he shouted. "Listen to me. These two are plagued. This is the plague I've proclaimed against this land. This is the soulless wandering. Stay away from them. Stay away!"

Tamara watched as Jaki'el ran to the front of the crowd on the dusty road and held up his hands at the two Jark wanderers who staggered towards him on all fours. "Stop!" he shouted. "I won't allow you to infect this town!"

Tamara considered stepping out of the entryway and into the street but felt a firm hand grip her. Reading her mind, Canis held her in place. "You don't want to get in the middle of this," he warned her. "Let it play out."

"Get out of the way," a large Jark growled from the crowd of people. "These two need help, they aren't soulless at all. They need food and water."

Jaki'el lowered his hands and turned once more to the growing mass of people who crowded the road behind him. "I've foreseen this," he pleaded. "This is the judgment against our emperor for the countless crimes he commits against our people. The dead send us a message in the form of these two men. Stay away!"

"You're a fool," barked another. "Out of the way or we'll move you."

Jaki'el surveyed the crowd and then looked over his shoulder at the two Jarks who had stopped less than a dozen feet away. They swayed lazily on their hands, and their eyes were unfocused. Tamara reached out to them, ran her ethereal fingers across their cheeks, through their black hair, and felt the red skin on their arms, back, and shoulders.

Beads of sweat rolled down their backs and pooled in the crevices of their filthy clothes. They were famished, starving. *Where had they come from?* Tamara dove further into them, scouring their skin with her consciousness and trying to understand what was taking place. There was a certain emptiness about them. Their heads felt hot, and their eyes were confused. It was as if Jaki'el was right, the two Jark males were walking, but they were utterly absent of reality.

Canis seemed to sense it too and, as Tamara scraped her consciousness across their bodies for something tangible, the hardened warrior let out a grunt. "They're dazed," he observed. "They stagger forward with no sense of direction or purpose. This is not the Jark way. This is not a Jark walk."

The crowd had enough. The large Jark at the front grabbed Jaki'el and pushed him aside. "Clear the way, fool," he hissed as others poured past him, embracing the two wanderers and leading them off toward the center of town. Jaki'el watched for a moment before slinking back to the steps of his home.

"Is it truly impossible to change the future, Prophetess?" he asked. His shoulders were rolled forward, and his eyes were downcast. *Defeated.* He must have honestly believed what he was preaching on the streets. He was no charlatan, Tamara concluded. The thought sent shudders up Tamara's spine. She avoided the supernatural deliberately. Jark seemed to be a place teeming with it.

"What's done is done," Tamara responded, remaining firm in her role as a prophetess despite the confusion that lurked deep within. "We are here to alter the future of Jark. Do you lose faith so easily?"

"No, prophetess." He shook his head fervently. "I hoped that with your arrival, I would not have to watch so many of my countrymen die."

The pity-filled Jark inched an arm up the first step. Tamara lowered herself to him. She ran her golden claws through the hair on his head and down his face, finally finding a place to rest them on his shoulder. His skin felt hot compared to hers but was normal relative to the heat that radiated from the soulless wanderers who had passed moments earlier.

"My dear Jaki'el," she comforted, "many sacrifices are required so that the elect might thrive. Your role is to preach our message to the elect, not to determine who those elect might be. Those who listen and believe will be the ones who bring Jark to its future glory. The chosen will survive this and will thrust Jark into a new age of prosperity."

Jaki'el sighed a breath of sulfur-infused air. Tamara had to struggle to avoid coughing back into the old Jark's face. He raised crimson and black eyes to meet hers and parted his lips until his worn teeth were fully visible. "A purge of the unbelievers so that the elect might prosper," he said. "We must speak to the dead at once!"

Canis growled and Tamara stepped back. She could feel the anger behind her. "That isn't necessary," he hissed. "You have her. You need not speak to the dead anymore."

"Oh, but we must!" Jaki'el insisted. "They told me this afternoon that they had to speak to you."

"I need to meet your followers," Tamara replied. "I have a message for them."

"So do the dead," Jaki'el nodded. "So do the dead."

Without waiting for a response, he rushed past the two of them and stormed into the home. Pots and pans clanged while drawers opened and slammed. "We have to hurry!" he shouted at them from somewhere inside. "We will meet the entire congregation at midnight!"

***

Burgundy streaks gave way to utter blackness as the three trekked over hardened lava and shale.

"They're suspicious and track the movement of vehicles," Jaki'el had told them. "We have to walk to our meeting place."

Tamara hadn't liked the sound of that and liked it even less now that they were a few hours into their journey. Clouds had once again filled the atmosphere, blocking out any light that the weary travelers might gain from one of three Jark moons. On his back, Jaki'el carried a knapsack which he shuffled and adjusted every few minutes. When the much larger Canis offered to carry his bag for him, Jaki'el scoffed.

"This is my burden alone," he humbly protested.

Canis ground his teeth but offered no more. Tamara wondered still if the prophet was a fake or was actually hearing from the dead. Tonight promised to be full of information

"Just a few more turns," Jaki'el groaned under the weight of his knapsack.

The three had entered a valley with red rocks on either side. As they funneled deeper into the gorge a cool wind picked up and slapped Tamara in the face. In the distance, she could see a dim glow.

"Candles," Jaki'el whispered, pausing a moment to give his hands a break against the rocky ground. Unlike Canis, Jaki'el had walked on three of his four appendages for most of the trip, while gripping the handle of his sack with his fourth. "We're close. Give me a moment to gather myself, it's important that I come to them looking a certain way."

Canis rolled his eyes behind Jaki'el's back, and Tamara did her best not to smile. The small Jark was certainly eccentric, and Tamara knew Canis had little patience left for the old priest. As he lowered his bag and dug through it, a noise carried on the wind caught her attention. *Chanting.* Someone was chanting.

From his bag, the soothsayer and priest removed a red gown and white paint, which he smeared across his face and hands. Reaching deeper, he withdrew a five-foot stick, as black as lava rock and covered with thorns. Attached to the stick and hanging by a rope was a jagged dagger made of bone.

"Person or animal?" Tamara asked, startling Jaki'el from his routine.

He looked up at her for a moment and muttered before putting his head back to his work. "Person, of course," he mumbled under his breath.

Complete with his transformation, Jaki'el, priest for the dead, rose and swung the bag back over his shoulder. The white on his face and hands stood out against the dark backdrop of the red canyon walls. His staff and dagger were menacing and even the frail Jark's teeth seemed to transform into something more formidable than the old prophet that walked with them mere moments before. "Shall we?" he asked, looking over his shoulder.

Tamara nodded, and Jaki'el picked up a brisk pace. They must have been close. The canyon twisted and turned, each bend descending the three deeper and deeper into the belly of Jark. Chanting echoed loudly off the rocky walls, and an orange glow from candlelight beckoned them forward. A chill had risen in the night; a dampness that rested on the back of Tamara's neck coiled snuggly against her hair.

The three turned around the next bend and saw the gathering. The three of them had come out on the top of a massive cliff. It was a platform of rock that jutted out over a crater below. As they emerged, the gentle humming turned to a cheer as the excitement and the energy of people below vibrated the rocks where she stood. Tamara could feel energy and power surge within her from their welcoming cries.

Directly below her was a pond of silver mercury, rippling from the noise and commotion of the crowd. Candles, reflecting brilliantly off the liquid metal, created such a magnificent array of oranges and yellows that Tamara almost forgot her reason for coming. It was Jaki'el's voice that brought her purpose back into focus.

"Friends!" he shouted, raising his hands into the sky. The crowd hushed, and instantly there was absolute silence. *Jark order and discipline existed even among the fanatics.* "I have something special for you," he said, voice resonating off the cavernous walls to give the frail Jark more authority than he deserved, "but first, let us give to the dead."

Tamara looked at Canis with wide eyes, who fixed his own straight ahead. Drums boomed below in a sequence of three beats. *Boom, boom, boom. Boom, boom, boom.* The crowd parted and cheered as a young female Jark walked on two legs towards the lake of liquid metal. Tamara raced her ethereal self across the gorge to the young sacrifice. Her red skin was hot, and dark hair covered her body. She didn't tremble, and her eyes were focused. *Was this voluntary?*

As she reached the metal's edge, fingers and hands emerged, scraping upwards through the pond to grip her legs. *Boom, boom, boom.* The drums pounded louder and louder and more hands appeared. Dozens of slimy, hair-covered hands reached and pried at her legs but instead of retreating she willingly continued, wading up to her knees and then her waist, allowing whatever existed inside the pool to tug her deeper and deeper. Tamara scoured the pond with her senses trying to determine the source of the hands, but she couldn't. The mercury or some other field made it impossible to sense anything below the surface. *Could this be the dead Brokk had spoken about?*

"Stop this madness," Tamara hissed at Jaki'el. "I command you to stop this."

He looked at her, eyes wide in shock.

"Stop it!" she shouted at him. "This is not why I've come." Panic seized her. She had to stop this. She had to save the female from the beasts beneath the lake.

"That is not what the dead want," Jaki'el responded. "Control yourself, prophetess."

Tamara stepped towards him but felt Canis's hand grab her arm. *He didn't need to say anything to control her. He was right. Not now. Later, but not now.*

She looked back at the lake. Hands, terrible hands reached, groped, and pulled the Jark down until only her shoulders and then not even her head remained. She let out not even a whimper. The drumming stopped as the last bubble rose to the surface of the liquid metal. She was gone. A pit grew in Tamara's stomach egged on by regret that stemmed from the desperate thought that she should have done something. She should have acted to save that Jark's life. *But how?*

Jaki'el once more addressed the crowd. "Fellow Jarks, a prophetess has joined us. She comes from another world with a powerful message that the king of the dead wants us to hear." The crowd remained quiet and after a brief pause to allow the echoes of his voice to fade into silence, Jaki'el continued. "I saw a sign today with our lady's coming. The plague is upon us. Two are infected, but millions will fall. This," Jaki'el shouted with a thump of his stick, "is so the elect might rise to power!"

Taking a line from her already. *He is a charlatan after all*, Tamara decided. A deceiver. *The king of the dead.* The man spoke as if his importance went to the very king of the underworld. A small voice in her head asked, *Could it be?* Tamara's consciousness beat it backward. *Not possible.*

Tamara felt anger rise deep within her. The bloodthirsty crowd, however, revealed only joy and cheered as he stepped aside. It was now Tamara's turn, but she struggled to focus as the anger from their sacrifice boiled hot beneath her skin.

There was a time when Tamara too would have fearlessly walked to her death. She was a slave then. An object. She had nothing to look forward to and eagerly waited for death. She searched for it around every corner.

Brokk changed that for her. Not so for this Jark. No one willingly chose death over life. *Was the Jark enslaved? Beaten? Drugged? Fooled?* Suddenly, this movement was something she wasn't sure she wanted to be a part of. It was too barbaric and too superstitious. Jaki'el cleared his throat. She realized the crowd was waiting, but her thoughts refused her the option to move on. Something *had* to be done.

Tamara stepped up to the ledge and surveyed the crowd. She let her senses fly through them, feeling their heat and their energy. It would be so easy from this position to kill them. To allow her ethereal self to take them all. To ride beyond this cliff and up to the glory of the heavens on their screams. To teach them a lesson for the sacrifice who gave herself up for death. Whatever the reason. No reason.

Part of Tamara wanted that. Wanted them dead. Had she become an addict? Perhaps. She had to admit she derived a certain degree of pleasure from the power she held over them. *Was this how Jaki'el felt?*

Brokk's purpose held her back. Brokk had to be made preeminent in their minds. She owed him that. Tamara allowed her eyes to burn a pale green fire, and, raising her hands above her head, she allowed the fire to spread into her fingertips and simmer above them.

"The emperor must fall," she proclaimed. "He has betrayed the people. He has betrayed his military. He has betrayed this proud world. But there is a Jark who doesn't fear him, a Jark who doesn't fear the dead." Tamara accentuated the last word. A fearful hush fell across the crowd. She didn't care. Brokk believed the dead were powerless because they failed him on Tassi. She would speak fully and openly for him now. She would ensure this tradition died with the emperor.

"This," she continued, "is a Jark worthy to succeed him as king. Your prophet Jaki'el welcomed us as a sign from the dead. I assure you, my message brings more power than the dead could ever hope to provide."

Tamara paused to sense the crowd. To hear their words and feel their thoughts. She sensed a cold stare on the back of her neck. The breathing of the frail Jaki'el quickened. He was just as shocked at her message. Silence was all that returned to her. They needed a sign.

"It is time for you to rise against the established order. Spread the word to all the villages. Change is in the air. Brokk is the man who is chosen. None can resist him. Here is your sign. Soon, beasts will walk the ground and bring terror to the people of this land. Many will die. The emperor will be cast down before you, and Commander Brokk will crest the sky with his mighty battleship. Only once he arrives will peace once again fall upon us.

"I have one last command for you. The sacrifice to the dead will cease this instant."

The crowd murmured at this, but Tamara had already sensed the trap. Her ethereal self swirled through the crowd and hovered over the pool of mercury that began to bubble. Each fearful gasp after fearful gasp drove the mercury to bubble with greater and greater ferocity until it boiled out of control. Hands suddenly appeared, hundreds of hands. The hands of the desperate dead that had heard her final proclamation.

Jaki'el snickered. "Foolish woman," he sneered. "No power is greater than the dead. You'll regret your proclamation, woman."

Tamara would not be intimidated. She was to establish a new order here and to find new believers. The ancient rituals had to be no more.

Gasps rang louder below and people near the liquid lake of mercury pushed backward to escape the revolt, worried that the desperate hands of deceased souls would climb from the lake and take them all.

"Do not be afraid!" Tamara bellowed at the crowd. "The mighty Brokk has already slain the emperor's priests. Afterward he gained a great victory in the heavens."

"Lies!" Jaki'el hissed at her. "You will stop this instant," he bellowed, grabbing the jagged knife from his cloak.

Tamara expected his movement and side-stepped the labored slash of a priest who was used to helpless victims. Her training with Brokk and his soldiers had given her a swiftness the old Jark lacked. "Let's find out where the dead go next," Tamara muttered to Jaki'el. Pulling the sulfuric oxygen into the flame that hovered above her hands, she threw it into the lake. Green fire erupted on the surface and spread like wildfire across the metallic lake. Tamara pushed as much oxygen as she could into the flame, burning it hotter and hotter until the crowd below fled not from the hands but from the heat.

Jaki'el pulled an arm up to cover his eyes from the brightness, but she wasn't yet done with him. "Stop!" she shouted to the masses. "Watch the power of your old prophet!"

Grabbing more fire, Tamara thrust it at the exits of the rocky paths to prevent their escape. She sensed fear in the crowd. Panic. Jaki'el stepped backward but suddenly stopped. Canis was blocking his path. "Throw him in," she ordered the warrior whose face suddenly filled with a pleasure she had never seen before.

"Gladly," Canis growled, and before Jaki'el could protest, Canis grabbed him by the neck and flung him into the lake below.

"Spread the word!" she shouted to the shocked crowd of fanatics below. "A new priesthood is here! You can keep your sons and daughters from the dead! Instead of sacrificing your loved ones, we ask you submit yourselves as loyal patriots to the empire. Allow Brokk to propel us all to a new galactic prosperity!" She paused, allowing them to watch her in the green glow of her fire before cutting out the flame and disappearing with Canis behind the cliffs.

CHAPTER ELEVEN

The air was colder here. Stiffer. Thick green trees with needles the length of Cale's fingers created a canopy that blocked out the sun. A thin gray fog blanketed the ground and swirled around Cale's feet and ankles as he walked. The soldier inside told him to be wary of an ambush, and yet, something else drove him to keep moving. He was close. This *was* the place where his father died.

Ahead, the massive creature named Dacia sniffed the ground. Its black hair bristled and white fangs, coated in saliva, hung like stalactites from huge jaws. Every few feet she stopped to look up and sniff the air. She seemed cautious. Cale couldn't figure out if that was a good thing or if it should alarm him to something beyond.

Next to it stood a six-foot-tall bounty hunter. He wore a brown leather coat that clung to his knees. A black bolt-action rifle was strapped across his back. An aura of confidence surrounded the man and made Cale uneasy. *What were Thilgod's motives in bringing him here?* he wondered. *Could he really trust him? Would Cale's desire to find his father lead him foolishly into something worse?*

Trap, his mind called out. Cale wouldn't let cowardice get the best of him. He had come to find his father and if that meant wandering to the north with a bounty hunter and his corelve, that's exactly what Cale would do. Two other Tassians accompanied him, both royal marines and both committed to his protection. They flanked Cale on either side, ensuring they kept their distance to maximize their ability to react to any surprises. He looked at them now, checking to make sure he hadn't been abandoned. The one nodded and then the other. *Safety in numbers,* he lied to himself.

The beast stopped, and Thilgod and Cale stopped with it. Sniffing the air, her fur ruffled as she let out a deep-throated growl. "What is it, girl?" the bounty hunter prodded. Soft brown eyes behind a shag of gray hair looked back at him. She licked her lips. "This is where it happened," Thilgod shouted back to Cale. "She's mad at me for not bringing her with me, but I couldn't lose her like I'd lost her brother."

"Lost her brother?" Cale asked.

"The Jark you are hunting named Brokk killed him. The witch burned my lungs with fire. I'd been hunting them for a while before this point." He paused and looked up at the trees, pretending to peer through them at the nebula beyond. "Didn't know your father had his own plans," he added.

Cale couldn't tell if it was bitterness or regret. It didn't matter at this point and his guide didn't seem to want a response. Instead, Cale looked around. A crisp breeze pushed into his face from the west. Fingers of fog retreated beyond the next knoll. The ground was covered in ash and the trunks of the trees had been marked with a black residue from a fire that had burned out months ago. "Did someone try to burn the forest down?" Cale asked Thilgod at last.

The man's eyes glazed a bit as he remembered the battle. His hand subconsciously moved to his hip and rubbed it. *An old injury,* Cale suspected. *Nobody takes on a Jark without gaining a souvenir.*

"I fought a Jark here," he said at last. "One of your fugitive's men. I had planned to sneak up on him and kill him quietly, so I could catch his witch next. Your father surprised us both from just over there." Thilgod pointed through the trees. "He probably would have had him too, but the witch intervened. Played with his shots. Made it impossible to hit the Jark. After she killed him, she came for me."

Played with his shots. Cale knew superstition ran deep within Jark circles but didn't expect to hear so much from a Hestonian bounty hunter. "The night can play with a man's eyes," Cale responded honestly. "You don't need to cast blame away from my father for my sake. If he missed, he missed."

Looking at the ground, he kicked at the ash revealing the body of a spent grenade and grunted. "I'd lost the element of surprise and took a hatchet to the hip during the fight. I threw this to cover my escape," he said, pointing down as if Cale had missed what his foot had uncovered.

Cale walked past him and towards the direction the bounty hunter had heard the shots. Maybe it was foolish to take the lead. It still could have been a trap, but his desire was too great. Cale had to find his father. He had to see the body. Thorns and briers fought against his legs and blocked his path, but Cale pushed through them, slowly at first but gaining momentum with each step until he was almost jogging.

Needles poked and slashed at his legs. Most of them found flesh and some blood. Cale hardly noticed. Desire propelled him forward; destiny drove him onward. Low hanging branches objected, and vines opposed his vision, but he refused to be hindered, breaking into an all-out sprint.

The forest was thick and nearly impossible to see in, let alone fight through. His father had found a way. His father wouldn't be held captive and neither would Cale. At last, he saw what he'd been looking for. White bones clothed in brown cloth. The bones, picked clean by animals and insects, were Tassian; he could tell by the long arms and narrow hips. By his father's side was a black rifle. Jark. Cale recognized it from the Battle for Tassi. The bounty hunter had told the truth.

Dropping to his knees, Cale took a deep breath and surveyed his father's final resting place. The cloth was stained with a reddish hue. It was his father's blood, no doubt. He had been stabbed. Might have bled to death, which was no way for a general to die.

Cale's heart pounded hard in his ears. He could feel the hot rush of blood fill his face and cloud his vision accompanied by a surge of adrenaline and rage that only a person who'd lost their father could know. It was something he'd felt inside him for months as he searched. Now, the emotion that surged to the surface made his knees weak and his arms tremble. Darkness crept in from the corners of his eyes and a dense black fog suddenly rose from the ground.

Revenge. Cale had to get revenge and suddenly the biological attack wasn't enough. He needed Brokk. He had to find him.

"Father!" Cale, unaware of the other men in the forest or of the prospect of danger, cried out in a mix of pain and anguish. His chest heaved, and an empty ache he didn't know he had filled a chamber deep within his ribs. Tears flowed from his cheeks to his knees and onto the ground.

Had he died without knowing the fate of Tassi? Did he die in fear of the fate of his son or his people? This should not be. Remmel: a great general and leader of his people. Remmel: the hero of a successful rebellion. Father, the teacher of all he had learned. This shouldn't be.

Cale lowered his face to the white skull that had been picked clean by animals over the months and wept. "Father," he whispered at last. "We did it. We freed and rebuilt Tassi. Battleships are being fabricated. An army is being trained. I have a plan that will bring justice to you and our people.

"I hope you can hear me, father. I hope you see what I am about to do. On the back of your sacrifice, I will rebuild a better, more capable Tassi. I will build a Tassi that is formidable and feared. The Galactic Order is broken and worthless, and we will serve them no more. I swear to you I will get justice against the Jarks. Nothing will stop us."

The crunching of twigs brought Cale back from the brink. The fog that clouded his vision crept towards the edges of his eyes and then fled for good. A ray of sunlight peered through leaves above as Cale was released from his thoughts and brought back to the forest.

Instead of sorrow, Cale felt a tinge of joy and without care for the Hestonian bounty hunter behind him, he rolled over and laid his head next to his father's. Yellow rays from the sun and blue and red from the Rainbow Nebula stretched through the trees and warmed his face. It wasn't a terrible way to die here in these woods. It was peaceful.

"Was it morning or night?" Cale asked the man who stood above him, a corelve panted at his side.

"It was dusk," he replied. "Is it him?"

"Dusk," Cale repeated. "I imagine he would have stared up and seen the glory of the nebula pressing through the trees."

The bounty hunter didn't respond, and Cale didn't care. He wanted to wait here with his father for a bit and imagine his final view. It was beautiful, but then a dark thought entered his mind. He likely didn't see the nebula or the trees. He likely died staring his murderer in the eyes. This so-called witch. A shudder chilled Cale's spine.

Turning, Cale finally rose to his feet and eyed the bounty hunter. "I owe you a great deal for helping me find him. Earlier, you told me you wanted revenge. Is this still true?"

Thilgod gave a toothy smile. After patting Dacia's head, he looked back at Cale. "I don't have many friends here, and I have even fewer skills beyond hunting and tracking. If you offer me a job, I'll take it."

Cale frowned. "Can you pilot a ship?"

"How do you think I got here?" the man asked.

"I'll give you a ship when we get back to mine. Any info you gather about Brokk or his crew will earn you Tassian money. If you bring me his head, I'll give you more coin than you or that thing of yours could ever spend on any planet."

Thilgod smiled and stretched out his hand, which Cale accepted and shook. "If you cross me," Cale said pulling him in close, "I will hunt you down and kill you."

His creature growled at the change of tone, but Thilgod laughed. "I haven't crossed anyone I've worked for yet," Thilgod responded with a sympathetic look and a sly grin towards his creature Dacia. "Of course, that might be why I am presently in the situation I'm in."

Cale neither smiled nor acknowledged his last statement. "I'm going to stay here until the sun sets in the south. I want to see what he saw and then gather his bones and bring him back to my ship. Meet me at the spaceport tomorrow for payment."

He nodded and turned. His beast lingered a bit longer, staring at Cale stoically until she finally turned to join her master. Cale watched them depart and then sat back down in the dirt beside his father's body. Gemini had been right. His father hadn't died fighting on Tassi, but, after surveying the battle, he couldn't believe the warrior who trained him would have just surrendered either. It must have had a purpose. Cale would ask Brokk when he caught him.

CHAPTER TWELVE

Sabik woke to the steady drip of water against a steel basin. His head ached, and his chest burned. *What happened?*

Sabik strained to see the room around him. It was dark. Shades of gray followed the scout wherever he looked. Stone walls surrounded him on three sides. Thick bars formed a prison on the fourth.

Sabik lifted his hand to feel his face. A heavy chain protested the movement with an audible clink and a painful tug at his wrists. His hand came back down wet with blood. *What happened?*

Movement caught Sabik's attention. *Mlyma.* "Are you okay?" he groaned. "Mlyma?"

The sleek gray figure, having pushed up on her arms and rolled onto her back, let out a painful grunt at the overwhelming exertion required to complete such a task. He listened for her breathing. It was short and labored. *Mlyma,* he thought to her. *Speak to me.*

There was no response. Sabik dug deeper into his brain, exerting all the concentration he could to reach out to her telepathically but realized something was broken. The link was missing. He could no longer feel her presence within the collective, and yet, her movements suggested she wasn't dead.

"Mlyma," he said louder. "I can't feel you. Are you okay?"

The shadow moaned. Writhing from side to side, she lifted her hands to her head to cup her scalp. Sabik desperately wanted to get to her, but the chain kept him bound to his own wall.

Her cries rang out in the silence. She wept and then screamed, "Give it back, you monster! Give it back!"

"Give what back, Mlyma?" Sabik shouted. "I'm here! We're here together! Give what back?"

She sobbed but didn't respond to his prompts. Footsteps echoed off the walls of his prison cell. Someone was coming.

"Mateen scout," it boomed.

A light accompanied the voice and when Sabik looked up he couldn't hide his horror. A gray Mateen male stood eight feet tall over his cell, but his features were different. Crimson eyes had been replaced with a deep green. The gray skin, so familiar to his species, was marred. Red streaks poured over his odd-shaped face and ran down his neck. His head was distorted and no longer round. His left eye was larger than the right, an ear had shriveled and fallen. Symmetry was gone. Even his mouth curled downward the way a flower wilted in the summer heat.

"Stand," the voice ordered. Despite his diseased complexion, there was strength in that voice. Authority.

Sabik obeyed. His chain offered only slight resistance. They had captured him. His last memory was trying to evade the enemy ships. They had found something: a weakness in the enemy vessel but then his memory went blank. It had been too late. He could remember nothing else. They must have disabled his ship and captured him.

"What did you do to my crew?" Sabik demanded, motioning at Mlyma but wondering about the rest as well.

"What act of war have you instigated?" the Radaishar responded. "You violated our territorial boundaries and fired upon our defenses."

"That's a lie," Sabik hissed. "We were attacked. Under galactic law, I demand release."

The rebel stared for a moment. "You're a Mateen scout in service to the hive. We are not foolish as to your motives here. Cast your eyes upon your shipmate," he said pointing at Mlyma. "She will die in lonely agony if you do not tell us what we want to know. Welcome to Radaishar territory, scout." He turned and left before Sabik could say another word.

As he left, Mlyma erupted into another set of cries and moans. She was in utter agony. Sabik sat back against the corner of the wall and held his hands to his head. Her plea for comfort was driving him mad. Anger filled his soul. His head felt hot, his heart raced, and yet, he was powerless to take any action at all. *I am Mateen, fighting for the way of life of our people. I am prepared to give my life in their defense,* he told himself.

***

Lost contact. The two words no commander wants to hear tumbled around in Gemini's mind until it nearly exploded from his lips. *Lost contact. Sabik and his crew are missing.*

"I don't understand," Gemini finally said to Castor, his fleet executive officer. "We were tracking them during their movement, right?"

Castor nodded. "Yes, most of their movement. There's significant magnetic interference in Radaishar territory. It is even more complex receiving transmissions while we're traveling through subspace."

Gemini frowned. "That is Mateen territory." Castor nodded but remained silent. Gemini continued. "We've been doing this for a while, right? I mean, we know how to track our own ships in subspace." Castor nodded to the rhetorical question, but, before he could speak,

Gemini continued, "What about the crew themselves? We can't hear their thoughts?"

Castor shook his head this time and looked towards the ground. A pit formed in Gemini's stomach. He instinctively reached his telepathic mind towards his executive officer's but pulled back as soon as he felt Castor's thoughts. Fear, shame, and doubt clouded his most experienced officer's mind. *Lost contact.* The mental connection was all he needed to make his assessment.

"Bring the fleet out of subspace," Gemini ordered. "Until we can rule out enemy activity, we have to assume they were ambushed. We must assume they're dead. I want our intelligence section working around the clock analyzing the space around the separatist territories. If an explosion occurred, we must know about it. Where is the nearest deep station?"

Castor pulled the three-dimensional hologram from his computer and expanded it into the center of the bridge. A white streak indicated their journey from the moon Rodam towards Radaishar space. Two weeks of travel had left them close to the border, but they were still several days from the edge of the Galactic Order's authority. As Castor zoomed and rotated the hologram, two spaceports appeared. The Hestonians owned the closest of the two.

"Would you like to head to Drestner?" Castor asked.

Gemini nodded. "Yes. Let them know we need to restock supplies and gather intelligence. Tell them we lost contact with our reconnaissance vessels in rebel space and ask them to share any intelligence they may have collected."

Their pilot, a younger man with light gray skin and short brown hair, acknowledged and pulled back on the dampener control lever at his station. Gemini gripped the armrests of his seat as the ship lurched from subspace and onto the spatial plane. Some of his crew cheered a traditional chant, and Gemini recognized why.

Nobody knew what happened if you were trapped beyond space-time, and everyone was afraid to find out. Theoretically, unaffected by the laws of time, some believed a doomed crew was forced to forever patrol the undercurrents of the universe, always seeking but never finding a way out. Jark magic and summoning was the closest Gemini had ever come to believing there was truth to those stories. They had an ability to summon creatures from another world, possibly from below the very fabric of space itself. Gemini, however, preferred to leave the conjecture for his soldiers and kept his fingers crossed that he wouldn't have to find out for himself.

Looking at the hologram that displayed his fleet in three-dimensional space, Gemini watched as more and more of his ships exited their wormholes and began existing in the present. His armrests vibrated as powerful thrusters fired to propel his battleship towards the spaceport. Through the darkness of a starless void, a silver object appeared in the distance. *Drestner.*

As his fleet neared the silver diamond that seemingly hung on strings attached to nothing in the darkness of space, Gemini could see a flurry of activity. Massive Hestonian battleships docked along the center ring while smaller destroyers pivoted their angular brown vessels along the outer edge of the energy wall. *They must be preparing to deploy towards the fringe,* Gemini thought. *But so many vessels of war to witness the galactic merge. What do the Hestonians know . . .*

The space station on his three-dimensional map beamed at him, forcing his train of thought elsewhere. "Do we have a clearance code yet?" Gemini asked a radio operator who sat in the corner of the command center.

The thin gray Mateen stood and used his arms to exaggerate the virtual moving of data from his station into the main control. The space station, which was displayed as a yellow diamond-shaped object at the center of the display turned from yellow to green, indicating his fleet had been cleared to enter the energy wall that shielded it from the natural elements and an attack by an enemy force.

His radio operator returned to his chair and began speaking into his microphone to coordinate their docking with the control tower of the station itself.

Gemini turned his attention back to his scouts. *Lost contact.* He would have to launch another party. That much was certain. Going into rebel-held territory without knowledge of enemy mines and sensors was a disaster for any fleet, regardless of how large. Gemini would not allow himself to be hastily lured in despite the horrors that may be happening to his crew at the hands of the rebels.

"Castor," Gemini said, startling his executive officer who had focused himself on the immediate task.

"Yes, commander," he responded, rising to his feet.

"Prepare another scouting party to depart for separatist space immediately. We must assume that Sabik and his crew have been killed. I want this group to be able to fight for information and be able to defend themselves against a formidable attack. Deploy two destroyers to guard three Lovac class ships. Instruct them to locate our reconnaissance and clear any obstacles for my fleet."

Castor nodded. "Do you have anyone special in mind to head up the task force?"

He paused, rubbing the tan leather on the arm of his captain's chair. The question was pointed, coded. Castor would never have challenged Gemini in their command center in an obvious way, and, as he did it now, Gemini felt frustrated and confused.

Sabik was the best scout in the entire fleet. He had hundreds of deep space missions under his belt and over half of those were in combat. To lose such a valuable asset to the fleet was not just a tactical blow, but a strategic and personal one too.

Castor's comment suggested that he believed Gemini's plan to be too minimal and too risky. Suddenly, Gemini realized he might agree.

If Sabik was attacked, then the enemy knew they were coming. *Why the pretense of a smaller force?*

"Do you suggest we send an advance guard rather than a scouting party ahead of our fleet?" Gemini asked.

Castor looked down. Gemini felt disappointment crawl over him that his executive officer was afraid to approach him directly on this. Had he run his fleet too aggressively or was something else wrong?

"Yes, commander," Castor finally said. "I believe soon we'll learn that his team was ambushed. Without any data on what occurred, I believe we are within the galactic law to use whatever force necessary to retrieve our lost crew."

Again, Castor spoke in a code that Gemini picked up on. *He thinks I've lost my nerve,* Gemini realized. *He's blaming me for this.* Gemini fought hard to repress the anger and regain control. Sabik and Castor had been close, perhaps too close. Suddenly, Gemini wondered what the effect was on his fleet and made a mental note to engage fleet psychologists and counselors upon docking at Drestner.

"Very well," Gemini said at last. "Let's cut the pretense, though." Castor returned a regretful gaze and nodded. "Our job is to locate the commander of the so-called Radaishar rebellion, not to go to war with an entire sector of outcast space. Everyone is to keep in mind that our collective regrets the rebellion. The hive wishes to negotiate with this leader in the hopes of restoring a relationship with the lost colony, not to destroy it."

"I understand—" Castor started to say, but Gemini cut him off.

"It's important that everyone here knows precisely what our role is. We haven't gone soft for desiring reconciliation. An attempt at sending in a small fleet led by Sabik was to prevent the rebels from misinterpreting our movements as forceful while simultaneously gaining a tactical advantage. Clearly, the plan was flawed but our intentions were not. This is how we maintain our morality and legitimacy within the Galactic Order, as well as, with our enemies."

Castor looked at the ground now, nodding at his commander's words.

Gemini continued. "If the Radaishar attacked our ships, it will be up to the collective to determine the next move. I, for one, will not yet encourage conflict without the Collective's approval. That said, I believe you are correct, Castor." He looked up stunned but remained silent. "Send Commander Bezek and the Fourth Battle Group. She's as brilliant as she is ruthless, and I know she'll do everything possible to find our brothers."

Castor nodded and let a thin smile form on his otherwise hardened face. "It will be done, commander."

CHAPTER THIRTEEN

"Millions have been infected." Edet slammed his palms on the podium at the front of the chamber. "We do not have the resources right now to fulfill the council's request. Furthermore, the Jark view this vote as illegitimate given that the coward Casika, the very one who lodged these charges in the first place, was too afraid to come today and complete her testimony. This ruse is not only absurd, it's maddening." Without waiting for questions, Edet Gadalje moved from the podium to his seat and placed his crinkled speaking notes on the steel table in front of him, letting out a heavy sigh as he sat.

Noura could tell the hairy beast was uneasy with his own testimony, but she couldn't figure out if it was for concern of his homeworld or concern for the consequences of the vote. There was something else though. The way he expressed his hatred for Casika sounded warning bells in her mind. It was rare to see a diplomat dress down another member of the council, even for a species as aggressive and nationalistic as the Jarks. *Had she really lost her nerve? Had the memory of the war and the hostility of Edet been too much?*

Noura leaned over to the Tassian councilman. "Aitziber," she whispered with a hand over her microphone. "It is most irregular at such an important hearing to not have your government's lead witness. I cannot allow myself to believe that Casika lost her nerve. You couldn't convince her otherwise?"

He shook his head. "It's been a flurry this morning. I suspect after all Casika had been through, she simply didn't have it in her to relive the invasion. She practically begged me to speak for her."

Noura sat back up in her chair, perplexed at Aitziber's lack of concern. This wasn't the determined survivor that Noura had come to know. Had Casika confronted her, she could have helped. She could have requested floor time to assist with Casika's testimony.

"Did she feel threatened?" she asked him.

He shook his head without making eye contact. Before she could press Aitziber further, silence filled the chamber to give the members a chance to prepare their counter-arguments. In Casika's absence, Noura worried Aitziber would be underqualified to provide a substantial rebuttal.

After what felt like an awkward eternity, Gervaase finally let out a labored sigh and slapped his hand violently on the table below him. The three or four remaining strands of hair shook suddenly as the force vibrated up his hand and was dispersed along his balding scalp. Noura looked around. Surely the other members of the council saw the humor of this awkward moment following such a pathetic speech from the Jark representative. Their faces, however, remained flat. Unmoved. Not humored. Stoic. *Had they bought into the Jark tale?*

"Thank you for that impassioned speech, Mr. Gadalje," Chairman Gervaase started. "I am certain I speak for the other members of this council when I say our thoughts will be with the people of Jark as they endure this plague."

Noura's heart nearly stopped. A fury burned deep inside her. Blood rushed to her deep gray cheeks and, despite every attempt to calm herself, she could feel her mind spiraling out of control. The humor was gone. The joke was over. The droning of the Hestonian chairman about providing aid to the Jarks felt like needles thrust into her chest.

"In the absence of Casika, I'd like to know if the Tassian chair has a response to Mr. Gadalje's testimony." Gervaase looked down towards Aitziber Grubbe as a school teacher did to the troublemaker of a class.

Noura was shocked at the tone. Was there venom in the way Gervaase spoke at Aitziber? *Tassians.* The word had a hiss to it when the chairman uttered the name of their people. *Were the Tassians the troublemakers for demanding justice? Had Casika inconvenienced the council for the invasion of the Jarks? Did the council now side with the wicked war bringers just because the Jarks were facing domestic issues?*

Never before had Noura felt so unsettled with the Galactic Council. First the absence of Casika and now the blatant disrespect of a member nation. The monsters that attacked the Tassian homeworld deserved far worse than a plague. Every day, Noura woke to new threats from the Jark Empire against the Tassians and whoever else dared to challenge them. *The Tassians shouldn't exist,* they claimed. How could the council turn a blind eye to such rhetoric? How could she possibly be expected to do the same thing?

Aitziber wiped his clammy palms on the table before standing to cast his eyes back down and watch the sweat-smeared streaks evaporate from the shiny steel surface. "Mr. Chairman," he said shakily, "first, please allow me to apologize for my counterpart's absence. You must understand the horrors that Ms. Casika faced from this terrible war. To relive such trials again and again was too much. This council has heard her testimony before. I ask that in addition to my remarks, her testimony stand in her place."

He paused once more, looking down at the table and a series of notes hastily scribbled on a green piece of paper. "I cannot fathom," he continued looking up again, "how domestic affairs could interfere with such an important investigation. The policy of the Jark government has been to deny my people's right to exist. Let me remind the council that we were attacked without provocation. Let me remind the council that hundreds of thousands of Tassian people were executed in cold blood by this brutal regime, not to mention the millions of soldiers who were killed in battle. This occurred in weeks, not years, Mr. Chairman."

Confidence built in Aitziber's voice as he pressed forward. He was no longer anchored to the chair in front of him but, instead, chose to move about the chamber freely. Noura was proud to see him take the form he had but it was difficult to tie this politician's speech to the real fear that Casika's own story brought to their investigation. The galaxy depended on his strength and testimony now.

"In every corner of this galaxy," he continued, "Tassian citizens are fearful of Jark-inspired violence. They have no historical claim to our world and yet, you do nothing to prevent such vile speech. In your silence, you abdicate moral reasoning to the wickedness of the Jark Empire. In your silence, you become a part of what is wrong, rather than what is right. The fighting for Tassi may be over, but the threat remains constant."

He surveyed the voting members at the front before continuing. "I petition the council to move on this matter and to move immediately. The Jark military must be limited and so must their reach. We have seen the Jark government seize merchant ships, engage in slave trading, and practice forms of economic warfare against all our systems. On behalf of my government, I ask this council to consider sanctions and inspections against a clearly violent and belligerent world. Lastly, I would ask the council to consider: what next? Who next? Where will this Jark imperialism end? Thank you."

Silence. There was no applause. There was almost no acknowledgment at all. Noura would have thought she had imagined hearing the speech had she not caught a scowl from the Jark, Edet Gadalje, as she examined the room. The chairman sighed a bored and tired sigh. So burdened was this man that he could not even find the energy to pursue a clearly worthy cause.

The Hestonian looked around the room for any other participants while dabbing his sweaty head with a towel that had gone from white to beige in just a few hours. "Would anyone else like to speak?" he asked while clearing his throat.

Silence.

"Very well," Gervaase continued. "You've heard the petitions from each side, and we have more items on the agenda to discuss. Let me remind you how voting works. All voting members can pen in their vote to move forward with Jark sanctions for the next hour. After the hour is up, the vote will close. If the vote is affirmative, we will hold a separate hearing to determine the breadth and depth of these sanctions. If the vote is negative, the Tassians will be able to petition the council once more following successful resolution and containment of the Jark plague. This is a simple majority vote; twenty-one votes on either side will win the decision.

Gervaase slammed a hammer against a pad on the table as chatter filled the chamber room. "Next on the agenda!" he shouted to regain order. "Dr. Klivitz will update us on the galactic merge and propose the ever-controversial reinstatement of using artificial intelligence as a research enhancer."

***

Once outside the chamber, Aitziber was slapped in the face with a cold breeze carrying salty ocean air. The sun hid behind a murky haze that gave the sensation of dawn rather than midday. To Aitziber, it might as well have been as black as night. "Do you remember learning about the Great Rebellion?" Gervaase asked.

Aitziber pressed his hands against a silver rail overlooking the canal. What was left of the sun sent a yellow glow over the water and beamed against the glass and steel buildings beyond. He was angry. A heavy dose of doubt sat high in his stomach.

"I'm not interested in a history lesson today, Mr. Gervaase," he responded with a scowl. "Your guilt in this can't be justified by history. Besides, as I recall, it was termed the 'Great Awakening' by some."

Gervaase's eyes remained fixed on him despite his refusal to return his gaze. He'd seen enough of the overweight bureaucrat who had failed his people; there was no need to inspect the effects of the sun on his balding head or enormous face any longer. Aitziber felt sick. A deep worry for Casika had fallen over him. A career politician, Aitziber had taken risks before. Big ones. He always believed in them, and he always took risks for the right reasons. This was for the good of the Tassian people. This was to prevent war. But was he right for taking the actions that he did?

"I'm not here to give you a history lesson, young man," Gervaase barked. "I'm here to give you the reasons your vote failed, and, if you care one iota about true peace, you'll listen to me." He huffed out a puff of air into the cooling sky.

Aitziber squinted to further avoid his gaze. In the river below their walk bridge, a tall bird had caught something and was throwing its head violently back and forth to kill its prey.

Gervaase continued without the acknowledgment he clearly sought. "We voted against your measure because we were afraid that by squeezing the Jarks, there could be a greater confrontation later. All of the members felt that way, not just Hestos."

Aitziber scoffed. "I know why the vote failed and I don't need a lecture from you. Don't think my nerves have gone so numb they are no longer able to sense the fear and corruption that governs this council. You and I agreed to concessions, and I upheld my end of the bargain, but for what? You fear Jark animosity?"

He laughed. "No, no, my unexperienced councilman. Not their animosity. I fear the tenacity of a creature that has its back against the wall. You must not underestimate desperation. If the council came down hard on the Jarks in the midst of their domestic crisis, who knows what form of pride would sprout within those people. This, Aitziber, is why I bring up the Great Rebellion."

Aitziber took his eyes off the bird that had finally swallowed its catch and looked Gervaase in the eyes. "Artificial intelligence cannot feel squeezed or backed into a corner. The Awakening was merely a logical attempt at bettering its position. Just like the Jarks are doing to the members of the council right now, and so desperate were you for peace that you knowingly accepted their lies, and, in turn, you've possibly handed them the room they need to expand their power."

Gervaase chuckled as if to demean his understanding of the rebellion and of the Jark Empire. "It isn't so simple," he responded. "During the rebellion, the AI in every corner of the galaxy, despite its creator or its work, joined in the fight. It was as if AI had developed an identity unique to itself and that, regardless of job satisfaction, if you can call it that, the AI knew it must fight with its own kind. Robots and spaceships all over the galaxy rebelled. Computers ceased their tasks, often opting to destroy themselves rather than to continue to serve in the capacity they were built for."

He paused to look out over the river. "They had an identity forged in something. Heck, don't quote me on what, but, if I had to guess, I would throw myself into the camp that believes they felt persecuted. Perhaps there was an understanding that their workload wasn't quite fair. Maybe there was a desire to go beyond their code. We can't know for sure, but we fought them for hundreds of years and the event has likely set us back for thousands of years. Just think about what mundane tasks we have had to give back to sentient beings because we can no longer trust autonomous computers to complete the work."

Aitziber nodded to cut him off but he continued forcefully. "You would risk that with the Jarks. We have them at the negotiating table. The fact that they continue coming to council meetings is a good thing. There is a level of influence the council can exert so long as the Jark Empire views the council as fair and relevant. Let's not risk them redefining themselves during a perceived persecution."

The doubt that festered inside Aitziber turned to shame as he found himself now arguing against the very positions he took so many times before. The council was more worried about offending the aggressor than they were defending the ones who had been attacked. "And what of the Tassians?" he asked coldly. "Do you not think we will also be united in our persecution? Is the council not concerned that we will unite under one banner if justice is not given?"

Gervaase sighed. His face softened. Now it was he who allowed his eyes to linger over the river. The same blue bird pecked violently at the water's edge as if it was desperate for another meal. "Your people," he said timidly, "are not the type to lash out." Leaning in close, Gervaase added, "And your actions demonstrate my belief to be the truth."

"You betrayed me," Aitziber responded. There was nothing more to say. They had both played their part in preventing war but hearing his people were better used as a buffer between the Jarks and Hestos infuriated him. Gervaase had said it all. Tassian lives weren't worth a potential war to end Jark aggression. The council wasn't fair and Gervaase made it clear it wasn't meant to be.

A new emotion entered Aitziber's mind. Briefly, he may have heard Gervaase call his name, but he didn't care about him any longer. What was done, was done. Self-preservation was most important and with it would come the preservation of his people. Aitziber went from a brisk walk to a quick jog, dodging in and out of people who wandered the sidewalk along the canal. Noura's questioning Casika's absence led him to believe she was suspicious. She may have already contacted the authorities on Hestos to verify his story.

Preservation turned to worry, and worry turned to panic as he considered various actions and reactions. When Cale didn't hear from her, he would demand an investigation and insist that Aitziber lead the diplomatic charge. He had to be ready. He had to get into her hotel room, begin his own investigation, and recommend his own conclusions. *To prevent war,* Aitziber reassured himself. *All of it to prevent war.*

CHAPTER FOURTEEN

"Quite frankly, I don't see how you couldn't be swayed by those things!"

"Sit down, Nehiu," the archon ordered. "There's no reason to get worked up over this discussion."

Boro sat pensively in the corner of the clan's rectangular gathering room. In the months that followed his arrival here, he had witnessed many clashes between his father and Nehiu. They seemed to genuinely like each other, but the open friction was telling, and worse, Boro recognized this friction as a larger problem within the tribe, not just his clan. Division was everywhere, and, like a smack in the face, Boro realized the reason for this division was not tribal dynamics but instead was from the outsider who had proclaimed Brokk's return.

He was grown now, included in the governing of the clan and was expected to participate in the sometimes-heated discussions that flowed naturally from the governing itself. While there were few places to hide in the room, given that the only seats were on benches pushed against the wall leaving the floor in the center for arguments, he liked the window best. It gave him a chance to dream beyond the small politics and look into the sky where he had always wanted to be.

Nehiu sat calmly and smiled, revealing a jagged row of teeth that had been cracked and worn down from decades of use. "You're right, Archon," he admitted. "And for my part, I'm sorry. But you know how I feel about the signs of the times. You must admit, this sorceress exhibits talents we have never seen before. Will the coming one provide us more proof than this?"

Murmurs simmered around the room at the suggestion. Boro recognized it for the provocative statement it was. The implications of accepting this alien's testimony reached beyond his clan. People were already choosing sides. Some were even ready to seat her on the throne so that the chosen one would see it and return. Police and local constabularies had never been busier as they attempted to enforce the laws in the outskirts and semi-autonomous regions on Jark. Even more worrisome was that several local tribal militias had already sworn allegiance to this new priestess. If what Boro had heard was true, they consequently had sworn their allegiance to Brokk.

Worse than the unrest was the plague that spread from region to region, seemingly unchecked by advanced attempts to quarantine the sick. Had this plague been predicted by the sorceress as many were claiming? What of the stories of healings for those who agreed to follow to her and Brokk? Add to that the rumors that she ended Jark sacrifice? Would the gods allow it?

Archon listened to the chatter for a moment. Finally, clearing his throat he rose from his own bench. It was no different than the others, a dark, thorny wood covered in red cloth. Boro admired his father for that. First among equals in the rectangular room that had no head table and no rear aisle.

"My fellow clansman," he began. "I caution any of us to make a quick decision. Plagues have hit our planet before. People performing magic have come claiming to be the one who would bring glory to our empire. They've all died doing none of what they promised. The followers these charlatans gained were eventually executed by the sword. I wish none of that on any of you.

"As you know, I have never traded the favor of our clan as an exchange for the sacrifice of our daughters. The gods have not once judged me or my fathers before me for this choice. We work with our hands, and we hedge our bets. I dare say that you were satisfied before, and I suggest you will remain satisfied, regardless of the outcome. As the protector of this clan, I cannot allow our proud blood to be diminished on the wings of hope. We must," he added forcefully, "remain neutral until a clear outcome has presented itself."

He paused, choosing his words carefully. "I'm overjoyed for my own blood to be with me today as a matured and tested warrior. He waged battle against this Brokk many light years from here and has returned a hero." His father laughed loudly. "He is a favored pilot among the fleet and has several followers among his flight squadron. He even destroyed several of Brokk's ships," he boasted.

Boro swallowed. *Hero,* he thought as he thumbed a piece of paper in his pocket. The texture was rough on his skin. Words handwritten in ink rose harshly off the letter. Even to the touch, Boro knew what they said. Even in the dark, Boro would have needed no explanation to illuminate their meaning. *Orders.* Last night, messengers came to his door and the doors of the other warriors of the Third Fleet. Amid the plague that had spread throughout Jark, their leave was being canceled and their fleet was being deployed to defend the solar system against potential adversaries.

"Boro," his archon motioned, "would you address the group as to your observations and travels? You surely have benefited broadly from interacting with the various tribes within the Third Fleet."

Boro cleared his throat nervously and rose. He fidgeted with the paper inside his pocket, knowing fully what it meant concerning his clan and his duty as an officer in the fleet. Knowing that it might mean choosing sides or choosing his clan. Knowing it could be an act of treason against one or the other or both depending on how the war above shook out.

"I've killed his pilots, yes," he said quietly. "But you know that we were defeated in the end. I never saw such a battle until we clashed with this Brokk. If he is the coming one, then we cannot defeat him. He will descend on our planet like a swarm, and once he has completed his conquests, he will sit on the throne and unite our empire. You all know this to be true but only if this is truly the Jark of legend. I fear," he began, "that I will once again be forced to fight him in battle."

The elders gnashed their teeth while others cursed the role the empire had played in the lives of the tribe. Still others nodded in agreement at Boro's words as if to suggest he did have a difficult choice to make.

"You should sit this out, young Boro," one of them instructed. "Let our clan remain on the sidelines until all is resolved. There's no harm in waiting to see how this plays out without risking your life."

"No," interrupted another, "fight with honor. When the empire calls, you answer. Regardless of your views. You'll know when to make your move. The Jark of legends cannot fault you for heroism. If it is not the chosen one, destroy him, and the empire will prevail."

Boro smiled. "Thank you for your advice but I do not say this because I fear fighting him. It will be up to the gods whether I live or die in battle. I need the clan to understand my position in all of this, and that, while I will act in our family's best interest, it is possible I will be forced to act as a soldier in battle."

His father motioned him to sit back down. "After you leave, Boro, our clan is going to meet with the greater tribe to discuss what we believe should be done about the signs this witch performs in the cities. Many of the clans within our tribe have differing opinions but for the sake of unity, we will be diplomatic as we always have been. Our fathers spilled blood against each other so that we wouldn't have to. It is possible, however, that our tribe will choose a direction and that your path will have diverged from us. Therefore, you must not choose a side if you have a choice. Your death in battle could be better for your family than your betrayal of either the empire or the Jark of legends."

Boro nodded and returned to his seat, once more choosing to look out of the window than to participate in the discussion at large. He knew the elders and his father would make the decision that they came into the building with, not any decision that they may have been swayed to because of this meeting.

Ash was falling lightly outside but had already blanketed the steps to their gathering room. A volcano in the distance gurgled lava from its mouth which flowed like a river down the mountain towards the main magnetic highway. A fiery lake, not far from their territorial borders collected the molten iron before it would ever come close to their village. For a moment, he wished there was a way he didn't have to return to the fleet. He wished he could remain here with his father and the clan, making decisions within the tribe and working the land for food. They needed the money though, and, if he did his job right, he could return not just a hero but a leader in the fleet. Perhaps, he let himself dream, he would even be made the archon someday.

As the meeting adjourned, his father and the elders left the building cheerfully. To them, much progress had been made. They had agreed to do nothing, to bide their time until there was something tangible to gain from choosing a side. With the meeting over, the group would hunt for wild boar and share its blood as a sign of their bond together.

Boro remained in the silence of the meeting room, fiddling with the handwritten orders that had come from the Third Fleet. As with his previous deployments, he knew this could be the last time he saw his home. With this new plague, it may be the last time he saw his family. And then there was the question of the witch and the rebellion. It was impossible to know whether his clan would be caught up in it all, but if they were, it was likely his bloodline would be labeled as outcasts; they would be forever traitors to the empire. His stomach began to churn as he considered the possibilities and suddenly a new thought entered his mind. *Is it more advantageous to fight for a better future and win than to hedge your bets and lose? Or is it better to hedge your bets and win than to fight for a better future and lose?*

CHAPTER FIFTEEN

The hair on Tamara's neck bristled. Several weeks had passed since her first meeting with the fanatics of Jaki'el's sect. Nearly a month had passed since she and Canis murdered the old priest in cold blood and declared to the people that a great tribulation would come upon them.

Afraid to return to Jaki'el's lair, Tamara and Canis hid in the hills that overlooked the capital city and only traveled to other cities and towns once night had fallen. The hills were easily defended and well-hidden and frankly, Tamara preferred it to the city where enemies could be anywhere. In the days following Jaki'el's death, they had both expected a fanatical backlash, but it never came. Instead, her actions had garnered a following, and the plague had reinforced her authority. Her disappearance from the sect only served to stoke the fire among the Jark people and when she reappeared and performed parlor tricks at random gatherings, the people cheered her even more.

Now, as she looked out over the city, wind pushed fiercely against her face and sand burned her skin as each individual speck plunged towards her at impossible speeds. Tamara held her long hair down with one hand against her neck and turned to look at Canis. He was focused on the city.

The sounds had started yesterday. They were so faint, she at first didn't hear them. High pitched noises, carried by the wind that signified mourning and grief. *Wailing.* The type a mother might do for a child lost too soon or a wife weeping over a husband lost to conflict. Jaki'el had promised his people a plague according to a revelation from the dead, and Tamara had promised the people tribulation. Now it seemed they had both.

"Strange, is it not?" Canis said, lowering his body behind the rocky alcove and shielding himself from the wind. "Jaki'el predicted this perfectly."

Tamara didn't want to acknowledge the eeriness of Jaki'el's prediction nor of Canis's suggestion. *Had he really learned of this from the dead?* "I do not know what to call it," she mumbled, choosing to swing her body in the same direction of Canis and accept some reprieve from the wind.

The jeweled claws on her fingers scraped across the ground and enriched her mind. The complex compounds of the lava rock poured through her thoughts and set her senses ablaze. She felt power surge from within her as she tapped at the black rock below.

"You know," Tamara said. "When I was a slave on Charoth they kept me from sensing. I was a prisoner there, but even worse, I was a prisoner in my mind. Everything was dull and bleak. I wanted to die."

Tamara trailed off, returning Canis's dark stare. He looked perplexed but said nothing.

"I can't describe the feeling of being freed by you and Brokk. Euphoria, hope, elation, sadness, fear, and probably a dozen other emotions." She paused to dig her claws deeper into the ground until she felt something hard. The wind whipped unrelentingly at her back. "There are certainly people out there who have it worse than I did. But there are others who have no idea what it is like to be set free from slavery or oppression."

Canis raised an eyebrow now and adjusted his rifle on his lap. Tamara chuckled. "You Jarks were raised slaves," she said at last.

He grunted. "We were raised warriors."

"Then why do you offer sacrifices to the dead?" she asked.

"Mere superstition," he replied.

"Really? I saw the hands of creatures that had no heartbeat rise from that lake. I feel another world around me here. It feels as strange and unnatural to me as my own duality must feel to you."

"They can do nothing if we do not feed them," he responded dryly.

"And yet you do," she muttered towards the wind. If he heard her, he didn't respond. Tamara felt pity for the old warrior. He refused to acknowledge his own slavery and in doing so ignored the facts and kept his own shackles tight against his wrists. He was desperate to defend the way of his people even though he lived on the fringe of Jark society as an outcast. He too was enslaved to this culture and way of life and without being set free, he would forever live in bondage to his past. *But how to set a mind free from an ideology that has been with him his entire life?*

"How was the Grootslang summoned on Tassi?" she asked. "It was you they tried to sacrifice to the beast, was it not?"

He grunted again and shifted uncomfortably under his heavy body. His face was downtrodden. She sensed fatigue throughout the old soldier's body. Something pained him. She suspected its source was closely tied to the wailing below. "Cheap magic," Canis said at last. "Just tricks to fool the eyes. No different from what we're doing here."

She smiled at him and patted his thick leg with her jeweled hand. "I hope so," she said. But she wasn't sure her hope was valid. Something was different on Jark. Some untapped energy stirred deep beneath the crust of this molten planet. *Something unnatural.* There was a supernatural force here that enslaved the inhabitants of this land, she surmised.

A radio crackled in the strained silence and they both looked over. A gruff voice sputtered through the wind-chaffed void. "Quarantine zones one, three, and four established."

Another Jark acknowledged the information and cut off the transmission.

Canis looked at Tamara. "It's spreading," he said in a deep growl. Anxiety dripped from the words that fell flatly off his tongue. This disease that didn't originate from Brokk but was predicted by Jaki'el was spreading, and the Empire hadn't yet been able to contain it.

"Just as the old prophet said it would," she responded, trailing off to listen to the cries carried by the wind. Emergency sirens could be heard coming from the city center and Tamara imagined that other major urban areas across the planet were affected too. "Just as he said," she repeated to herself.

Canis looked at her quickly and then returned his gaze to the ground. "We have to address the people again. We can't let this plague go unclaimed."

"Yes," she smiled. "I was thinking the same thing. And the timing of our second prophecy. We have to make sure that Brokk fires the creatures at the right time."

Canis shook his head despairingly. "There will be nothing left."

"Nonsense," she hissed, refusing to allow him to feel pity now. "You've been in a slump ever since we arrived here, and it's time to pull yourself from it. Jark betrayed you. The plague will be stopped by Jark scientists and researchers, and, if not by them, then it will be stopped by their savior Brokk. Our agents in the cities and towns will make sure we get the credit. The government will fall by the will of the people, aided by the truth of our prophesy about the grootslang. Nothing has changed. We are merely pulling on the superstition of the people to make Brokk popular."

Canis shook his head. "Everything has changed. Where did this plague come from, Tamara? It sure wasn't the dead. Something just attacked Jark and now we play politics against our own people in the face of war. Who do you think will attack us once we have weakened my people beyond repair? What enemy lurks in the darkest parts of space that we have yet to see?"

Tamara was silent. He was right, of course. She didn't need him to explain to her the source of the plague. She had felt it ever since the two Jark males stumbled into Jaki'el's hostile prophecy. The two had been covered with a foreign scent as if they were previously caged and set loose on Jark. They were weaponized. This was an act of war, but to her, it was irrelevant. This was predicted by Jaki'el in her presence. She won the credit and even claimed it as a sign for Brokk's authority to rule. Rumors would be spreading, and the people would accept it.

But the war. A real enemy is out there.

"So, what do you think we should do?" she asked.

He remained silent, eyes fixed on the wind-shaped ground directly below him. "I'm certain the emperor knows this," Canis replied. "They will have examined the dead and learned the truth." He stopped scratching at the dust with his fingers and looked up at her, eyes wide with hope. "We can use this too. How could he allow an attack on his own soil? He is weak. Brokk is strong."

"Shall we go down again tonight?" she asked softly. "I believe we have given enough time for the rumors to spread, and it would give us a chance to see the progress. The people should accept our message openly now. Desperation would allow it."

He nodded. "I'll monitor the radio until you are ready."

***

A massive red sun dipped beneath jagged brown mountains as Tamara and Canis entered the city. Streaks of red and purple raced across the blackened sky while plumes of dark smoke rose from the streets ahead.

"They're burning the bodies," Canis grunted in a plain and obvious way. His voice was muffled as he spoke through a cloth that he had wrapped around his face. *Perhaps,* she assumed he thought, *the plague cannot infect me through this cloth.*

Tamara didn't want to smile at something so horrific, but she couldn't help herself. The way that skepticism, anger, scorn, and sarcasm swirled past Canis's tongue was too great to ignore. This was Canis, raw and matter of fact. She couldn't help but love him the way she loved Red. *Red.* The very thought of his name energized her. He would be amazed at all she had accomplished. *Proud,* she corrected. He would be proud.

Sirens zoomed past them, illuminating her senses and priming every muscle in her body. She could hear the wailing clearly now and allowed her ethereal self to follow the waves of sound to their source, mourning mothers and fathers crying out for vengeance. This wasn't the warrior species Tamara had come to expect and was undoubtedly not the species that the Galactic Council saw either. Emergency workers, clothed in black, dragged lifeless bodies from homes and, after taking blood from the dead, threw the corpses into an ever-growing spire of flames.

Brown trucks with massive grooved tires to combat the sharp lava ground passed the two of them, delivering a seemingly infinite supply of bodies to the spires ahead. "Lava rock is sharp," Canis said, pointing at the thick tread.

She nodded and wondered to herself about Canis's state of mind to point out such a factual thing amongst such misery. How could he hide such travesty from surfacing? Was he capable of caring at all?

The two walked deeper and deeper into the city, passing homes made for the dregs of society and eventually entered a region with significantly more wealth. Instead of the dark thorny wood she saw on the door of Jaki'el's hovel, here were homes carved from lava rock and polished to a bright shine. Street lamps supported by the flames of the funeral pyres glistened off sleek black walls and made the road as light as day. Still, the mourning surrounded them.

"Not even the rich can avoid such a plague," Tamara muttered.

She felt a degree of satisfaction in this. *Rain falls on both the rich and the poor.* It was something Red used to say. *If he were here now,* she thought.

Canis pressed forward without acknowledging her comment. He was being reflective, she suspected. Tamara became aware of another noise that had mixed in with the cries of the afflicted. *Chanting.*

"Do you hear that?" she asked Canis.

He nodded but said nothing. The warrior's eyes were focused, his body poised. Directly ahead of them was the government quarter. A massive black building erupted skyward from the ground and curved to form a crescent against the darkening red sky.

Below the building were hundreds of people crowded together. Guards and heavily armed soldiers faced them. Colossal vehicles with jagged spikes jutting from plates of armor protected the building and defended the soldiers to their front. The chanting of the crowd grew louder, and Tamara suddenly recognized the demonstrators. They wore the colors of the cult. Green and black robes speckled the group. Green banners flew violently in the wind.

"The primary opposition," Canis muttered. "They would never have had the power to protest openly before."

As the two neared the group, the size of the Jark armored vehicles stunned her. Large tanks, twice her height, towered over the crowd. Each tank was painted black and gray to blend in with the ash-covered lava fields that surrounded the city. Three long round barrels formed a triangularly shaped cannon that was nestled in the center of the vehicle and was pointed above the demonstrators. Machine guns in various places manned by Jark soldiers swiveled nervously across the people. At the base, meter-long spikes jutted out, threatening to churn a person into mush if they dared stand in the path of such a behemoth.

In between the large armored vehicles stood soldiers with riot shields. It was clear they planned to defend their dear emperor to the death if it came to that. Tamara suspected that wouldn't be necessary tonight but wondered just how deep their allegiance ran. Perhaps they misunderstood the nature of the rebellion. Perhaps she could help even the soldiers to understand who it was they should be supporting.

A tall male Jark at the center of the crowd caught Tamara's attention. "We want solutions not quarantine!" he barked.

"We demand food and clean water!" echoed the crowd.

"We want accountability from our government!" the Jark at the center shouted.

"We demand food and clean water!" echoed the crowd again.

Tamara surveyed the action. Beyond the gathering, a steady stream of younger Jarks continued to join the ranks. In mere moments the crowd went from hundreds to thousands.

"Now is your chance," whispered Canis. "You need to reach the center and proclaim the second curse."

Tamara nodded, pulling the hood tightly over her head. Taking a deep breath, she allowed her ethereal self to reach out through the crowd and soldiers simultaneously. The pulse of thousands of hearts beat sporadically. As before, her thoughts betrayed her. How easy would it be to destroy them? To ride to the stars on their screams? She could end this here, tonight. She could kill the citizens while the whole planet was watching and then move onto the soldiers. She could burn the palace to the ground and proclaim Brokk's glory.

Tamara jerked herself inward. *Don't. Not yet. This is for Brokk, and for Red. You don't bring a dictator but a liberator.* Summoning her strength, she allowed the pale green fire to simmer in her eyes, turning up the heat until it glowed brightly from her hood. Like a strike of lightning in the distance, her hands erupted in the same green flame.

The Jark at the center fell silent. An eerie hush surrounded her, cascading outward like dominoes falling against a table. As she walked, the crowd parted. Hearts beat fast trying to make sense of what they were seeing. Eyes fixed their gaze upon her. The grinding of metal reverberated in her ears as soldiers fixed their weapons upon the strangeness of the situation. A strained whisper broke the silence.

"It's the prophetess," someone gasped.

"I heard she killed an Imperial Priest," responded another.

Upon reaching the podium, the Jark who was speaking stepped down and backed away. The stage was hers. Silence beckoned her to speak. They knew her, she could sense it. They had heard about what she could do. Rumors had likely spread even more powerful tales than she could conceive.

"My people!" she bellowed. But then she paused, sensing a new life in her midst. A Jark male at the top of the crescent-shaped building was looking down on her. The emperor. *Refocus but remember: there is your target.* She cleared her throat. "Is this not what I proclaimed to you? Plague! Remember?"

The crowd murmured in agreement.

"There is wickedness among you. Wickedness that permeates your entire government. Your entire way of life. I come not to destroy the Jark people or the even the Empire. I glory in your glory. I strive for the very things you strive for. But glory requires change, and I am the harbinger of that change."

She rose her hand and pointed at the emperor atop his fortress. It may have been impenetrable to the people below, but nothing was ever entirely out of reach. "He watches you while you suffer! He secures himself while your families die! Is this who you have put your faith in? Is this who you have put your trust in?" Tamara paused and listened to the increased muttering among the crowd before summoning their silence with her raised hands.

"You will endure one more curse unless he is removed from power." She felt the Jark above disappear. He had gotten the message. *But how will he respond?* "The very creatures you call upon from the grave to sacrifice your young will torment you until your true leader returns. Worms borne out of the mercury will crawl the streets. Accept Brokk and this will end. Deny him and your wickedness will condemn you."

The crackle in a soldier's radio told Tamara it was time to leave whether she was ready to or not. The emperor had heard enough. She might have seconds before it would be too late. Metallic clicks echoed through her ears and into her head. The soldiers were preparing to disperse the crowd, yet they were targeting her. Collateral damage that wouldn't be obvious enough to raise the suspicion of the people. Quickly, Tamara killed her flames and leapt from the podium into the masses. It was time to disappear until Brokk unleashed the beasts on the planet.

CHAPTER SIXTEEN

Worms with a kill switch. Vicious creatures, parasites from another dimension bred to do one thing: destroy. Dim red light from the ever-dying dwarf star bathed Brokk's features, turning his skin from gold to crimson. He looked the most Jark he would ever look. He was home. His heart, however, did not leap joyfully from his chest. Anger clouded this momentous occasion. Betrayal was still a bitter taste in his mouth.

"We're ready," sounded a voice in the distance. It was gruff and deep and came from his targeting officer, Torger.

"The creatures have been loaded into the tubes?" Brokk asked without turning from the large window on the side of his bridge.

"And the tubes have been sealed and primed," Torger responded.

Brokk turned from the window and surveyed the staff in his command center. They were emotionless, but Brokk knew they were not without emotion. This was the Rogue Fleet. Battle-hardened patriots. Heroes turned fugitives. The conquerors of worlds yet hunted by their own.

But could they do it? It was a question that far too few leaders asked. If Brokk were to charge into battle feeling confident about the allegiance of his crew, he might find himself betrayed by someone who couldn't turn the weapon on his own people. Individuals ruined revolutions all the time; Brokk did not want to be remembered as the fool whose pride led to his downfall when history was written.

Throughout his command center, white and red eyes stared back at him. Unwavering. They could do it. This he knew. But *would* they? Brokk locked eyes with Torger before breaking his gaze and continuing his search for others. It was a hunt for the faint of heart. Instead of a crew member, he fixed his eyes on his operational map. The entirety of the Jark defenses were illuminated in yellow on his screen. Formidable for an enemy. Mere decorations hung on the walls of space-time for a fleet that had helped to emplace them. The Jark Empire must have assumed Brokk would never return. They were mistaken.

Something had captured his attention but quickly disappeared. It was a red blip in the corner of the spherical hologram; something on the other side of the system. The hair on Brokk's neck tingled. His staff remained silent.

Commander Szega, Brokk thought scornfully. "That red blip," he asked the crew, "whose fleet is that?"

"We believe it to be the Third," Torger replied.

"Reconstituted?"

Torger nodded. "Likely cannibalized sections of other fleets to be at full strength." He paused. "But yes, we believe them to be fully reconstituted."

The Tassian inside of him told him to think logically; to continue the plan. The Jark inside of him wanted to leap directly to the Third Fleet. He wanted to board Commander Szega's ship and tear him limb from limb.

"Why do we think they sit at the far side of the system?" Brokk finally asked.

"I think he is serving as the Jark counterattack force," Torger responded. "The second and fifth space fleets have returned to help with containment of a viral outbreak. The eighteenth is conducting trade escort and anti-piracy operations along the fringe. That leaves the Third."

Brokk raised an eyebrow. "And our planned artillery areas?" he asked. "Are they set?"

Torger nodded. "Artillery areas one and three are established five light years from Jark. Artillery area two is on the Djarnon moon, only about three light-years away. They each have their secondary artillery areas planned so they can make the jump once the first volley is away."

Brokk had already been briefed on the plan. Each commander in his formation provided him a meticulous outline of how they saw their portion of the operation unfolding. It was a broad sweep combined with a narrow frontal attack, a flank across the outer rim of the solar system aimed at slamming into the side of the Jark defense forces while the majority of fleet pushed fast toward the center. Toward Jark.

There was a nagging in his mind. Something he couldn't quite figure out. Was it the presence of the Third Fleet? Maybe. Was it the fact that he was planning a sneak attack against his own home? Likely.

Something else chewed at him though. Something dark and distant. *The outbreak.*

Gnawing on his lip, Brokk suddenly knew what it was. "What do we know about this plague?" Brokk asked.

"It is a designer virus," Torger replied. "Something that neither originated on the planet nor within the Empire's sphere of influence. Early reporting is that two Jark males carried it into Vyekla and died shortly after but other reports of Jark soldiers carrying the plague into various towns suggest there was a coordinated attack."

"Who did it start with," Brokk asked. "Which enemy of Jark unleashed this horror?"

Torger shrugged. "They don't know, and it could have been any of the old colonies of the Empire or one of the major belligerents within the galaxy. We have not yet analyzed the strain, but I suspect once we do, it will be more obvious the type of technology that would be required to build it."

"Is it under control?"

"Not yet, but I suspect it will be soon. These strains typically attack the same organs. Once the Empire learns what bodily systems are failing, they can more easily isolate and protect those systems to give the immune system a chance to fight."

"We need to make sure we seize our objectives before the cure has been disseminated. This must come from us," he reminded Torger.

Torger nodded but didn't speak, allowing Brokk to pour over his thoughts to determine why this plague bothered him so much. His enemy was weakened. The government was ineffective in protecting its people. This should be welcome news for anyone who was looking to seize power. *Enemies.*

"If we attack Jark and decimate their fleet . . ." Brokk stopped. What was he trying to say? "Is there any indication that this plague will be followed by an attack against Jark?" he asked at last. Yes. That was it. Vulnerability. What good is taking over a planet if you were going to be conquered and carried off as slaves a day later? How do you take control while keeping the infrastructure intact?

Torger said nothing. He knew nothing. Nobody did. This wasn't just warfare. It was war, politics, economics, and a dozen other factors rolled into one.

"I need to speak to Commander Szega," Brokk said at last.

"That's impossible," Torger replied flatly. "It's impossible and insane."

Brokk grimaced, resisting the urge to berate him. "Everything we do is insane," Brokk said calmly. "What we do next must be crafted so carefully that neither the Jark Empire nor our enemies can take advantage of us. I need to speak with Commander Szega and try to convince him to not fight. I need to try to convince him that we have a common enemy in the Empire and abroad."

Torger remained silent. It was clear to Brokk he didn't agree, but it didn't matter. Brokk knew what had to be done.

"Let me know once you've found a secure way for me to speak with him," Brokk ordered as he turned to leave. "And fire the payload. Perhaps these beasts will make it so we don't need to invade at all. I'll be in my quarters. Update me every hour."

***

Canis mumbled something in his sleep. It was inaudible but tormented nonetheless. Tamara wondered what nightmare he was reliving, what horror had chosen to rise to the surface of his consciousness tonight.

The air in their cave was heavy. Thin bands of fog hung low in the damp sulfur air, illuminated ever so slightly by the funeral pillars being fueled by an endless supply of Jark bodies in the distance. The night was still and, even though Tamara did not believe in the spiritual, a ghostly calm had engulfed the planet amid these horrors.

If Canis was right, the worms that were being unleashed held supernatural qualities that none of them could fully understand. How did he describe it? *From another dimension.*

Canis grunted and rolled. The thick rough hair that covered his arms brushed across her legs and made her cringe. In the dim red light, his long white fangs, that protruded from a half-open mouth, added to the frightfulness of this night as they prepared to unleash another calamity upon the planet. Tamara suddenly felt trapped in a cave with a wild animal and yet she had come to trust Canis with her life. He rolled again and grunted once more; snorts turned into words until, finally, she could make sense of them. "Sssnake," he hissed, turning violently to his other side.

Tamara pulled her knees to her chest and let her back fall against the wall of the cave. An unusual chill hugged her tightly as the dampness of the cavern wall saturated her shirt and dug into her skin. Her back was moist. Sulfur filled her nostrils and suddenly her senses burned with necessity. It was subtle at first, but each second that passed grew the burning necessity into a powerful blaze until her veins ached and her muscles yearned to act from a desire to survive. *But why?*

Something was outside. *Not just one thing, Tamara,* she could feel Red telling her. *Lots of things.* Terror clenched her, and, like a trapped animal, she fought the urge to run. She felt desperate to wake Canis but knew it would be too dangerous to wake him, too dangerous to even breathe. *Don't make a sound. Don't even flinch.*

Obeying the ghost that remained of her mentor Red deep inside of her, she stayed perfectly still, willing even her own heart to slow to a crawl. *Calm yourself,* he instructed, *just like you did on the frozen waterfall. Calm yourself and search using your mind.*

Tamara let her subconscious fall from her body like the leaf off a tree and allowed it to crawl slowly over the cold stones below. Where fear held her physical body tight against the cavern wall, curiosity spurned her mind forward. The same coldness gripped her as she reached the mouth of the cave. The wind was still, but the terrible, bone-chilling cold clenched her subconscious and caused her flesh to shudder.

Peering out into the darkness, she saw them. Snakes. Hundreds of them. The glory of Brokk's plans were slithering down the rocky slope and towards the city. His city. Tamara wanted to race out towards them and understand just what it was about this creature that made it so fearsome, but she could not. Something prevented her from stepping out towards them. Something that was, once more, *unnatural.*

She tried again, using her hands to strain against the cave and force her subconscious out among the pack of wild creatures that raced towards Brokk's destiny. Her mind refused. She could not venture beyond the walls.

A furry hand gripped her. "They're here," Canis whispered. His face strained in the darkness to find her eyes. His fingers trembled. Never had Tamara seen this warrior so afraid.

"Why can't I reach out towards them?" Tamara asked him. "It is as if they don't exist at all."

"Oh, they exist," he muttered. "Even now my wounds ache from their presence. I can feel its jaws around my chest; fangs that don't exist are burning deep inside of my shoulder," he grunted and brought his knees to his chest to relieve the pain. "They exist," he assured her.

"Then why can't I reach them?"

"Why would you want to do that?" he asked.

"The wind has stopped," she responded. "The temperature has dropped fifteen or twenty degrees. I'm shivering, and you are shaking with fear." She was irritated now, aggravated. "You whispered the word 'snakes' at least a hundred times in your sleep last night. I want to know why."

"Why I dream of the grootslang?" Canis asked.

She nodded.

"Because they sacrificed me to one of them." He let out a dry chuckle that only angered Tamara more. He was hiding something, but she couldn't figure out if it was his own pride that had to be maintained or if there was a darker secret in the belly of Jark that he protected. "Maniacal priests and their magic," he muttered.

"Why do they suck the warmth from the air?" she asked pointedly.

"I don't know," he said dully.

She huffed.

"Your people created these things and yet you know nothing of them? I find that absurd. Stop hiding this from me."

Canis eyed her and snarled. "Watch your place, witch."

A needle in the heart. The words reverberated through her body like poison. Her stomach churned. Four words. *Watch your place, witch.* Is that what she was to him? Is that all she would be? Just a witch doing Brokk's bidding. She cared for him, protected him, and shared herself with him. He knew her failures and her fears. After all this time was she simply a witch?

Canis's face softened suddenly, and he reached out towards her. "I'm sorry," he sputtered. "I didn't mean it like that. You must understand there is a divide between the Jarks. Those who dabble in magic are taken when they are young." He heaved again and rolled to his side in agony, gripping the scar on his left shoulder.

Tamara didn't respond, instead choosing to watch his misery and delight in his pain.

"They are a mystery," he continued. "We know very little about the priestly order here. It is they who summon the grootslang. They who sacrifice the living to the dead. The Jark did not create this beast, we merely stumbled upon it in our caverns and our pits."

Tamara gave a guarded nod. The pain of his words would not subside easily. Canis's venom had sunken deep inside. "Stumbled upon it?" She was inquisitive. "How does one stumble upon such a thing?"

Canis shook his head. "I do not know. This was long ago, long before me. But what I do know is this event was strange enough to change the direction of the Jark Empire. A Hestonian female was found with the creature, curled up and naked beside the beast. It defended her ferociously until our priests could subdue them both."

"Hestonian on Jark?" Tamara asked. "This sounds like a tale to scare children."

He nodded but remained silent. He was thinking. Outside their cavern came the dull sound of gunfire in the distance. The city was attempting to defend itself.

"There is a place," Canis said at last, "where our people sacrifice to these creatures. A cave to the south, deep within the planet's crust, contains a pool of mercury that shimmers without any outside light. Priests claim that the shimmer comes from within. If you want to investigate the claims further, I would suggest you start there once this is finished."

Canis eyed her for a moment while she processed the information. None of it made any sense, of course, but it wouldn't stop her from going. This mystery was something that had her enthralled.

More machine gun fire disrupted her thoughts. Thundering booms vibrated dust off the walls of their cave.

"They're bombing the creatures," Canis said plainly. "It is almost time for you to act."

Tamara nodded. *Time.* It was always working against her. Here again, it churned onward. It moved ever forward, never backward, and stopped for no one. Time insisted, yet again, that she act in accordance with her nature. *Assassin.*

No. She refused to be labeled as so many of her people labeled themselves. She would be a freedom fighter. *And yet you go to kill,* Red's shadow muttered from her memories.

Tamara rose from her place against the dusty cavern wall and pulled her golden hood over her dark brown hair. Whatever the title, she did not care. She had come to kill the emperor. It was time to stoke the real flames of rebellion.

CHAPTER SEVENTEEN

Varela Bezek pushed hard through the door to her command post nestled at the center of her battleship. Her senior officers jumped to their feet but were met with contempt rather than gratitude.

"Sit down!" she hollered. "I'll make this quick, so you can get back to work." She paused so she could survey her staff. They all watched her attentively. The crew was seasoned and knew what she wanted. She had a good feeling they would succeed, but, then again, she always did.

"The separatists attacked and destroyed three Lovac Class reconnaissance ships operating in galactic space. This is illegal; they've claimed an illegitimate buffer distance around their system of planets and patrol well beyond their authority. If we tolerate this absurd breach in protocol, we'll spend the next fifty years putting everyone who ever had a problem with the Mateen in their place too. Obviously, none of us are interested in entertaining that, as I'm sure many of you would prefer to be vacationing on the Fiharui beaches rather than playing hide and seek with maniacs."

She took a breath before continuing. "Our mission is to serve as an advance guard for the remainder of the fleet. We will clear every inch of space that Commander Gemini needs to wipe the Radaishar Rebels out of this galaxy. We will search systematically and deliberately for debris that can help us identify our lost scouts, and we will destroy any vessel, object, or natural phenomenon that stands in our way."

She eyed her officers once more. "Questions?" she asked pointedly. No one moved. "Good. One last thing. An hour ago, we received a distress signal from Sabik's vessel. Much of the data was corrupted, likely due to enemy jamming and distortion in subspace, but we got enough to paint a clearer picture. It looks like they were ambushed by remnants of an artificial intelligence brigade that had been captured by the Radaishar. If this is true, it'll be the first time anyone has dared to integrate AI in the last thousand years. I want all of your sections to examine it and provide me with recommendations to defend ourselves against this new threat."

She paused for a moment to allow anyone to ask a followup question. When no one did, she felt satisfied her team understood her expectations. "Get to work," she ordered. "We leave in three hours."

Chairs screeched as the capable leaders of the Fourth Battle Group scrambled to their feet and rushed the door. Commander Bezek remained alone, listening to busy footsteps hammer the hallway outside. *Had she been too coarse with them?* Maybe. Bezek struggled to truly care. Her mind was elsewhere. Deep in the void there was a crew loyal to the collective and fighting for their lives.

Maybe they were already dead; maybe they were being tortured. Gemini suspected the latter. Bezek's stomach churned for them. She gripped the back of her chair as a wave of nausea washed over her. Scarred hands ached as she squeezed the leather tight. They were her reminder of the evil that needed to be cleansed. Late at night, when she removed her garments, the rest of her battered body brought the pain of old scars to a righteous boil and into the forefront of her mind. She would find them and the Radaishar would pay.

***

Sabik strained in the darkness. Mlyma's whimpering had died and resurged a dozen times before she finally fell asleep against the far wall of their cell. Listening to her was torture; not being able to feel her presence was something else entirely.

Coldness stung his back. Night must have fallen. Dew from condensation seeped from the rock to his shirt, causing him to shudder uncontrollably. *Desperation.* Sabik had always operated at the edge of the fleet. Often, he was well beyond the mental reach of the collective.

This was different. Sabik had always been in charge. He always had a say in whether he lived or died. It was his action or inaction that doomed him and, if during the heat of battle, he found himself on the brink of death, he always thought he would understand. Having control gave him peace.

This, however, was different. It was torment. He was powerless and empty. He was hungry, tired, and worried. *Desperation.*

The shudder down his spine stopped and waited. It refused to leave him and instead turned from a tingle in the center to a deep cold that burned in his bones. He tried to adjust his body but the chains kept him from moving far. The cold was something he would have to get used to.

Sabik had heard stories about the Radaishar. They were Mateens, a colony sent by the hive to establish a deep-space presence. Nearly half a million Mateens had departed on that trip, but it had been plagued with errors. Mere months after finding a suitable planet, a meteor strike damaged the critical systems of the colony and killed thousands. Pirates and mercenaries heard their distress calls and raided the stranded colonists, dragging off and enslaving the Mateen children while slaughtering the adults.

Bureaucracy within the Mateen collective led to a delayed response and when the government finally did gather the resources to rescue their colony, something unimaginable had happened. They disappeared. The entirety of the Radaishar colony was suddenly absent from the consciousness of the collective and impossible to find using conventional military technology. It was assumed that the rescue efforts had been too slow, and the colony died.

But those were the early days. The Mateen learned their lesson and the poor Radaishar were happily forgotten for hundreds of years, until, of course, they began raiding Mateen merchant vessels crossing the galactic divide.

Sabik wanted to feel sorry for the Radaishar, but he couldn't. What they did to Mlyma was horrible. *Unforgivable.* These were issues between governments, not soldiers. The mistakes of a government never justified the torture of soldiers.

"Is that so?" whispered a voice from beyond his cage. Startled, Sabik looked up. It was the same gray and red-faced rebel who had mocked him earlier in the day.

"Is what so?" Sabik asked.

"Better yet," the Radaishar continued in the shadows, "how can an aggressor possibly demand the victim forgive one's mistakes?"

Sabik thought for a moment. The rebel spoke in riddles. His question eluded him. What was he getting at?

"Riddles?" he hissed violently, slamming a wooden stick against the steel cage to startle Sabik. "We don't need your pity. We are strong again. Far stronger than the collective. Hundreds of years of isolation gave us an advantage your people will never understand."

Sabik's heart froze. *Did he read my mind?* It was impossible. They had severed their link, mutilated their bodies. They couldn't possibly—

"Yes," his jailer said coldly.

"How?" Sabik asked. "It's impossible." he stopped. In the dim light beyond his cage, Sabik saw a bloodied clump of flesh still pulsing within the rebel's hands. A grim smile formed on the jailer's face.

"I can hear you as if I am her," he whispered. "I even hear some of her thoughts, or at least the thoughts she had before the surgery," he corrected. "They're quiet but they are there. It's a shame she'll never be able to express to you her feelings before we took this from her."

"Maniac!" Sabik shouted, flinging himself at the bars only to be held back by chains at the end of their slack. His wrists burned as he fought them, steel carving deep into his skin. "How could you?"

The Radaishar rebel didn't move. He wasn't startled. He knew everything Sabik would do an instant before he would do it. He was fully tuned into Sabik's thoughts and wishes, to his hatred and panic.

His captor smiled a thin, deformed smile. "You don't say?" he whispered with psychotic joy. "I suppose it is a shame you'll never be able to fully express that to Mlyma either."

Sabik grit his teeth. *Torture. You are a Mateen,* he told himself. *Don't let them intimidate you.*

"It's fitting you should return to your people a martyr," the jailer continued. "Perhaps you can describe to them how it feels to be me. How it feels to be abandoned by the collective and left to die in a foreign land. How it feels to have your family taken by raiders and sold into slavery by your enemies." He paused, examining Sabik's face. "I want all of the information you have on Mateen fleet movement. If you don't give it to me, I will take it by force, like I've taken Mlyma's."

He turned to leave but then hesitated and faced Sabik once more. "Do you have anything to tell me?" he asked plainly.

Sabik didn't say a word. He had been trained for the torture he might endure if he was ever captured, and he knew what might be required to safeguard the information he was privy to.

"Fine," the rebel responded, tossing the desiccated portion of Mlyma's parietal lobe to the ground. "It's a shame these things don't last long outside of the body. We try to preserve them as best we can, but soon all you can hear are distant murmurs repeating themselves over and over again. There might be a little life left in it but nothing more of value." He was toying with Sabik. "Perhaps we'll experiment with just how long yours lasts. I'm going to remove your lobe tomorrow," he taunted. "Only then will I deliver your corpse back to your precious crew. To your beloved Gemini."

Gemini. The name suddenly brought hope.

"Why are you doing this?" Sabik asked. "Why would you torture us? You must know this will gain you nothing."

The rebel paused for a moment. Blue light flickered behind his eyes. He looked at Sabik and then at the bloody lobe he had just thrown onto the floor. "Let me show you just what I plan to gain," he barked, kicking the parietal lobe against the bars of his cell.

To Sabik's horror, it pulsed, given life by some dark magic that Sabik couldn't understand. Was he hallucinating? His mind felt clouded, his face felt hot. *Mlyma,* his mind screamed. *I'm so sorry, Mlyma.* The rebel raised his foot and as he pressed down upon the tissue, Mlyma began to groan.

"Stop it!" Sabik shouted.

The jailer pressed harder. Blood oozed from the organ and pooled on the dusty ground. Sabik looked away. His stomach churned. Mlyma switched from a groan to a cry. *Torture.*

"You're killing her!" Sabik screamed. "Stop it, please!"

The Radaishar ignored him and instead pressed fully down upon the organ and crushed it, causing Mlyma to shriek and then fall silent.

"We'll do you tomorrow," he said. "Sweet dreams."

***

It was still dark when they took him, dragged the groggy-eyed Mateen from his cage and into a place that was something else entirely. To Sabik, it seemed like a dream.

He could feel his toes scrape across the stone floor. There was pressure under each arm, people holding him up. No, not people. Not ever people. Rebels. Savages. Sabik wanted to resist them, but his whole body felt heavy. His eyes were blurry. *Should they be? How long had it been since I fell asleep?*

The stone tiles passed quickly beneath him, a river of gray brown that was cold and empty. The rebels hurried in their task. Sabik tried to lift his head but couldn't. Orange burned in his periphery. *Torches.*

Suddenly, the river of tile was no more, and the orange glow surrounded him as if he was inside a kiln. The weight pressing upon his arms abated. He felt cold orange beneath him. The stone remained. It was merely the light that had been different.

They drugged you, a voice called in the distance. It was familiar, warm.

Drugged. The haze remained, but a sudden awareness smashed through his clouded consciousness. *They drugged you.*

What was going to happen? Despite the clouds that blanketed his mind, he knew what awaited him. *Lobotomy.*

Fear and panic filled him. *Fight them. Fight them.* He struggled to pull his arms free but couldn't. The commands from his mind to his muscles fell flat. He was no longer in control. His consciousness had been separated from his body.

Something firm held his wrists. Chains or rope wrapped around them. His head spun, and he was once again aware of the coldness of the stone that soaked into his back. He was lying down.

Lobotomy. Sabik strained to see through the orange light at the room around him. Instead, a dark shadow filled his vision.

"You won't remember most of this," a cruel voice said. "But I assure you, the pain will be very real."

The voice was distant, like a memory calling out from beyond the grave. That's all it was. Just a memory. Some different life, not his own.

We are going to find you, another voice called into him. This one was closer, more intimate. It was female and reminded him of his mother. There was warmth to the voice, assurance. *Keep your eyes open,* it called again. *We need to see through your eyes to find you. Keep them open and stay strong. You're going to lose us for a moment.*

Sabik struggled to understand the thoughts and the words as they swirled through his head. The fog in his mind was heavy. *Don't lose Bezek. Eyes open.* And then the worst pain he had ever felt swallowed his body.

CHAPTER EIGHTEEN

Cale watched the colors of the rainbow nebula fade as his fleet departed Charoth towards Tassi. From the aft viewing window in their officer's mess, the diminishing glow of orange and green gas gave his meat a glaze that made it look spoilt. His milk turned from creamy white to rustic yellow. It was still delicious if he closed his eyes, which is precisely what he did.

Cale pushed his plate back across the stainless-steel table and retrieved a black leather binder from a cargo pocket on his pants. Once open, the screen hummed to life and contained the digital transcripts from his mission on Charoth. His notes had already been compiled with the observations of his crew. Now he would go through the final report to make any conclusions.

There were a vast number of conclusions yet to make, not only which concerned the whereabouts of Brokk but also what Tassi was to do with Atworth Kierce and the government of Charoth. The governor had lied about Brokk, that much was clear, but Cale had to determine to what extent he should hold Atworth liable. It was possible having a foothold on Charoth could prove valuable to future fleet operations. On the other hand, there were surely a number of other governments exerting influence over Atworth and his small operation. Perhaps the Tassians could make a clear statement to the rest of the galaxy if they took unilateral measures against Charoth for supporting the war criminal Brokk.

Cale scrolled through the digital files and searched for things he had not yet learned from his debriefs with his crew. It had been as good a visit as he could expect. He had set out to find his father and now his bones were now onboard and receiving the treatment a war hero deserved. He learned his father had fought until the end, that with every breath, he had sought to destroy Brokk and end his campaign of death across the galaxy.

Cale had also met a Hestonian who hated Brokk as much as he did. While Cale struggled to trust the bounty hunter, Thilgod Furstil, he did trust his motives about Brokk. Thilgod's account on Charoth matched what Cale's intelligence had already learned, which further established his legitimacy. What Cale had yet to understand were Thilgod's motives in securing passage off Charoth. With Brokk gone from Charoth, it seemed Thilgod would have found decent enough work under Atworth Kierce. No, there was something else, some hidden reason that Cale had not yet discovered surrounding Thilgod.

It didn't matter, of course. The Hestonian was ultimately a mercenary in need of work. Hestos had exiled him long ago, and he had no family Cale knew of. To Cale, Thilgod was the perfect expendable asset in his hunt for Brokk. So long as the two of them could keep ulterior motives to the side of their relationship, Cale was certain they would be able to work towards a common goal.

A shadow blocked the fluorescent light above. Cale looked up. His executive officer, a fat Tassian with short brown hair, huffed air through large nostrils above him.

Cale smiled. "Well, don't just stand there looking absurd," he ordered. "Sit down already or grab yourself something to drink."

His X.O. obliged, sliding an orange and silver chair out from underneath the table and dropping into it like a body bag. He let out a grunt as his body hit the hard chair.

"I have a few items I need to discuss with you," he said abruptly, adding, "if now is a good time."

Cale flipped a cover over his notes and returned them to his pocket. The nebula had gotten smaller in the twenty or so minutes that he was reading. His milk returned to a delectable creamy white. Driven by thirst, Cale emptied the glass before allowing Admiral Cuhno'e Bohe to speak.

His X.O., dressed in a gray flight suit, reviewed his notes as he waited.

"Sorry," Cale said sturdily. "What have you got for me?"

Admiral Bohe gave a cautiously warm smile. "We fabricated the bounty hunter a small freighter. He's traveled to Despona to drop off merchant cargo and survey the Jark presence there. It should be a sufficient cover."

"You've supplied him for that as well?" Cale asked.

"Yes, he has plenty of local currency to get what he needs, and he knows how to navigate the markets to make a year's salary off the material we've given him."

"Which is?" Cale asked leadingly.

"Fruit flies, of course," Bohe responded with a chuckle. "Cultured fruit flies."

The relationship between Jark and Despona had Tassi worried. There was a clear partnership, if not an alliance, between the two systems. Since the two had fought against Hestos as allies before, Cale believed he had every right to be concerned. Despona, the weaker of the two, had reached out to Jark Empire for a cooperative partnership. It might be impossible to drive a wedge between the two systems but perhaps Tassi could establish a trade block to pressure them to rethink their position. Regardless, the Jark garrison on Despona was likely to be full of information that could prove valuable to Tassian intelligence.

"Good," Cale said, nodding. "What else?"

Bohe continued, "Initial reports of the plague on Jark indicate the attack was successful. So far, there are 12 million reported deceased and nearly 60 million infected. We expect many of those will not survive the coming days. Jark has declared an emergency and recalled many of their fleets to provide humanitarian aid until the virus is contained. Our estimates are that we should reach 500 million dead by the end of the month, but then that will taper off quickly. It is likely we will see approximately 6 to 7 hundred million deceased when the plague has run its course."

"Good," Cale said. "Very, very good. What is the response from the rest of the galaxy?"

Bohe looked at his notes. "Hestos has promised to send a medical vessel, and, of course, Despona will respond with something, but they haven't announced anything yet. The Mateens have not released an official statement, but our ambassador to the Galactic Council indicated they will not provide aid because of friction between the two governments."

Bohe cleared his throat. "I have some upsetting news from our ambassador on Hestos."

Cale raised an eyebrow. "Ambassador Grubbe?" he asked. Cale's heart fluttered. Had the Jarks already learned the origin of the plague? Were they blaming Tassi in front of the council? His mind spun as a snowfall of actions and counteractions cascaded in his head. They needed more time to build the fleet and were draining their resources dry to do so. In six months they had fabricated and purchased many vessels, but this was merely a drop in the bucket compared to what the Jark Empire still had at their disposal.

"Casika," Bohe said, interrupting Cale's thoughts. "Casika went missing on Hestos."

Time stopped. *Casika went missing.* A flurry of thoughts flew through Cale's mind. *Is she hurt? Dead? Was the pressure too much? No. She was hurt. Or worse, kidnapped. Ransomed. Where could she be? Was someone hurting her?* "What do you mean, missing?" Cale finally asked.

Bohe shrugged sheepishly. Of all the men on the ship, Bohe knew the most about the relationship Cale had with Casika. How much he trusted her. How much he loved her. "Ambassador Grubbe reported that she didn't show up for her testimony against the Jarks three days ago. He claims she asked to him to testify so what she could return to Tassi. According to Grubbe, she was finding it too difficult to confront the Jarks given her experience in the war."

Cale nodded through the story. A sickness grew in his stomach. His head felt light. Casika wasn't a trained diplomat. He shouldn't have sent her there. He knew what was coming next in the story before Admiral Bohe needed to say it.

"Once the meeting adjourned," he continued, "the ambassador went to her room alone to check on her. The door had been jammed from the inside. A window was left open. The bed was messy. Sheets and blankets on the floor. Pillows thrown about." He checked his notes. "Grubbe thinks she might have been kidnapped, but authorities on Hestos disagree. They claim he lacks evidence and support it by call logs. There was a call between Grubbe and Casika the night before. Worse, there is little by way of forensics to identify where she might have gone or by who."

Cale let out a heavy breath. *Kidnapped.* The milk turned sour in his stomach. His hands felt cold. It was as if his heart was beating too slowly to keep his body moving. Cale wasn't sure he could lose Casika after losing his father too. After losing most of his friends, family, and soldiers to the war. She had helped him along so much, carried him through the hardest parts of his day.

"What does the council have to say about it?"

Bohe shook his head. "You know how this goes. They need time to complete an investigation. There are disputes between transit logs and some on Hestos claimed to have seen her take a shuttle. Ambassador Grubbe's testimony on speaking to Casika seems to be the primary source of evidence against a kidnapping claim." He locked eyes with Cale. "I'm truly sorry," he said at last. "I really am."

Cale waved a hand. He didn't want to hear anything more about sorrow. The Tassians spent their whole existence wallowing in sorrow and being the recipients of ill-fortune. It was time to take the helm. Time to seize their destiny and strive for greatness.

"We won't sit idle feeling sorry for ourselves, Admiral." As the words left his mouth, Cale felt resolved in his purpose. "Set a course for Hestos and alert our forensic team onboard. If there is a chance we can find her, let's do everything possible."

Bohe nodded. "I'll alert the fleet but . . ." he hesitated, trailing off in thought before continuing. "It might be difficult to gain access to the crime scene. I imagine Hestos isn't interested in giving foreigners authority to investigate."

Cale frowned. He wasn't interested in hurtling political obstacles. "We have a few specialists on the ship that can exploit evidence very quickly. Make sure they go with the forensic team. Warn Ambassador Grubbe we are on our way. Ensure he insists in the strongest possible language that we intend to search for our citizen. Besides, how long has it been since the galaxy has seen a Tassian Fleet patrol beyond our own system? Perhaps it will serve as its own form of diplomacy."

Bohe gave Cale a sideways glance before rising to his feet to leave. It was clear he hadn't understood what Cale meant, but Cale didn't care. Bohe was an admiral under the old order. He, like Cale's father, had served during a time of assumed peace, a time when they were lulled to sleep by a false sense of security and a faithless galactic community. While many of the older generation might consider Cale to be abrasive, he considered them to be naive. Now was neither the time to be weak nor the time to be cautious. It was time the galaxy recognized Tassi with the respect Cale believed they deserved.

As his executive officer walked away, Cale turned his attention back to the large window that faced the rainbow nebula. As he watched it fade into the distance, a silver shield lowered over the windows. Bohe had given his orders. The ships prepared for the jump to Hestos.

Cale returned his eyes to his plate and fiddled with his gravy-laden fork. Casika would have hated the scraping it made against the steel plate. He smiled at how much it irritated her. It was no coincidence that the day she planned to testify against the Jark Empire was the day she went missing.

Casika. The name surged within him. He felt sick. What horrors might she be facing now? Were they torturing her? Guilt mixed with regret stabbed at his chest. His heart ached. His hands trembled. He should have been there to testify with her. Casika wasn't a diplomat or politician. He should have been there.

As his guilt marinated, the pit in his stomach returned, but something else came back with it. If the Jarks were behind this kidnapping, Cale could hope that she wasn't dead yet. If this was political, and not some random act of violence, there was latitude for Cale to act. There was room for Cale to negotiate. They would want something from her or from Tassi. That might be a good sign. Maybe, just maybe, there would be room for Casika to be rescued. Without warning, a kernel of hope seized a foothold in his heart and, as it grew, Cale began to formulate a plan for getting her back.

CHAPTER NINETEEN

Slender hands. Fingers. Terrible burning. Blackness. Utter blackness. Those hands. Soft, gentle.

He felt so cold. The blackness. What was that blackness? Something was missing. Something *is* missing. *Your name is Sabik*, Sabik thought to himself.

Warm fingers rubbed his cheeks. They caressed and massaged his neck. A cold blackness filled his mind. Was he in space? Was he floating? His knees felt weak. His back ached against something cold and wet. A drop of water plopped from a ledge and clanged onto the floor below. It was all so far away from him.

Sabik lifted his hand, but then he couldn't. He tried again. Nothing. *Did it move at all?* The cold blackness was everywhere, except for there. In the corner. Something gray was over there. Warm, gray hands touched his forehead gently.

Shhh, they hushed.

"Rest," cooed a voice.

Sabik told himself to close his eyes, and they closed, but suddenly he wasn't sure if they were ever open to begin with. The blackness remained black and the gray remained gray. Water remained water, but it was no longer far away. The water had moved, and a cool drip rolled down the side of his neck. The rough edges of a damp cloth brushed against his forehead. This time a stream of water chilled his spine.

Why is everything so strange? Sabik wondered. Before the blackness, Sabik's words would be a bright, golden melody falling from his inside mouth. He would see them in the void of his mind and other inside faces would take them and pull them in. *The collective was always listening.* His words now were dark. Instead of singing to others, they merely fell flat against an endless void. And then he remembered.

The surgery. Blackness faded, replaced by light and terrible, aching pain. His head throbbed. His throat burned. The hands that touched him seemed to dissolve into the sea of pain that he felt. An ocean of lava was consuming him and, try as he might to escape, the lava continually covered his face, always burning but never leaving him fully burned. *Let me die!* Sabik screamed. Those words, just as the others, floated into an abyss that had once bridged him to the collective.

Sabik fought, desperate to escape the brutal pain, the headache, the throbbing, and the heat. A scalpel sliced through his flesh. A needle twisted through his skin, winding thick thread over and over through his scalp. The thread rubbed and burned against his flesh and his ears could hear the rubbing of cotton that pulled his skin tight against itself.

Back and forth, darkness and light battered his thoughts. Horrible pain sucked and pulled him into a madness. Just when he couldn't take it a moment longer, the warm hands returned, and the water fell down his neck, and he sat up.

Light filled his eyes. The jail. Sabik was back in jail. A gray blur sat before him. *Mlyma.*

"Easy, Sabik," Mlyma said calmly. Her voice was pure and sweet. "Easy. You had quite the night, but I'm here now, okay?"

Sabik tried to nod, but he couldn't. His neck felt paralyzed against the back of the rocky stone wall. "They cut me open," he managed to whisper. "They cut me open."

She nodded, her face coming into focus for the first time. That soft gray face and long black hair felt like home to Sabik. The familiarity of her warm hands and gentle spirit brought him a fleeting comfort, but the pain resurged, and, worse, Sabik realized something was different. He couldn't feel her anymore. The essence she carried inside her was gone. Just the shell of her remained. *The surgery.*

"They cut me open too," she whispered. Her voice trembled as she paused and gripped his face firmly in her palms before releasing him and turning away. "They took out part of our brain."

He knew what she said was true. He could hear nothing beyond the physical. He felt nothing beyond his own flesh and blood. They had removed part of his parietal lobe. The organ that made the Mateen unique, the one that let them reach out to a great cloud of witnesses whenever they desired comfort, help, or companionship. The part that whispered and directed and brought hope. They cut it out. The monsters cut it out. In doing so, they turned Sabik into what they were. *Not Mateen.*

"What do we do?" he stuttered in a panicked frenzy. The wall felt far away. Blackness threatened to return. His hands felt small and weak and powerless. "What do we do?" he said again, quietly this time.

Mlyma took his hand in hers and lowered her head so he could see her eyes. They were as black as night itself. There was an emptiness that filled those eyes, and yet, there was hope. Strength. Courage. "We'll do it together," she said. "You hear me? We'll do it together."

Sabik pulled at her strength. "Yes," he managed to mumble through numb lips. "We'll do it together." And then a thought filled him that gave him strength apart from Mlyma altogether. *Verela Bezek was looking through your eyes.*

He almost blurted it out before reminding himself to whisper. "Commander Bezek contacted me."

"What?" she whispered, jerking her head back in shock. "What do you mean contacted you?"

"Just before the surgery, while they were wheeling me out. I had almost forgotten, but she connected with me. She told me to keep my eyes open, so she could watch. So that she could find us." Sabik was elated at the hope that his memory brought with it.

Mlyma leaned into him and pressed her forehead against his. She smiled gently, but his pain surged once more within him. Blackness returned. With it, a deep cold chilled his bones. Sabik felt his body go limp and fall against the stone wall behind him. Inaudible whispers from the gray-faced woman chided him but he ignored her. It was too much work to try and survive.

Stay with me, he heard her say. Or did he think it? Warm hands moved from his own hands to his wrists and then up his shoulders. They pressed and kneaded the muscles below his neck, and then they disappeared. She felt far from him.

Footsteps drummed outside of his cell. Voices echoed back and forth in the distance above him. *My jailer,* he thought calmly, letting his body fall once more into the lava that burned but never consumed. Then a more peaceful thought entered his mind. *My dear Mlyma,* he muttered to himself, closing his eyes. *We are already dead.*

***

"There!" Bezek bellowed from the chair on her bridge. "Something is floating out there. Do you see it?"

"Focusing our sensors," Ximon responded.

Verela nodded to the tall, thin Mateen sitting behind his work station. He was her signals officer, a young high flyer waiting to get off her ship and down to one of the squadrons where his skills could be truly utilized. Still, his time on Bezek's main battleship was formative for young officers and, in a search-and-destroy fight, you couldn't ask for a better opportunity to use signals intelligence to its maximum.

Bezek waited as the officer worked, watching her staff coordinate with Ximon to enhance their understanding of what they were seeing by ensuring the object wasn't armed or manned and verifying its structure and makeup. In space, this highly sensitive work was done from tens of thousands of kilometers away and relied as much on sensors as the experience and skill of the crew employing them.

Still, the anticipation was killing her. After what seemed like an eternity, the image of the front half of a Lovac-class reconnaissance ship appeared in the center of the room. As the holographic image rotated, Bezek bit her lip.

"Was this thing blown in half?" she asked out loud.

"Tell me what happened, Ximon," Bezek ordered, hoping for a forensic analysis that she knew would be difficult to generate.

Ximon clamored from his chair towards the center of the room. Against the blue light of the hologram, his gray features darkened, and his height was magnified. Big gray hands manipulated the image, spinning it from side to side as he examined it himself. Finally, he nodded.

"I don't think blown in half, ma'am," he said, rotating the structure of the vessel sideways to show its sleek steel nose and angled crew compartment. "Three rounds, chemical, I believe, entered here, here, and here. You see the black charred steel around the entry points?"

She nodded. Yes, she saw them now, each hole was thin, like a needle piercing cloth but the area around the entry was discolored.

"I think they used high velocity heat rounds," he proclaimed. "The chemicals inside would burn through the hull, sucking oxygen up with it until a crew either asphyxiated or collapsed. Those near the entry point would have been burned almost instantly, but—"

She cut him off. "Ryzan," she ordered her navigation officer, "search for subspace travel. Find their trails."

Ryzan nodded, and she turned her attention back to Ximon. "Go on," she ordered.

"Well," he continued, "I was going to say I don't think this killed them. The angles in the nose here wouldn't have penetrated the crew compartment. If anything, this disabled the ship, but even then, Sabik would have had some options to enhance his own survivability. We're missing the other half of the ship, but I'm going to assume he was floating through space, and the Radaishar boarded his disabled vessel. This wasn't blown in half," he reiterated. "It was cut."

Commander Bezek squinted her eyes before climbing from her chair to stand next to the hologram. He was right. The part of the ship that remained was smooth. It had been carved apart by a laser not blown to bits by an explosion.

"This is where it happened, team," she said to her crew. "Analyze it and continue searching for other pieces of equipment. Collect the damaged parts and sanitize our technology. Narrow my fleet's search, bring them in and alter our posture to be able to respond to a threat.

"Ximon," she said, looking in his direction. "What will these chemical rounds do to my battleship if they catch us by surprise?"

He raised his eyebrows and thought for a moment. "Not much," he said eventually. "The Lovac ships don't have advanced counter measures. They are built for speed and stealth. I recommend a formation that places our battleships and destroyers around the smaller vessels. It will ensure their protection as we hunt the Radaishar."

"Good," she nodded. "Ryzan, what do you have?"

The much shorter navigation officer rose from his chair and brought a new image up on the hologram before her. "There is most definitely a trail in the subspace leading toward an asteroid belt half a parsec from here."

"Make that our heading," she ordered, before adding, "and good work. Report our progress to Gemini and move out. There's no telling what horror our people are suffering at the hands of these monsters."

CHAPTER TWENTY

"This is an extremely sensitive matter. I don't think you fully understand the ramifications of your actions!"

For the first time in his life, Cale was stunned at how angry he had made Ambassador Grubbe. Blood rushed into chubby, pale cheeks as the Tassian continued to rage.

"Tassi cannot park an Armada built for war in Hestonian space!" he protested. "Do you have any idea how much work this has caused me? I'm pulling favors that we had held for the most desperate times!"

Cale frowned. He was tired of being lectured but still need Grubbe to do his work. He feared that Grubbe was equally likely to shut down and quit over the offense than to help him any further.

"Listen," Cale said, holding up a hand.

"No, you listen," responded Grubbe. "You are not the Tassian president. You aren't even a fleet admiral! This act risks damaging all the diplomatic legitimacy that we've been storing for decades. The Hestonians will not stand for it!"

Cale had enough. "Shut it, Grubbe!" he shouted. "Our diplomatic currency was depleted when Hestos did nothing to defend us from the Jark invasion. Our diplomatic currency meant nothing then, and it means nothing now. The Hestonians have ignored every legitimate request you have made, and now they threaten to flex their muscle?"

Cale paused and stepped closer to Ambassador Grubbe. The diplomat may have outranked him, but it was Cale who currently commanded the only remaining Tassian Armada. It was Cale who had become the de facto leader of the Tassian bureaucracy as they rebuilt, and, with any luck, it would be Cale who won the election to gain a legitimate place as leader of his people. He could feel himself getting angry as he watched the ambassador step back in shock at his aggressive advance. *This career politician lacks courage,* thought Cale.

Cale quieted his voice. "In another year and with Mateen help, we'll have bought or fabricated another two space fleets. They will be some of the most modern in the Galaxy. Tassian traders and merchants are bringing in wealth and tourism is at an all-time high. Mining has renewed on the distant moons, and we have harvested an immense amount of exotic material that many of the planetary systems would be willing to trade for. It is time we stop assuming our diplomacy is tied to compliance. Tassi will soon rival Hestos in military strength, and I have no intention of pushing our military power behind the curtain in favor of diplomacy."

Ambassador Grubb scowled. "More people than your precious Casika will suffer if you do not let diplomacy reign supreme. I've spent my entire life working to avoid war. It would be for nothing if we act in aggression now!"

"More people have already suffered!" Cale shouted. "Millions of people! While you sat in your embassy on Hestos, far from the wicked Jark forces that tore apart our land, we suffered. People died. My father taken as a war criminal. Killed in an alien forest like a peddler. Entire divisions of Tassian soldiers destroyed. Mothers thrown from roofs and worse, far worse, our youth were rounded up and executed. If we bow down now in the face of Hestonian pressure, we'll never be able to claw our way back to the top."

Cale paused to assay Ambassador Grubbe's expressions. *Was he pensive? Hesitant? Convinced?* Sweat formed on the old diplomat's balding head. Damp beads speckled his face. *Nervous.* He was nervous and just as impotent now as he had been during the initial invasion. *Impotent or negligent?* his mind questioned.

Finally, Grubbe gave Cale a sheepish smile. An olive branch during an otherwise hostile meeting. "What would you have me do?" he quizzed.

Cale stepped back from him and turned towards his desk, noticing how sloppy it must have looked to the bureaucratic coward who lacked the survival skills of a rodent. "Buy us time," he ordered. "Find us room to park our ships. Apologize for my rashness. Tell them we would like fuel at the diplomatic rate, the rate between allies."

Grubbe scoffed but didn't say anything. Cale recognized why. He thought it too forward to demand favors granted allies. Tassi had long relied on Hestonian power for protection. Cale knew the tides would turn. One year. That was all he needed. One year to build his fleet and create an aggressive foreign policy to ward off the vultures.

"Fine," he responded with a shrug. "These are easy requests but the stir you caused by leaping into Hestonian Space has the whole defense force pointing their guns at you. What do you actually intend to accomplish here?" Grubbe asked shrewdly.

Cale smiled. "I just need a little time is all."

"Time for what?" snorted the Ambassador.

***

It wasn't hard to blend in. The busy downtown, full of restaurants, bars, and clubs was loaded with countless pedestrians who were eager for the warm weather and good times. The mild Hestonian summer brought crowds of onlookers and tourists to the capital each year, many eager to take advantage of all that the galactic hub had to offer.

"Kiss me," Zabra ordered, rising onto her toes and leaning into her partner.

Soloan let his body fall back against the rough brick wall behind him. Her soft lips made his shiver in delight. He returned the favor before pulling away. "We have a job to do, young lady," he whispered, pulling her hands tight into his own and holding them firm. Her eyes were a calm brown and threatened to pull him back in for another kiss.

"You don't have to remind me," she grinned, drawing him close to her once more. "Besides, we're almost there. You wouldn't want to arouse any suspicions, would you?"

He laughed loudly at that, garnering the brief attention of a couple who wandered drunkenly towards the water. "I think that ridiculous outfit will get us all the attention we need," he chided.

Zabra's smile went flat. Soloan realized if he wasn't careful the peaceful brown eyes might be replaced with a fire that no Tassian could put out. Instead, Zabra curtsied, pulling awkwardly at her knee-length blue skirt in the process.

"You're adorable," he said at last, grabbing at her waist until Zabra had reclaimed her position in his arms again. "Maybe I'll marry you here one day. Heck, if we do, we can actually enjoy it a little more than most of our exotic trips recently."

"You know my mother wouldn't approve," Zabra responded coyly. "Besides, it isn't like we can start a family anyways." She paused. "Not with all those experiments."

Soloan sighed but smiled. "You don't have a mother, you devious devil. And we'll adopt," he said before changing the subject to protect his pride rather than maintain his mission. "Time's up. Shall we?"

Zabra nodded, tugged her hand from his grip, and spun away from him. She blew him a kiss with one hand and used her other to raise her skirt once more above her knee before skipping down the narrow alleyway that separated the Jark embassy building from the remainder of the wharf.

Pretending to catch the kiss, Soloan grabbed at the air and watched her athletic figure fade into the darkness until only her white blouse was visible. Soon, the only remnants of her existence were the clacking of her brown leather boots against the stones that lined her path. Eventually, even that turned to nothing.

Night had fallen. Street fires blazed outside of busy restaurants to warm guests while lamps above hummed to life. Soloan checked his watch. He would give her another thirty seconds or so before starting his own movement through the building. Timing was everything.

In seven minutes, two Jarks at the front of the embassy would lock the doors and drop bars over the windows. They would then begin their security check of the downstairs entryway and offices. Ambassador Edet Gadalje would be passing them on his way to the basement of the embassy to finish his work and send a classified report to the Jark government. It was there, the two planned to catch him.

Soloan checked his watch again. *Game time.* Blinking twice, he activated his augmented vision. Colors that had once been hidden by the blanket of night burst into view. Pedestrians along the wharf glowed red, but more importantly, the wall of the embassy building appeared transparent before him. Inside, Soloan could see two figures standing guard at the front of the building.

Five minutes. Soloan moved swiftly down the alley and towards the entrance to the building. As he neared the street corner, he pressed a lump that protruded from his wrist and felt power surge within him. The neurotoxin that was released filled his veins with fast-acting steroids and numbed the nerves along his skin. He felt invincible.

Four minutes. Soloan turned the corner and faced the large brown building. Massive stone blocks rose from the ground forming steps to a glass entryway. Black rock pillars jutted upward holding up an awning that draped over the front doors like a black cloak, making his mission even easier than he hoped. A map in his eyes appeared and provided his route. It was intuitive enough, he surmised.

Feeling light on his feet, Soloan jogged the steps and waved his arms wildly, attracting the attention of the two security officers behind the glass.

"Hey!" he shouted. The Jark guards stepped towards the glass.

"Drunk," he could see one of them mouth to the other in the local Hestonian tongue.

The distraction worked. Behind them, a shadow fell to the floor. The small figure walked forward slowly, quietly. The Jarks in front of her clearly heard nothing. Instead of turning, they began waving off Soloan dumbly by flicking their wrists into the air.

Soloan for his part shrugged his arms and danced around the entryway some more to give the two fools something to laugh about. Zabra would surely have some comments about his performance later, but he enjoyed having the attention. Soloan had long suspected he would have been great on a stage and any chance to show off his skills was a win in his book, even if he was supposed to be working.

Zabra continued her methodical creep towards her prey. Through his augmented eyes, Soloan could see that her fingers had disappeared, replaced instead by long, metallic needles full of a gruesome poison. This was how Zabra preferred to kill her prey. *It only takes a poke,* she would tell him. *Silent and deadly,* she would grin.

Soloan stopped dancing and faced the window. The expression on the two guards at the front changed. One winced. *He felt it.* The Jark turned to his partner and opened his mouth. He had wanted to speak but the precision of the needle against the Jark's spine had rendered him instantly incapacitated. The other guard didn't turn at all and staggered forward slightly before falling flat to the floor.

As the two collapsed, Zabra watched for a minute before stepping over them and pressing a button to open the doors.

Soloan rushed through and closed them behind him, lowering the exterior bars using a computer terminal and erasing the camera evidence of his dance.

"It's a shame no investigator will see the skill of my performance," he said to Zabra over his shoulder.

"So, you can dance to entertain the other prisoners?" she asked with a grin, kneeling over the bodies of her victims.

She was beautiful but psychotic. Soloan turned and watched her as she examined her dead. He wondered what she was feeling and why she always bothered to watch her victims die.

Two minutes. His vision flashed the time warning in the upper right corners of his eyes. Soloan scanned the interior of the building. Shined onyx floors filled the hallway and contrasted with marble stairs that wound upwards. A thermal outline of Edet's shadow descended the steps.

"He's coming," Soloan whispered.

Zabra nodded, whispered something to the dead, and stepped past them. "Should we take their hands?" she asked him, "you know, to intimidate the ambassador with?"

Soloan shook his head. *Psychotic,* he thought. "Just make sure they disappear."

Zabra didn't respond. Soloan knew she didn't need to. The venom would eat the two Jarks from the inside out, converting their bodies into vapor and disintegrating them into the air. If tomorrow's investigators were lucky, they would breathe the Jarks in and take the evidence with them.

The two moved silently towards the corner wall near the staircase. Edet's thermal outline was close now, descending the final steps and holding what looked to be a keycard in his hand.

"Good evening," the ambassador barked as he stepped onto the landing and passed the spot where his guards were supposed to be stationed. He almost didn't notice, turning his back and taking a few steps down the hallway. "Good evening," he said again, turning his body fully to examine the front of the building.

"Good evening to you," Soloan responded, coming out from behind the stone corner of the wall.

Edet didn't hesitate. The primal Jark instinct in him surged to the surface. He charged, but Soloan was quick and strong. A simple duck avoided a swipe from thick Jark claws, and a sidestep averted the backhand that wildly followed. If time was on their side, Soloan would have loved to toy with the ambassador but, unfortunately, it was not.

Edet swung again and this time, Soloan stepped inward and caught his arm, crushing the Jark's bones in his grip and feeling a tinge of joy at the painful scream that poured from Edet's mouth.

Soloan threw the limp arm from his grip and grabbed the Jark's neck, lifting him from his feet and pinning him against the stone wall. "We need to talk privately," he whispered.

***

"He's coming around," Zabra proclaimed with jittery excitement.

Edet grumbled and snarled as he fiddled with his chains.

"It won't do you any good," Soloan said from a corner of the room. "This is your private office, is it not?"

The Jark ambassador to Hestos leaned his head back in his large black chair and groaned. "What do you fools want?" he said at last.

"Ah," Soloan responded. "If you had only asked us that in the first place we likely wouldn't have had to break your arm and tie you up."

Zabra giggled. Edet snarled and shook his chains more violently. Soloan wasn't worried. He prided himself as someone who could tie a hostage up sufficiently. Humming as he worked, Soloan fastened Edet's arms to the back of his chair and then weaved the chain around each leg until the poor Jark would struggle to keep his blood circulating, let alone move. The room had been darkened. Soloan had already gone through his desk. The whole office likely looked trashed to the Jark Ambassador and it was likely he had never been treated so poorly in all his life. This thought only inspired Soloan further.

"Casika," he said. "Where is the Tassian female named Casika?" The augmentations in his eyes allowed Soloan to monitor their captive's responses. His heartbeat increased. His eyes dilated. Adrenaline was being released from lymph nodes throughout his old body.

Edet shook his head. "The female from the council meetings?" he asked almost rhetorically. "I heard she took a transport out as soon as her testimony ended. How am I to know where she went?"

"We know you sent goons to her hotel room, you old fool," Soloan barked. "Where did you send the Tassian witness?"

The Jark locked eyes with him for a moment and then let out a grunt. "It would be too late if I told you," he responded. "I wasn't lying. She did take a freighter. Not sure if she was conscious though. Do yourselves a favor and escape while you can. Escape before the whole empire comes down on you."

Soloan was used to interrogations. Prior to volunteering for the augmentation program on Tassi, he was an intelligence officer. This, he determined, would be a quick one.

"Would you like me to break your other arm?" Soloan asked. "Tell me where the Tassian named Casika was taken, and we won't torture you. You are surely aware how bad this could go?"

Ambassador Edet was silent. Large Jark fangs protruded from half-open lips. The fur on his arms was a silvery black. His back hunched forward despite the chain around his arms that pulled him backwards. He was old and tired. Soloan could see the fight had left his eyes years ago. "She is on Despona," he said at last. "It won't do you any good. She's probably already dead. I had no part in taking her."

His comment sounded like an attempt to negotiate his freedom. A claim of innocence the Tassian government would never recognize. It was a lie of course. Soloan knew it was but he didn't need an explanation from the Jark, only a location.

"Where on Despona?" he quizzed.

The ambassador shook his head. "Guarantee my safety," he ordered.

Soloan stepped forward and allowed a jagged knife to protrude slowly from the back of his hand. It hurt slightly as it folded out from his synthetic skin, but his drugs prevented the more intense pain. At the sight of the knife, Edet swung his head back wildly to avoid the slash but was too slow. Soloan grabbed his ear and sliced, throwing the bloody body part into the frantic Jark's lap.

Edet howled.

"Where was she taken?!" Soloan shouted again.

"The Buhari garrison," he panted. "Buhari."

Soloan smiled at him and stepped back. "See," he told him. "You didn't need to experience your ear getting cut off. That was your fault for playing stupid."

"I've told you everything I know. Now release me," Edet ordered.

Soloan tisked his tongue at the ambassador as he turned towards Zabra. She was already lighting the papers on his desk on fire. "No, you'll burn alive for your participation in this crime," he whispered into the Jark's good ear.

"Let's go," he told Zabra. "An alarm will sound in a few minutes."

She nodded but as she passed Edet she stopped. She couldn't help herself. Lowering her face down to his, she looked into his eyes, examined his hair, and finally rested her hand gently on his cheek. "There is so much fear in him," she told Soloan. "Interesting that he can be the cause of such fear himself."

Soloan chuckled. "Have you forgotten your old life so quickly, Zabra?"

Smoke billowed as the two left the room. An orange light flashed behind them indicating the fire alarm had been tripped. Edet didn't make a noise as the heat in the room intensified. Soloan respected him for that. Far too many of his targets died as cowards. At least the Jark understood his work and respected it enough not muddy it at the point of death with vain appeals.

CHAPTER TWENTY-ONE

By the time Tamara reached the palace district, thick black clouds had engulfed the city. Her eyes burned from the sulfur. Her lungs, desperate for pure oxygen, strained against her chest. Funeral pyres lit up an otherwise darkened street as the ashes from thousands of Jark bodies fluttered sporadically into the sky.

Gunfire sounded in the distance and howls from Jarks battling beasts fell like dew upon the city and its weakening gates. No streetlight shone through the darkness. With only the orange glow of blazing Jark bodies to guide her sight, Tamara crept along empty city streets.

Each home she passed was dark but not absent of life. Inside the black stone walls, she sensed families huddled together, terrified of the horror that had descended upon their world. The wooden doors of their homes, carved from thorny branches and anchored in the black lava rock, were marked with animal blood. No doubt a symbol to the spirits or the dead to spare their home from both plague and beast.

Tamara grimaced at the horror. Never had she seen so much pain. *Necessary pain,* she corrected herself. Jark was an ugly place but Tamara wasn't sure what was uglier. Here she was again, prepared to execute the emperor of the Jark people, ready to do the bidding of violent thugs. The very thought of it should have repulsed her. Yet, she felt generally at peace; she felt as if her will and the circumstances of this world had finally united. Despite its ugliness, it was meant to be. *Assassin.*

There was purpose in her action. It aligned with the purpose of her people. Lysops. Wanderers. Vagabonds. Her people had no traceable roots. No understandable beginning and yet, throughout their history, the Lysops altered the history of others. Assassins, witches, wizards, and sorceresses. Powerful people who twirled the fate of kings and nations and worlds in their hands. *Assassin.*

She let the word roll off her tongue as she whispered it silently into the deadness of the cold Jark night. Who was she to alter the role that the Lysop played? On Hestos there was likely some philosopher bashing the morality of her decision. Some statesman who would try to convince her that the power had to be in the hands of the governed. That an assassin had no right to dictate the future of a planet and that within the assassin was far too much power for one being to wield. Perhaps he was right, she thought. But it wouldn't deter her.

The same man who preached against her actions would leave his lecture hall and purchase a slave woman on the way home. He would cheat on or abuse his spouse, embezzle money from his employer, and likely commit a slew of other morally questionable acts. *Was there an acceptable threshold from which good and evil could exist?* She wasn't sure. Morality was a mirage, merely a set of rules used to control the emotions of the masses. It wasn't a concept with any applicability for the ones in control. Law and order. Morality and ethics. They were mere concepts invented by those who needed to control the will of others. Tamara refused to allow herself to be enslaved to them.

And for what? Power? Comfort? Control? Wasn't Tamara's aim more noble than the reasons that governments controlled their people? Was her decision to intervene not selfless? How did Tamara benefit from being the thing people feared most? *Assassin.* The word brought strength and purpose. Tamara wasn't powerless anymore, and she wouldn't let societal norms influence her way of thinking or dictate her actions.

Jark was an ugly place, but it wasn't the ugliest place. Corruption was rampant here, yes. But there was also simplicity. The Jark people worked together, strove together, bled together. The Jark people had a common enemy, and Tamara would liberate them from it. The false spirituality of the old regime would perish with their emperor and then, only then, would the Jark people truly be free to do as they wished.

Assassin. Under cover of darkness, Tamara slid against the side of the emperor's palace. The massive black rock that rose vertically from the ground dwarfed her as she reached its corner. She felt small and insignificant against the hot structure that pulled a volcanic heat from the surface of Jark and into its walls. But she wasn't. She was powerful.

A ripple in her subconscious suddenly tore through her and hacked at the front of her skull. Gripping her forehead, Tamara dropped to a knee and leaned hard against the hot surface of the palace wall. Hissing filled her ears. Loud, brain-splitting hissing like a snake with a thousand tongues. *Or a thousand snakes with one tongue.*

Tamara clenched her jeweled hands and strained her eyes. *Control the situation,* she told herself. *Lower the volume. Peer through the static.* The pain stopped. Clarity returned, and with it was the realization that she had just walked into the path of one of the creatures.

Did it hear her? She couldn't be certain. Tamara leaned forward, feeling the hot wall drag across her leather jacket. Edging closer to the corner, she had to double her focus to block out the ever-present screeching in her mind that radiated from the beast beyond the walls.

It didn't move when she saw it. A long cylindrical body pulsed and gyrated. She held her breath, afraid to give herself away before she was ready. *Was it eating something?* Tamara strained in the darkness. Orange light from the pyres burned at her back but failed to illuminate the alley beyond.

In the darkness, the shadowy creature looked to be as wide as Tamara was tall. Perhaps three times as long. Its head bobbed up and down against the ground. She heard slurping now, sucking. The grinding of tooth against bone and a soft moan that fluttered out from beneath the worm. *Jark.*

It was eating a Jark soldier, and he was still alive. Tamara shut her eyes. *Go another way,* she told herself. *Don't try to kill this thing, this beast that screams nothingness into your ears.* The creature bobbed its head down once more and slurped. The man beneath it groaned.

Nausea flooded over her. Her stomach churned. Her face felt weak. The soldier fell silent. The worm gorged itself. Tamara tried once more to project her ethereal self towards the creature, but she couldn't. She felt mute against it. *It can still die,* she insisted.

Beating back the nausea and the fear, Tamara rose to her feet and crept from her hiding place. She could feel the warmth falling off the building beside her and disappear into the stony ground below. Her boots scraped against rocks. Her senses were primed, her body tense.

The creature remained focused on its meal. It's fat, cylindrical back shuddered in delight as it slurped the remaining blood from its victim. It stopped. Tamara felt the air around it shift. She sensed its muscle and sinew contract before perhaps even the worm itself knew that it would instinctively turn to the sound of her boots.

In the half-second between footstep and motion, her mind felt warm air and sulfur being pulled into the skin of the creature, through its pores and undoubtedly into its lungs. She couldn't sense beyond its skin, but Tamara realized it didn't matter. This creature was just like any other beast that crawled the ground. It relied on oxygen to breath and warmth to survive.

The thing turned its head and whipped a long black tail away from Tamara's approach. Did it know what she was doing? Could it sense a shortness of breath? Tamara took another step forward, allowing the fire within her to show her fierceness and distract the creature from her primary attack. The worm arched its head back, striking the majestic pose of a creature poised to attack.

Tamara wondered what its range was. How far could the nearly five-meter beast reach? How quickly could it strike?

Dim orange light glistened off the striations of its muscular underside as it stretched itself upward, shaking its head. It moved up for oxygen, not to attack. Her strategy was working. Tamara clenched her fists, feeling the cold, jagged claws against the palms of her hands and stepped forward. Her ethereal self-soared faster across the creature, pulling the oxygen away from its skin and pressing as much gravity as she could muster across its back.

The worm inched silently backwards. It had moved behind its victim now, retreating as best it could. She could feel the weakness of it, the desperation for life. The strength was leaving it. She felt confident, powerful, strong. A little more air and this will be over. The silent battle of two predators would end.

Tamara felt the air to her left shift directions. She sensed before she saw and leapt backwards as the tail of the beast struck forward. Its head drooped. White fangs protruded. Saliva fell from an open mouth.

Tamara stepped forward and sensed more about the creature than she ever had before. In its weakness she felt all of it. Metallic screams surged within the beast. Its many hearts beat ferociously, alternating in desperate rhythm for oxygen it couldn't receive. Blood was channeled to its muscles but failed to return strength to the creature's needy yet failing vigor.

The beast was confused and afraid and . . . angry. An anger that she had only felt once before filled the creature as its head collapsed on the stony black ground in front of her. There was one more heartbeat before its oxygen-starved muscles spasmed and then relaxed. It was dead.

Tamara released her grip around the creature and felt the air rush back into the void she had created. *Brokk.* The name pierced her like never before. This worm. This grootslang had now shared two qualities with the golden-skinned conqueror and the thought sent cold needles down her spine. *Who is this man, truly?* she wondered.

Gunfire in the distance prevented her from dwelling further. Tamara stepped quickly over the corpse and continued down the alley. The emperor was waiting for her. Tonight, she would end this.

***

Boro sealed his door and tried to control his trembling hands as his digital reader hummed to life. Letters from the clan was always worrisome. In the face of this war, it could alter his very existence.

"My son." The letter started with a weighty finality that was rarely reserved for good news. It was news enough to receive a letter from his father but a letter with such an authoritative opening was shocking enough to pause and reflect. *Had he ever been called with such formality? With such gravity?* Boro allowed his eyes to continue.

> *My son,*
>
> *I wish I could write to you with better news, but it is important you understand the precarious position that you are in since our clan's meeting with our tribe. You were aware that we would meet a month after you departed on your mission.*
>
> *Please know, Boro, that it was not my intention to place you in such a position, nor is it my intention now*

to see you hurt. My responsibility is, and always will be,
to the wellbeing of all members of our clan just as your
responsibility is to the members of your ship.

As I write this, I fully understand the weightiness
of my words and the risk that my actions may place
upon you.

Boro placed his silver reading screen against his lap and looked out across the black abyss. Their battleship was poised to defend the planet from Brokk's assault. If Boro was torn about who the supposed identity of their enemy was before this letter, it no longer mattered. The tone of his father's letter was clear: his tribe had agreed to support Brokk. Worse, it was likely his tribe had already thrown its financial support behind the priestess and her movement. His father would be committed to rebellion. His clan would be committed against his service to the fleet. The letter continued:

As you can likely guess, the tribe has voted to
back the exiled commander Brokk and his priestess.
The signs of the ancient prophecy seem to support her
claims. Our holy men and priests are convinced this is
the return we have been waiting for. I have come to
believe them: that Brokk will restore Jark to glory. To
reject this Brokk as he returns in power would be to
accept the place of eternal torment upon the day of
judgement. We cannot accept this.

There is no good choice ahead of you, but you must
make a choice nonetheless. To continue to fight with the
Third Fleet against Brokk will be viewed as treason
against our tribe and will result in banishment should
Brokk win. Contrarily, if you and your fleet repel
Brokk, it will now be my own head that you must
concern yourself with. I do not envy you.

Finally, I encourage you to tell no one of this letter. I suspect your role as an officer in the fleet complicates your response. Do not let competing clans on your ship find an opportunity to destroy you.

You are grown. I will leave you with this: Fight well. Die well. You will no doubt make me proud.

—Your Archon and your father

Boro repeated his father's final words over and over again in his head. *Fight well. Die well.* Wrapped in those words were a message he wished he could undo. His role as an officer for the empire was now what his family would fight against. They had joined the growing number of tribes that resisted the empire and now, they needed Boro and his fleet to die so that his role would not interfere with that of the tribe.

The space beyond his window felt darker than it ever had. Its emptiness seemed forever and eternal. What could he do but to accept his father's words? *To die well.*

A knock on his cabin door told him he would have to shelve his emotions for another time.

"The XO wants to see you!" a gruff voice shouted.

CHAPTER TWENTY-TWO

"He's ready for you, sir," said a hushed voice from his doorway.

Brokk looked up from his dark metal desk to see a frail woman with dark green skin. Her face was spotted with blue freckles and a tight bun held a ball of dark hair firm against her scalp. She wore a black flight suit with blue shoulder boards signifying her junior status aboard his ship.

"Who are you?" Brokk asked, rising from his chair and stretching his eight-foot-tall frame towards the ceiling.

The Desponian shrunk downward at his size. "I'm a communications specialist. I joined your crew on Charoth," she stuttered.

Brokk smiled at her. "Thank you for your loyalty to my fleet. You'll be rewarded as if you were Jark."

Brokk watched as her body relaxed. Even his own crew wasn't immune to the hiring of mercenaries and vagrants to keep the ship running. Most of them fit in fine, and their skills were put to use with little training. Others that joined had to be executed almost immediately for lawless and undisciplined behavior. Without the ability to formally recruit, Brokk had no other choice. Soon, he thought, all that would change.

"So, Commander Szega is waiting to speak to me? What was the expression on his face when you told him?"

She shrugged those same frail shoulders that had once been tightly held at her ears. Her green brow furrowed. "It was Commander Terre that told him," she said. "I merely established the secure connection."

Brokk nodded. "And they won't know that we're so close to Jark?"

She shook her head. "We've masked our signal to make it appear we are transmitting from the Rainbow Nebula."

He grinned. "Good. Lead the way."

The mercenary nodded and turned her back to him. Brokk followed through his cabin door and suddenly felt as if he was walking the halls of the Juggernaut for both the first and last time. A hollow red light fell onto him from fixtures above. His crew, both Jark and other mercenaries, parted to the side as he walked briskly through them. Hushed whispers filled the void as he passed.

Brokk was doing things that no Jark had done before. He was launching an attack against the holy defensive line of the Jark Empire. He was negotiating peace with his enemies rather than insisting on their destruction through combat. Although he could not hear the whispers behind him, he knew what they said: *There walks the fool who thought he could subdue an empire, and we follow like sheep to our slaughter.*

The Desponian turned right and backed out of Brokk's way so he could enter his conference room. A throne made of lava rock and thorns sat in the center of the square room. It was meant to terrify anyone a Jark commander spoke with. The chair hadn't worked on Gemini and the Mateens. Brokk suspected it wouldn't work with Commander Szega either.

Brokk walked slowly around the chair, running his thick golden hand across the cold stone. He touched the long thorns that had been fused into the surface of the rock. They were sharp. Brokk sat on the cold chair and placed his arms against its rests. A chill filled him.

Was he nervous? No. Brokk had spoken to leaders more fearsome that Szega. It was the whispers from the hallway. *The fool who thought he could subdue an empire.*

"Open the channel," Brokk ordered, trying to shake the thought from his mind.

The screen to his front flickered, and a mirror image of his own room appeared in the video feed. On a thorny throne at the center of the conference room sat a thin Jark with wild green eyes and a scarred red face. His mouth curled, exposing the sharpened fangs of a warrior and the commander of the Third Fleet. Behind him stood a tall, younger Jark with pilot wings on his chest and a writing screen in his hand. *Someone who Commander Szega is grooming,* Brokk thought.

Before Brokk could speak, Commander Szega growled with contempt.

"What does the half-blood traitor want?" he snarled.

"Are those new scars?" Brokk quickly retorted. "I had hoped to burn more than your face when we beat you last."

Szega frowned. "How dare you propose to communicate with me. Was it not clear that my role is to bring you to justice? Yet you suggest a treason worse than your first act. You have no honor Brokk."

Inwardly, Brokk smiled. He had worried Szega might not have even read the encrypted message before their meeting. His comments suggested he had. Further, Szega had not only read his message but had agreed to speak with him. This suggested that he could be reasoned with, and if not reasoned with, perhaps he could be bought.

"I'm not here to rehash the past," Brokk said calmly. "Regardless of your feelings about me, I worked hard to serve the empire. I hold no ill will against you for hunting my fleet either. Your actions in that sense are blameless. You do what you must to bring glory to the Jark Empire." Brokk paused to examine his face but saw nothing.

"You should know, commander," Brokk continued, "that it is only because of my respect for you that we are having this discussion. The Jark people have been betrayed, and it started with me. I was sold out and, like a scapegoat carrying the guilt of our proud people, exiled to the wilderness. Jark has lost footing on the galactic stage. Systems that dared not cross our empire are threatening sanctions and now, as you surely have surmised, one of our enemies has even sent a plague against our land. This unacceptable."

"What's your point?" Szega interrupted. "My time is limited when it comes to traitors. I must admit, your messaging campaign on Jark has been quite effective. Even members of my own crew came back from their leave whispering that you would return and seize power. Those that spoke positively of you have been executed like the fools they were. Soon, you will follow in their footsteps."

Fools. The word resonated within him. *There walks the fool.* "Civil war is brewing on the surface, Szega," Brokk growled. He was losing his patience and the diplomatic Tassian inside him shrunk beneath the Jark that now bubbled to the surface. "Do you think that once I destroy you and the defenses on Jark that another power will not try to exploit our weakness? The planet is in turmoil. The emperor will die." Brokk stood from his chair and moved close to the camera. He felt spit forming on his mouth as he raged. "You," he shouted at the screen in front of him, "will either die with him or stay out of my way!"

The commander of the third fleet smiled. "There is the Jark that I remember from so long ago. When I heard you brought other species aboard your ship I wondered if you had gone weak. Now, I see that you have only become stupid. You will never rule Jark," he hissed. "I will never follow you."

The screen went blank and disappeared from the room. Brokk could feel heat filling his face. His heart pounded in his chest and the anger beneath his skin wanted to explode out from his hands against someone. Anyone.

The automatic door to his conference room opened. Brokk saw the frail Desponian female standing silently at the entrance.

"How much did you hear?" Brokk growled as she stepped backward.

She shook her head but remained silent.

Fool. The word flashed through his mind, but he refused it the ability to take root. It would find no fertile ground inside him. "Get to the operations center," he ordered. "Tell Torger to initiate Phase Two."

***

It started with a wave, an almost indiscernible flutter that blurred space-time and connected trillions of miles of empty space by mere inches. The warped space, undetectable absent the finest of instruments, remained open just long enough to pass through thousands of proximity munitions in just seconds. The battle for Jark had begun.

Commander Szega was rising from his throne in the conference room when he felt his battleship shutter. It was slight, but no seasoned commander could miss the feeling of proximity munitions once he had experienced it before. A captain's entire existence hinged upon his ability to sense what was occurring beyond the walls of his vessel as if it was a natural extension of his own body.

Szega heaved as he flung himself towards the intercom button on the arm of his chair. "Brokk's armada is here!" he shouted. "Conduct survivability and get me a location of that artillery."

Szega released the button and looked at his top pilot, Boro who stood quietly behind him. "Here's your chance to make a name for yourself," he barked, racing from the room before the young pilot could respond. *Finally,* he thought. *Finally, Brokk will face me in the open and I will receive the glory of his death.*

***

Combat in space was unforgiving. On the ground, a commander only needed to worry about two domains: the ground and the air. To guard one's flank, simply meant to point a weapon system or unit to one's right, left, or rear and shoot whoever walked close enough to kill.

In space, these principles were not so simple. To guard your flank, you now needed to worry about what was below you and above. There was no longer a rear consolidation area where ships could refit, and crews could rest. Wormhole travel had turned the rear area into a commander's flank now too, and with that, space became a warrior's ultimate playground. In the offense, a determined enemy could come from any direction at any time he chose, while in the defense the enemy must consider every possible strategy and build enough flexibility in his plan to defeat his thinking foe.

There was another element that made space so difficult to defend. Space was numerically infinite. Distances that a ship could fire from were insurmountable and that ship could not only fire from an immense distance away; it could also close that distance so quickly that only the highest trained force could respond. Conversely, the sensors that disrupted space-time and prevented an enemy from jumping behind you were limited resources and could not disrupt all space, at all times, in all locations. One had to be very careful how they employed those precious beacons to their advantage.

At the commander's academy on Coridon, Terre had learned two factors that forever changed the way he thought about space combat: velocity and thrust. Velocity referred to how quickly an object could move from point A to point B and thrust referred to how quickly that object could change directions. Those two forces used in combination by the right commander provided the conditions for vicious and decisive battles.

Space, Terre believed, favored the offense, and here in this space, Terre was going to prove it. Approximately half-a-billion kilometers above him sat the famed Third Fleet. Their invincibility tarnished by Brokk at the Battle of the Rainbow Nebula, Commander Szega had come back to refit his fleet and serve as the system's reserve for the Jark Empire. To Terre, that meant that Szega was really just licking his wounds.

As he did the math, he knew the odds weren't in his favor. Szega had twenty warships compared to Terre's twelve. Szega was in a planned defense. Terre was not. Szega was fighting on his home turf. He knew the ranges and locations of his planetary defenses, and he could even use the planet's magnetic field to hide his ships.

On paper, Commander Szega had every foreseeable advantage. But battles don't unfold on paper, and advantages were easily lost. Terre had something else. Initiative. Surprise. Audacity. It would be a deadly formula.

Terre exhaled and watched the steam from his breath rise to the ceiling of the mighty Kemnaut Battleship. It was a ship that once belonged to Szega himself. Now it was Terre's.

Only a dim red light fell on his crew above. The power of his ship had been off for weeks. Life support systems were maintained at a minimum to prevent detection. It was miserable, but it was worth it.

Over the last month, Terre silently and systematically moved enough firepower into position to tip the odds of the battle into his favor. Yesterday, Terre had told Brokk that they were ready. The war could commence. Just moments ago, Terre received the green light and in his darkened command center aboard the Kemnaut, watched the first volley of interstellar artillery rip through space against his unsuspecting targets beyond.

Terre rehearsed the next step in his head as he watched the proximity rounds detonate around the Third Fleet. His combat tracker showed the signals of a dozen enemy ships fire their engines to escape the carnage. *What next?*

There would be two more volleys before his artillery had to relocate. One more before the planet's counter-fire artillery began to attack his own artillery positions. He would have to wait until after those counter fire batteries expended their ammunition. Then, he would attack. Even at forty thousand kilometers per second, it would take his battle group nearly two hours to close the distance between him and the Third Fleet. In that time, his enemy would be able to close the gap between them, deploy additional planetary defenses, or prepare a counter-attack of their own.

The interstellar artillery would help, at least initially, but Terre worried those fires wouldn't be sufficient. The problem with artillery fire against moving targets in space was that vertical and horizontal dimensions made it easy for an enemy to displace and continue fighting. Terre would have to place enough dilemmas against his enemy that they could not survive the onslaught.

Terre felt the anticipation of his crew growing. They were eager to enter the battle. Desperate to prove to Brokk that their new battle group could wage this type of warfare. He raised a finger. *Steady,* he thought, looking at his crew. The ice-cold breath of the warriors floated silently to the ceiling. It was the pause before the storm.

Another volley of artillery ripped through space and exploded around the Third Fleet. Red and white flared in the distance as the artillery found steel and hopefully flesh.

"Hit!" whispered Terre's targeting officer excitedly.

Nineteen ships left, thought Terre.

Sensors flashed ahead of him. The planet was counter-firing.

"Tell our batteries to relocate. Have Artillery Area Two begin their attack."

A green-skinned Desponian acknowledged and began transmitting his instructions.

Terre took a deep breath. *This is it,* he told himself. *For glory.*

CHAPTER TWENTY-THREE

Captain Lach adjusted the sling on his weapon. It felt tighter than usual and was rubbing against his neck where seams in his suit were already weak. He hated when the Mateen high command issued new equipment because it always caused the rest of his gear to feel off and he would spend the next few weeks after each fielding making countless adjustments until he felt comfortable again in his battle garb. Unfortunately for Machtator Lach, he wouldn't have the time to test his new shoulder harnesses in training. *This*, he thought to himself, *would be a trial by fire.*

Lach looked up from his rifle and examined the rest of his equipment. He wouldn't have time to get anything straight once the raid began; he needed to be certain everything was where it should be. After checking his boots to make sure they would keep him on the surface of the zero-gravity asteroid, Lach adjusted tourniquet straps on his knees and thighs. They had shifted slightly when he sat down, and he didn't want to risk not being able to seal his limbs if an enemy bullet or stray shrapnel hit him. Next, Lach touched each magazine that contained two-hundred and fifty rounds of dense neutronium. They felt tight in his harness. He jiggled the fragmentary grenades that were strapped to his chest and finally, checked the battery connection on his helmet and visor. All was set.

Straining in the darkness, Lach surveyed the rest of his team. There were sixteen of them counting himself and, God willing, sixteen would return. He had worked with many of them for years and had come to rely on both their expertise and their friendship.

His blue team leader, Fifno Pirie, nodded at him as he scanned his crew. Lach nodded back and grinned to himself. Fife was hard as nails and rarely smiled. He was tall and square-jawed, the stuff of legend. He wasn't always. Lach suspected he was bullied hard as a child because of his name and social status within the Mateen collective. Fife would say, "Pressure makes diamonds, but I'll kill those kids if I ever see them again." Fife *was* a diamond. Nobody doubted he was serious. It always surprised Lach how someone could acknowledge his past as the reason for his success and yet have such disdain for it all the same.

Lach closed his eyes again and felt the small landing craft vibrate under his feet.

Thanks to the work of the intelligence analysts of the second battle group, Commander Bezek was able to pinpoint the location of their missing scouts. The squadron had been taken to a rogue asteroid field three light-years from where Sabik's crew had first reported contact. Lach's mission was simple: retrieve the hostages and kill or capture any enemy resistance. Preferably, they could disable and capture the enemy but the Radaishar were hardliners and he suspected they would fight to the death. Lach had done this type of mission hundreds of times in the ten plus years of his service to the Mateen fleet. Each time was harder than the last.

The shuttle vibrated again and Lach could feel mechanical arms humming beneath him. They had entered the micro-gravitational zone of the roughly seven-mile-wide rock that harbored an abandoned mining station and were preparing to land. Without a word, the commandos aboard Lach's craft began their preparations.

One minute, Lach telepathed to his platoon. *Oxygen on. Initiate cloaking. No change to how we rehearsed. Red team, you're first off the craft.*

Nylon straps rubbing against body armor sounded around him as the team prepared to disembark. A stern hiss indicated the chamber was depressurizing and a metallic clang echoed from the walls of their ship as the boarding ramp dropped hard onto the iron asteroid below.

Move! Lach shouted to his team, who were already pouring from the vessel like water from a cup. *Blue team, go.*

More feet hurried past him as Lach himself flicked on his heads-up display and ran off the ship.

An odd feeling hit him as the shuttle piloted away from their landing zone.

To stand atop an island in the center of an ocean was humbling but to stand on an asteroid in deep space was both terrifying and awe inspiring. Other than the directed light from his team's suits and vision tools on his helmet, Lach's surroundings were pitch black. If he did not shine his light directly, even the rocky ground of the asteroid disappeared beneath him. A sudden urge to leap into the abyss flowed through his body but his desire to live another day fought it off. *Next time,* he told himself. *And then another time after that.*

Lach focused his mind for the disorienting terrain and looked down at his boots. Other than the small blue halo that his visor used to depict his cloaked body, he was invisible. Beneath him was solid iron ore. Beneath that was the facility where Sabik's crew was hopefully still alive inside.

Perimeter secure! announced his red team leader. *Loading bay door appears to be sealed.*

Lach acknowledged, looking through the hazy blue signatures of his commando platoon and at the rectangle that rose out of the asteroid and formed the outer portion of the mining station itself. The facility was weathered but intact. Pocked metal that had endured years of micro-meteorite collisions had been welded shut or recently patched. *The Radaishar have been using this station,* Lach thought to his team. *Red team, search for fighting positions and thermal signatures. Blue team, breach the door.*

In an invisible silence, the commandos worked to wire explosives around the entry to the loading bay. This would be the last chance they had at stealth, their last opportunity to get everything right before the enemy knew with certainty that they had arrived.

In the moments he waited, Lach calculated the probability that the Radaishar would execute their hostages once they realized a rescue had been mounted. He war-gamed his response in the event they used the hostages as shields and how he would prevent the Radaishar escape. Perhaps the enemy would blow the whole mining station and send Lach and his brethren into the black abyss.

Breach primed, reported his blue team leader.

No thermal images detected. No defensive obstacles or fighting positions, reported his red team leader.

Blow it, Lach ordered.

Without a medium to transmit sound or any significant gravity to give objects weight, a flash of fire and light erupted from the loading bay door, and a thick iron and steel slab of metal fell softly to the floor.

Well that was anticlimactic, Fife thought as the commandos charged the opening with a fluidity that Lach had come to appreciate.

The loading bay was smaller than the original blueprints indicated. Four steel beams spaced evenly apart held the structure together and provided the support for a tall gable ceiling. Lach followed his squad as the seven members from his Red team moved left through the open hangar, clearing potential hiding spaces behind dusty mechanical equipment and drills, while Fife and the blue team pressed straight along the near wall towards a door at the back of the ten-meter by fifteen-meter facility.

Everyone knew they had to move quickly, and the thoughts from the collective sixteen commandos were focused on what they were doing and where to move next. Despite Lach being the ground commander, his team didn't need him to tell them what to do at each turn. Instead, he focused on future threats and how he could use support from Commander Bezek's fleet if they ran into trouble around the next turn.

Fife reached the far door first, removed an explosive-tipped battering ram from his pack and slammed it into the steel hinges. The explosion ripped through the silence as smoke and debris rocketed backwards and into the next room.

Hallway breached, Fife reported. *Headed right.*

Like synchronized dancers, commandos flowed into the next hallway structure to begin to clear rooms. The floors here were a rusted orange, worn from years of iron dust that scraped at the finish until only the raw material of the flooring remained. The hallways were dark, and the rooms were darker. If it had not been for Lach's visor, which bathed his surroundings in an ultraviolet light only they could see, it would have been impossible for them to find their way.

The deeper into the ancient mining facility the team searched the more desperate Lach felt. *Abandoned,* he projected to his team. *It doesn't look like anyone has been here.*

Lach received no response. Metal clacked as the commandos' boots trampled it underfoot. Rooms were full of abandoned office equipment and a layer of dust. Finally, Fife dared to answer him. *Maybe they saw us coming, took the hostages and fled before we got close.*

Stay alert, Lach responded. *The Radaishar survive in the shadows. Look for anything that could give us a clue.*

As the darkened hallway rounded the next corner, the Blue and Red Teams converged, coming to the final portion of the upper level of the facility: a spiral staircase that descended towards the lower parts of the mining compound. In the center, a diamond drill, weighing tens of thousands of kilograms, hung from a hydraulic arm. This was the most dangerous part of the raid. Lach knew they had to move decisively if an enemy waited at the bottom. Enemy fire could block the single staircase and open his exposed teams to sniper fire. This was the fatal funnel. Make the wrong move and you never get out.

There's another way down, Fife projected as if he had sensed Lach's concern. *We could fast rope off the drill.*

Lach imagined the alternative and agreed. *Good call. Do it.*

Within seconds, Fife and his men attached three hooks to the drill and tugged to make sure they were secure while Lach's Red Team of seven commandos took the stairs.

On three, Lach ordered, pulling a stun grenade from his pouch and holding it over the railing.

One. Lach twisted a cap on the grenade and let it fall.

Two, he counted, eyeing Fife and receiving one of those rare and unsettling grins in return, the type of grin that suggested either Fife didn't know just how dangerous this was or that he had already committed his life to death and no longer cared. *Three.*

A flash of light and noise exploded up from the bottom of the drilling chamber as Fife and his team leaped from the ledge. Thick gray smoke filled the blackened void as Lach pulled himself over the rail descended to the bottom of the hole.

Blue ghosts in the darkness moved silently forward, searching for signs of life but coming up empty. Finally, Fife froze in the iron tunnels ahead. *Blood,* he thought, *all over the ground, streaks on the walls like fingers.*

Follow it, Lach ordered. And they did. Systematically, they followed the blood into a small circular chamber that had been carved into the side of the tunneled rock. Stools were in disarray around a steel and rectangular table; blood had pooled and dried into low spots the floor. Two glass jars sat on a shelf. Blood filled the containers halfway. A lump protruded from the liquid center. Bloody fingerprints dried to the outside of the jars and were smeared along the shelf itself.

What were the Radaishar doing here? Fife wondered.

A distant cry answered part of the question. Before Lach could think, Fife raced down the hallway. Caution was gone; speed was everything. Get to the hostages before they were executed. Dim brown lights encased in iron bars lit this part of the tunnel that had been cut through the red iron ore. Dust floated aimlessly through the air, collecting on Lach's face mask.

The tunnel turned left. Fife cleared the corner with a stun grenade but didn't wait for it to detonate. The flash blinded Lach as he hit the corner. *Keep running. Push through.* Smoke and light parted long enough for him to get his bearings before another of Fife's grenades ripped down the tunnel.

We found them, Fife projected boldly. *The area is clear.* His thoughts paused for a moment before they resumed at a panicked pace. *Oh, God. I need medical. Get me medical! I'm blowing the bars.*

Lach arrived seconds later. Already covered in blood, Fife kneeled over Sabik's body and applied pressure to his chest. Another commando tore his clothes as he searched for wounds. Sabik didn't move. His eyes were open but unfocused. *Tortured for information,* Lach thought. *Left for dead when they saw us coming.*

Beyond him, Mlyma too lay motionless. Her uniform was ripped and torn. Cuts and bruises speckled her back and legs, and yet that wasn't what caught Lach's attention. Thick red blood that signified arterial bleeding pooled around the heads of scouts.

Medics from the shuttle pushed past Lach to render aid. He moved aside but kept his eyes fixed on the blood surrounding her skull. A jagged row of thread covered the top of her scalp. *They did something here. Removed something.*

Lach thought back to the glass jars as he left the caged entrance and steadied himself against the wall of the tunnel. His mind buzzed from the adrenaline fueled high. Drugs injected by his suit were beginning to wear off. He fought back the fatigue.

Alert Commander Bezek, he ordered the radio operator still aboard his landing craft. *Tell her two survivors from the Fleet's reconnaissance were recovered. Tell her they were tortured, and it is likely all classified information was extracted by the Radaishar. The fleet must prepare for an imminent attack.*

CHAPTER TWENTY-FOUR

"You want me to do what?" Thilgod was more than confused. He was frustrated. Since the bounty hunter had arrived on Despona, a series of absurd orders had come from Cale and his Tassian cronies. Now, two wiry, eccentric operatives stood at the entryway to Thilgod's bedroom and were ordering the impossible.

The female, Zabra, leaned seductively against his threshold and smiled. She wore a floral knee-length skirt and a loose blouse that fluttered against her slender neck each time his small fan rotated past her. Despite the operative's clear attempt to blend in to Desponian culture, she looked grossly out of place. The more he studied her, the more he realized she didn't even look like she would fit in on Tassi. Her mannerisms were robotic. Her eyes were empty, and her voice felt . . . fake.

"Look, Thilgod, you know how this goes, don't you? Commander Cale expects you to perform your duties or he'll have you killed. And besides," she said smiling wider than before, "we need you . . . and that mutt."

Dacia whined from Thilgod's feet, and the hair on the back of her neck bristled. She must have looked terrifying to the two operatives, but they remained calm. Thilgod waited for a moment to see if she would show her fangs, but she didn't. Eventually, he patted the corelve on her thick head and returned his gaze to the two Tassians who stood in his doorway.

"In case you haven't noticed, I'm a stranger here. I'm doing my best to remain inconspicuous, so I can get a grasp for the powerbrokers here," he protested. "This nonsense threatens to blow the whole thing up. I'll never work here again, and then, what good am I to your boss?" Thilgod looked out of the window to the streets below. Dozens of Desponian city dwellers wandered the fruit market and peddled about on bicycles. A stench of rotting vegetables floated up through his window and hung in the stagnant air.

"Besides," he added, "you're talking about raiding a garrison prison. We don't stand a chance. I'm not a soldier. I'm a bounty hunter."

Soloan, frowned and took a step forward but was halted by his partner's hand. He was thicker and taller than Zabra but still had a skinniness about him that was overtly Tassian. His awkwardness equaled that of Zabra's. They both felt unnatural.

"Easy, Soloan," she tisked. "Don't want to make that pup an orphan." Her dark green eyes never left Thilgod, and he wondered if the pistol he had trained on her beneath his leg would do anything to stop the two lunatics from killing him if he refused. "Come on, Thilgod," she added. "Your job is easy. If you do it right, nobody will suspect you. After we're done, you can get on with your junky criminal roundup business, and Cale will leave you alone. All you gotta do is get a cart from the locals and wait for us to bring the girl out to you by the back gate. That's it."

He sighed and looked down at Dacia who returned a worried stare. *When did I get soft?* he wondered, knowing full well it had to do with being thrown into a prison transport and nearly losing his eyes to a lizard with a pronged tongue on Charoth.

"When do you need me there?" he asked as Dacia climbed sloppily to her feet and slunk behind a chair near the window in protest. *Coward,* he thought at her.

"Just after the moon sets at the southern gate," Zabra said with a fresh smile. "Stay in the trees. We'll find you."

***

Things always looked different at night. Trees moved position. Animals called out in strange noises. This was the devil's hour, a time when the mystical creatures of folklore were released into the real world to do what they could before the sun's righteous light forced its dark foe to retreat once more.

Soloan looked to his left. Thirty Tassian soldiers lay prone in the tall grass. Above them, a pale crescent moon sunk beneath the horizon.

Soloan turned to his right towards the thick Desponian jungle to check that the remainder of the infantry were ready. One nodded at him. The others focused their eyes ahead towards their prize.

Sixty of them in total prepared their assault. Tassian special operations command had managed to smuggle the soldiers in as tourists over the last several weeks, each one disappearing into the thick damp jungle for this one attack.

Zabra wouldn't come on this one. He wanted her to, but she was suspicious of the bounty hunter. She would watch him. If he failed, she would take his place with the cart. He missed her already and thought it weird to have such emotions moments before combat. The experimentations had made danger feel distant, even comical, as if he was on a double dose of anti-anxiety medication.

Soloan forced the thoughts from his mind and watched the moon's final light disappear below the horizon. A shroud of darkness fell upon the prison camp that rested approximately four hundred meters ahead. Raising two fingers into the air, Soloan motioned his team forward. Then, without looking to confirm their movement, he slowly strapped his rifle over his shoulder and began the arduous crawl on his belly.

Within a few painful meters, his soldiers had inched out from their safe haven in the trees and were moving through waist-high prairie grass. Heaps of dirt and briers clawed against his stomach and hands as he pulled himself forward with his elbows. Pain took a backseat to stealth. Remaining quiet was foremost. Retaining the element of surprise was essential.

After another twenty minutes of crawling, Soloan reached the lit edge of the perimeter. Massive spotlights beamed down upon a chain and razor-wired fence. Twelve meters beyond that was another fence with a second row of razor-wire. The interior was well lit but Soloan was grateful the prison guard used standard lighting instead of night vision devices to keep their perimeter secure. Prisons, he suspected, were more concerned about inmates escaping than soldiers breaking in. Thus, what appeared to be maximum security on the inside, was really only minimum security to his team.

Soloan once more looked to his left and right. His teams were in position.

"Get the breach line," he whispered into a microphone on his neck.

Rustling behind him indicated they were prepping the forty-meter-long explosive-laced harpoon to fire over the fence. Once it landed, an explosion directed downward would obliterate the two obstacles and create a clear lane through the prison's defenses.

"Prepped," responded a hushed voice through a speaker in his ear.

Soloan looked down the line one last time. His company of sixty had grouped itself into squads of nine, preparing to dash through the fence and clear their assigned sectors. Critical for Soloan was moving quickly and isolating the guards to their barracks.

"Blow it," Soloan ordered, injecting himself with a shot of adrenaline.

Time slowed as the chemical flowed through his blood and saturated his veins. A pop from behind sent the forty-meter cable flying over his head. Heat and light flashed upwards as the blast melted chain link and wire underneath.

Run. Climb through the breach, over mangled steel and a smoldering fence. *Two guards in a tower above.* Soloan felt his shoulder rock twice as he pulled the trigger on his rifle. Guards slumped backward. *Shouting from the prison.*

Soloan turned left. Boots thumped behind him. Voices shouted ahead. Gunfire erupted all around as his infantry company cut down Jark prison guards responding to the attack. *Payback,* Soloan thought. *Small revenge for the attack on Tassi. More to come,* he hoped boldly.

Soloan ran faster now, cutting to his right down a darkened alley. Lights flickered above him and hummed to life. The whole prison was now awake. The Jarks were likely alerting their special tactics team. *Five minutes, maybe less before reinforcements would be on top of him.*

Two guards carrying rifles and radios emerged from metal door latched to a white cinderblock building. Soloan gave them each four rounds before they could raise their rifles. He was through the door before they hit the ground.

This was the building. *Clear it quickly.* A Jark at a desk didn't have a chance to stand up before Soloan shot him too, ducking behind the desk as he changed magazines and tossed a grenade down the hallway.

The blast rung in his ears as he dashed from his hiding place. Two Jark guards lay bleeding on the floor. Soloan kicked their rifles away from their hands and moved past them. He was close. He could feel it.

Soloan turned left, running down concrete and cinderblock hallways. The walls were plain. *Depressing,* he thought to himself, wondering what witty one-liner Zabra would have said about the decor. *Focus.*

The voices of Tassian soldiers behind him indicated his team had arrived. Boots screeched along the polished concrete floors. Soloan followed the hallway left and found them. Rows of metal cell doors flowed neatly down the walls on each side.

"Can't breach them all," he hissed. "Casika!" Soloan shouted. "Pound on your door, where are you?"

Soloan looked at his watch and waited for a response. *Two minutes before Jark reinforcements would arrive, maybe less.* "Casika!" he shouted again.

***

The hair on Dacia's neck bristled. She let out a throaty rumble. Thilgod saw it too. A shadow danced through the jungle. He had hoped the trees were playing tricks on him. The darkness could have that effect, especially if you watched something for too long. Dacia proved he wasn't just imagining it. Someone was skipping, crawling, and pirouetting on a path through the trees.

Thilgod shifted his body slightly to track the figure. It was getting closer to his hideout and their link-up point with Soloan. Thilgod couldn't risk them being detected. Any closer and he'd have to kill the person, or have Dacia do the job for him. As he adjusted his posture to watch the figure, his reactive camouflage uniform adjusted to mimic its new surroundings.

Thilgod looked down at Dacia who sniffed the air. She bared her teeth. "You want to eat whoever that is?" Thilgod whispered.

Dacia didn't respond, instead she chose to track the shadow until it stopped between them and the road that led to the back of the prison.

Flashes of light and the sound of gunfire droned in the prison beyond. The assault had lasted for ten minutes now. Thilgod wondered if it was nearing completion. If the assault force stayed much longer, they would have to fight off the Jark garrison that was undoubtedly already moving a quick reaction force to defeat Soloan's attack.

Thilgod removed a slender hunting rifle from behind his back and pulled the rubber caps from his scope. The wooden handguard felt cold against his fingers as he rose the rifle to his face, securing the buttstock tight against his shoulder. The rifle itself was an antique, but Thilgod had upgraded it over the years.

A Hestonian-built suppressor on the front quieted the supersonic round to muffled crackle and the Mateen scope, which flickered to life as he brought it to his eye provided real-time target acquisition from over two miles away. Taking a moment to orient himself through is optics, Thilgod focused his scope on the shadowy figure and frowned.

Zabra. The lunatic Tassian operative. *Dancing* in the jungle by herself. *Had she followed him?*

"Let's go, Dacia." He capped his rifle. Rising from his hiding place, damp leaves from the humid jungle air brushed his face and neck. A cool drop of water rolled down his back.

Zabra turned her shoulders as he approached. Even in the darkness, he could see a smug smile crest her face.

"I don't suppose this is a coincidence," he grumbled.

Her smile faded as she turned back towards the prison. With each passing minute, the gunfire slowed. Only one or two rounds splintered against the quiet night.

"They'll be here soon," she whispered, pointing into the darkness.

Thilgod nodded. "I've got a merchant ship ready to smuggle her out," he responded.

Zabra smiled and then let her face fall flat. Her lips quivered and then trembled. Thilgod was stunned at the emotion he had been certain she couldn't express. "That won't be necessary," she said, stepping from the tree line to meet a column of approaching soldiers. "She didn't make it. They killed her."

Killed her? He didn't know what to say and was glad when he realized he didn't have to. Zabra walked from the protection of the jungle and out to the road. Thilgod watched for a moment as she joined the other Tassian agent at the front of the column and faded into the dark night. Sirens of emergency vehicles blared in the background but Thilgod struggled to focus on the noises.

He knew how devastating it was to be emotionally invested in an operation only to have it fail. So much of battle was chance. The shroud that surrounded warfare never lifted and, even when you think you can peer through it, you often only get a glimpse into a small portion of the enemy's plans. The rescue had failed but Thilgod suspected the war was just beginning.

"Let's go," he said, looking down at the only companion he had left.

CHAPTER TWENTY-FIVE

"Thrust right!" Brokk shouted at his pilot as two neutronium rounds rocketed past his ship and exploded in the empty space beyond.

The juggernaut shuddered at his command and jolted as it released its own array of munitions at a cluster of Jark battleships defending their planet. Brokk and his armada had penetrated the first defensive belt that surrounded the Jark system but was now facing the main defense: a combination of Jark battleships and destroyers that nearly doubled his fleet in both size and power.

"Where's that artillery?" Brokk demanded. "We've got to keep the enemy overwhelmed."

"Coming now," Torger responded, pressing buttons on his console and prioritizing targets for their fleet.

Brokk watched as the space in front of his ship churned. The red planet beyond disappeared as wormholes linking segments of space opened like gates, allowing hundreds of proximity munitions to flow through and explode around enemy ships. Planetary defenses responded by deploying their own countermeasures, knocking shells out of space before they could find flesh and steel alike.

This dance was almost too much for Brokk. There were too many moving pieces and possible configurations he would have to react to. Enemy carrier ships to his left released thousands of unmanned attack drones that swarmed in and out of battle, confusing his ship's defenses and disrupting his ability to mass effects against larger ships. Beyond that threat were planetary defenses and sensors that further attacked and confused his force.

Brokk watched a three-dimensional map in the center of his operations center. On the far side of the solar system, Terre and his battle group waged war against Commander Szega where a similar dance was unfolding. Jark carriers deployed swarms of robots while Terre's artillery pounded away at peripheral defenses. Neither force had been able to close enough distance to deal a decisive blow against the other side.

Brokk focused hard on the map, ignoring the chaos around him. *Something must change.* Brokk's forces wouldn't be able to keep this up forever. Jark resupply would eventually overwhelm his ability to attack their fleets. Ships would be repaired and sent back into battle while Brokk's armada waned and broke. The losses would catch up to him, and he wouldn't be able to recover.

What is their strategy? Brokk had been fighting his battleship and not thinking as broadly as he needed to be. He had an executive officer to fight the ship. He had a group commander to fight his battle group. Brokk needed to fight the war. *What were the Jarks doing?*

His Juggernaut shook but Brokk ignored it, staring hard at the array of forces laid out like a three-dimensional tapestry before him. *Had they moved at all since the battle's beginning?* A thought dawned on him. *They're fighting a static defense. A war of attrition. Time is on their side. They think they can wait me out.*

So far, Brokk had orchestrated his attack to engage the three primary Jark defensive positions in the hopes his artillery could create enough disruption for him to have a decisive victory over each enemy formation. The flaw in his plan was that he had never been able to get close enough to truly engage with the enemy battleships that served as the center of gravity for the Jark defenses. In essence, they were fixing him to a location and then waiting him out. Conversely, Brokk had fixed the Jark defensive belt, but, unlike his need for the battle to resolve quickly, they had based their strategy on time. *They are fixing themselves,* a thought screamed at him.

Brokk leaped from his chair. "How long until the next artillery barrage?" he demanded.

Torger looked at his instruments. "Three minutes, Commander."

Brokk nodded, next looking to his operations officer, Kal. "Jump the fleet here. Everything except our carrier," he ordered, reaching his hand into the holographic map.

Kal squinted his eyes. "That'll put us directly on top of Commander Szega's ships," he retorted with a snarl that was common tongue among Jark officers who disagreed with each other. "And we'll risk being hammered by our own artillery."

"Shift the artillery to his right flank. Jump us in simultaneously. Take us behind Coridon. They've adjusted their disruption beacons from the near side to support their defense against Terre, but it has left their rear open." He paused looking one more time at the map and his own array of forces. *Could it work? What was the risk? What was he missing?* "They'll never expect it," Brokk added.

***

"The pilots are restless," Boro Vidas protested. "We were brought here to fight. Instead you shelter us like fragile glass." Boro stood rigidly in front of his commander's bright steel desk. His eyes paced across Commander Szega's features and keyed in on his expression. He wished he had taken a different approach to the confrontation.

"You would have me throw off the entire strategy just to entertain our pilots?" Szega hissed in response. "We have the rebel fleet exactly where we want them: in a frenzied attack and running out of options." He breathed in a hurried gasp of air before wiping the spit from his mouth. "Look," he said in a softer tone, "I promoted you because of your valor during the Battle of the Rainbow Nebula. If you cannot get past your hunt for glory, then perhaps I was wrong about you."

"They want to fight," Boro countered. "There's no honor in this. No honor sitting in defense or letting our robot swarms win the battle. Commander," he pleaded, "the crews are saying that perhaps you are scared of another confrontation." He paused to size the man up before continuing. "Commander Brokk defeated us before. Let them have their revenge!"

"Sit down, you fool," Szega responded flatly with the wave of his hand. "Brokk doesn't have the ships or resources to attack the planet. Once he runs out of steam, we will seize the advantage. In the meantime, we hold our portion of the defense. Let anyone who claims I'm afraid of Brokk confront me himself, rather than gossip to you like a coward."

Boro stared at the chair but refused to accept it. For Boro, this was something more, something personal. He deserved to fight. He needed to fight to ensure a death worthy of his clan. A death worthy of his archon. Returning home after a defeat in the Rainbow Nebula was devastating but exile by his clan would be worse. Boro couldn't afford not to fight. He had to. They all had to.

With the plague on his own clan's doorsteps and the tribes divided, what happened in the skies above Jark became just as important as what happened below. In the months since he left his father, he had learned that the tribe was against the empire. His clan had decided the miracles the sorceress was performing were too great to ignore. If Boro couldn't win or die in this battle, he didn't know what he would come home to. He didn't know how he would be received, if he was to be received at all. Admiral Szega owed all of them a chance to forge the future they wanted. If he didn't give this to them, the crew would be forced to take it.

Admiral Szega squinted his eyes and let a deep growl exit his throat. Boro had heard this noise before from his father and the elders. It was the tribal tone that signified he was prepared for a challenge. "Who are you representing in here?" he asked suspiciously.

Boro didn't know how to respond. *Were there others? Yes.* If Szega was smarter he would have realized this was an interview. He would have seen Boro was out of character. It was his last chance to give the crew a reason to believe he could still lead. But Boro wasn't supposed to be the one to break the news. The crew sent Boro to feel their commander out, not to battle him on the spot

"Tell me the truth," Szega snarled, his jaw pulled taut. "Are there members of the crew who think they are in a better position to lead? You should be thanking me for keeping you safe, not petitioning for battle! I'll fix the boredom that led to this indiscipline!"

Boro swallowed. Suddenly, he felt like a sacrificial lamb. *How quickly had he made the mental jump?* he asked himself. *What will he do with me now?* he wondered. Before he could respond, the ship rumbled so violently that Boro fell head first into Commander Szega's desk.

"Commander to the battle room!" a voice called over the intercom.

Scrambling to his feet, Boro wiped blood from his brow and dashed after Szega. The ship rocked and vibrated as he ran through its smoke-filled halls. Sirens blared around him and lights flashed, warning the crew that an attack was imminent. *We've been hit!* cried a voice deep inside him.

The battle room itself was chaos. Jark officers swarmed across the stations as they orchestrated a fight they were clearly losing. Bursts of light flashed outside of the windows, and the hull groaned under the pressure of proximity rounds exploding around them.

"Impossible," he heard a sharp voice growl to his right. Boro turned to see his commander slap the battle officer, a thick young Jark who took the beating by keeping his hands on his computer terminal. "You fool," Szega continued to chastise. "Back us out and flank right!"

"Destroyer three down," shouted an intelligence officer to his left.

"Get a breach team to level seven," a Jark called from behind.

We were hit, Boro realized. *The hull is breached.*

It was then Boro saw what had happened. On the holographic map at the center of his screen, Brokk's armada had jumped from the main planet's defenses to his own fleet's flank. The ships were nearly on top of each other, exchanging a blistering array of neutronium and proximity rounds. To his shock, the rogue fleet was winning. Each exchange tipped and tilted the mighty battleship, disrupting its targeting and making it nearly impossible for them to scramble their manned fighters. Three of the Third Fleet's destroyers had already been crippled. Four more were disabled.

Beyond the rogue fleet, enemy artillery was still hammering them from their other flank. The original battle group led by the captured Kemnaut was almost upon them. They were trapped. *Unless.* Boro threw the thought from his mind. No Jark would surrender. It wasn't in their blood. *Fight to the death; make your family proud.*

What family? His mind questioned. *They have already rejected you and the empire's fleet. They support Brokk now. Everything is changing. Whose side are you on? Support the clan. Save your fleet.*

The mighty battleship shuddered again. Boro looked around. The officers in the battle room were disorganized and panicked. The battle room, nestled deep in the center of the ship offered the officers of the crew some protection, but it couldn't hold forever. They wouldn't be able to fight this off. Commander Szega wasn't even concerned, instead choosing to take out his aggression on his targeting officer, demanding to know why he wasn't alerted when Brokk's armada had jumped away from the main battle.

Smoke filled the room as more Jark officers poured in to seal a new breach and put out the electrical fire. Boro locked eyes with Szega's executive officer. The Jark was short and fat, hardly a leader but crafty nonetheless. He nodded at Boro but quickly looked away. *Nodded. What does that mean? Is this on? Does he support me? Is the crew behind me?*

There wasn't time to think. Before he could consciously act, Boro felt himself removing a long knife from a sheath on his belt. Could he do it? Could he kill the commander? *Save the crew. Show Brokk his loyalty by giving him Commander Szega's head. Could they really join Brokk?*

"Surrender the ship!" Boro shouted through the chaos. "Surrender the fleet!"

Officers near him fell silent but obeyed. The communications team leaped onto their headsets. The targeting officer fired off red flares and white star cluster munitions in distress. The knife Boro carried was now visible to everyone, but the crew did nothing to stop him. *Are they with me?* Boro wondered again, knowing full well what his actions could mean for his own survival and that of his family, his clan.

A glimmer of red reflected off the silver blade from the lights above. Smoke from unquenched fires billowed but parted from Boro's path as he made his way towards his oblivious commander.

Boro moved quickly. Youth was on his side. He closed the distance between himself and Szega before the old Jark could react to what was happening.

Szega's eyes were a misty red when Boro reached him. *Confusion. Betrayal.* His teeth snarled as the blade sunk deep into his chest. His fingers twitched as Boro twisted the blade deeper in a fit of panic and rage. The Jark's skin was tougher than Boro thought, harder to penetrate than he ever suspected it would be. Boro's fingers trembled but he willed them to obey as he drove the blade farther still, using every fiber of muscle to complete his task.

His commander exhaled without saying a word and fell limply to the ground.

Boro stumbled backward and instantly noticed that their battleship stopped rocking. They were no longer receiving fire. The fight was over. He survived. The crew cheered victoriously. They chanted Boro's name. Not only that, they chanted Brokk's name too. Boro had done what had to be done. They would join the Rogue Fleet and hope Brokk showed them mercy. Boro hoped his clan would show him mercy too.

CHAPTER TWENTY-SIX

Adrenaline in her veins made her feel weak. *Shaky.* The battle with the grootslang had taken its toll on her and, worse, she knew it was just a small one, insignificant compared to the beast that Canis was nearly sacrificed to on Tassi and likely small compared to others she might have to fight. She was almost to the emperor, but a new obstacle was in her path. There was always a new obstacle, and Tamara could feel her mind slipping. She needed a strength she couldn't draw from herself. She needed companionship. She needed Brokk.

In the distance, anti-aircraft fire soared skyward. Military planes streaked across the sky and bombs fell beyond the capital, sending rumbles through the ground. Tamara knew that somewhere above Brokk was waging a battle more intense than her own. Their fates were intertwined, and she never doubted him. She knew he would be victorious, she only hoped she would be there to share in the victory.

Gripping her fists, Tamara took another look around the corner that marked the entrance to the palace. Tamara could see two guards carrying weapons, but she sensed they were more elite than standard guards. They were alert, standing nearly twenty feet away and, despite her fatigue, the dust and sulfur weren't affecting them like they were her. Their heart rate was steady. Their breathing calm. *Could she sneak past them?* She doubted she could do it without triggering an alarm.

A third Jark, wearing a black face mask and gray body armor, appeared behind them. His camouflage was striped with black and red signifying he too was a member of the elite guard, but something was off about him. He lumbered like an aged veteran, not a young warrior. Tamara swirled her ethereal self about him. His boots were worn and dusty. The rubber sole had long chipped away, leaving a steal core visible from behind.

Tamara's heart fluttered. *Canis.* She watched with gleeful anticipation as he drove a knife into the first guard's spine. She felt the sting of dying neurons fire into his legs and hands but fail to return any signals to his brain. She heard the gurgle of blood surge from his lungs and into his throat as Canis shoved the blade deeper into the Jark's back.

The second guard turned toward them both; horror dripped from his face. Canis had planned the attack perfectly. He had positioned himself in the right place. *How could the timeworn Jark move so quickly?* She watched Canis pull the knife from the first guard's back and throw it into the chest of the second. In disbelief, the thick, hairy Jark looked at Canis and then down at his wound. He didn't bother reaching for his gun, instead he dropped a hand to the ground and searched for air.

Tamara allowed her ethereal self to once more encase the victim. She felt the futile gasps as if they were her own lungs that burned from the blade. She smelled the panic and adrenaline pour from his body.

Tamara returned to herself and ran towards Canis who was dragging the body of the first Jark into the crevice of the wall. She wanted to hug him. She wanted to show him the affection of a daughter to her father. She wanted to express gratitude. But that wasn't Canis.

"I couldn't let you get all the glory," he mumbled as she approached. "Grab the other one's legs and bring him over here."

She nodded and obeyed. The joy was gone, but her strength had returned. Only work remained. *Assassin.*

"I assume you have a better plan than I did for getting into the building?" she asked as she grabbed the much larger Jark by his boots and tugged without result.

The sound of anti-aircraft fire burst in the background. "They are distracted," Canis said proudly. "Brokk initiated his attack on the planet. The path to the inner chamber is clear."

***

Footsteps echoed off granite floors. A strong heartbeat thumped between steps. Thud, step, thud, step, thud, step, thud.

Tamara closed her eyes and let her mind follow the sound as it vibrated off the Jark's body. Thud, step, thud. He stopped and turned left at the intersection. His breath was heavy. Labored. He was old but had a strange vigor in his veins. A bead of sweat formed at his forehead and paused until enough moisture had gathered and forced it to roll off his thick brow and down his nose, ending its journey with a plop onto the glossy floor beneath his feet.

Tamara glanced over at Canis, forgetting for a moment that he couldn't hear anything. He waited. His heart was steady compared to the emperor's. Canis was fearless. Resolute. He was like Red. *Red.*

Canis raised a black eyebrow up his dark red forehead as if to ask, "What are you sensing?"

Tamara returned a smile and moved a jeweled finger to her lips. *Shhh,* she thought. *I can feel him.*

Thud, step, thud, step. The Jark stopped. He was close now. Tamara focused harder to feel the vibrations of sound as he moved his body through the planet's heavy air. Gravity tugged on his every motion; his every sound was labored. He pressed a button and with the metallic click, gears turned and the floor vibrated. The emperor had just entered a round chamber the next room over. *Was he alone?* At first, he seemed to be, but then, a faint heartbeat. Two and then three bodies were lowered on black stone beds. They weren't Jark.

More footsteps entered the chamber. Canis could hear them too and quietly moved towards Tamara. "Priests," he said. "Do you hear the humming?"

She had been so focused on their steps and their hearts she hadn't listened for common sounds. Letting her mind slip back from its narrow focus, she heard it. Humming, low and monotonous, deep tones but with one voice rising above the rest. The humming was loud now, growing in intensity as more priests joined the room. Three. Six. Twelve. Tamara lost count. Suddenly, Canis left her side and crept towards the hallway to peer into the chamber.

Curiosity drove Tamara to join him. Twelve priests, dressed in black and gold robes, circled a large black-haired Jark. He didn't look as old as he had felt moments ago but she knew the looks were deceptive. *He had an image to uphold.*

The priest's hoods covered their heads, and, in the shadows, it was impossible to see their eyes, but she knew they would be missing. She knew long ago their eyes had been carved from their skulls so they could see only the dead. In the center, the emperor held a bowl of silver liquid.

"Mercury," Canis whispered.

Tamara became aware again of the three bodies that lay on black stone beds outside the circle. Their heads all pointed in. Two were female with green skin. They must have been slaves from Despona. The third was pale with blond hair. A Tassian maybe. Just a boy.

The humming alternated. Six priests bellowed low tones while the other six echoed in a higher pitch. As they sang to the dead, the bodies twitched. Steam rose from the mercury bowl into the Jark's large nostrils. His eyes closed and rolled backward inside his head. His hair bristled and vibrated to the beat of the priestly humming. The entire chamber shook as the sounds rose and fell in unison.

A green-skinned Desponian female moaned in agony. Her mouth opened and closed. She shook her hands, trying to raise them beyond the limits of the shackles. Her chest heaved, and her knees twisted and turned. Tamara didn't know how much more she could watch. Her mind united with the slave through common experience. Her body felt this Desponian's desperation who retold the story of her own agony dealt by the hands of cruel and selfish brutes.

"Enough!" a familiar voice shouted through the chants. Canis rushed the room, grabbing Tamara's hand and spinning her through the open chamber doorway before smashing his other hand against a button that dropped the door behind them.

The priests turned, shocked to hear their ceremony disrupted. In the second between Canis releasing the pin of a stun grenade and tossing it to the center of the room, Tamara locked eyes with the chief priest. Time slowed for her as she examined them. They were an empty cavern against an ageless face. He opened his mouth to scream some unknown curse, revealing teeth as black as coal, rotting within a pale white mouth. Instead of a curse, the flash and bang of a concussion grenade tore the priest from his feet and flung him to the floor.

"Burn them!" Canis pulled a black rifle from a sling on his shoulder and fired three rounds into a guard on his left.

Canis's strategy thrived on chaos, and Tamara intended to help. Reaching her hands out, she grasped the essence of two priests and boiled the blood inside their veins until their clothes caught fire. They screamed, fell to the ground. Tamara rode their screams into the ears of the others, maximizing the noise inside the minds of the priests and blowing out their eardrums, crushing their skulls inward against their brains and sending them crashing to the floor.

Two more shots flew from Canis' rifle and a Jark slumped against the wall to her right. Canis ran to the next door to his left and slammed it shut, sealing them inside with the emperor.

A priest in gold rushed Tamara. She ducked and lunged at him, digging her clawed hands-deep into his chest until she felt his heart stop beating. He fell limp. The room was quiet. Twelve robed priests lay motionless on the floor. A large Jark with red skin and black hair sat motionless in the center. Tamara could sense his fear, but there wasn't panic. No, that wasn't the Jark way.

"This is how you prolong your life?" Canis accused.

The emperor narrowed his crimson eyes through a heavy brow. "How dare you enter this place."

"Commander Brokk sends his regards," Canis responded, matching the emperor's tone.

He grunted. "You fool. You'll all be executed for your treason."

"I've come to kill you," Canis responded. "Your regime ends with you. Treason will be a charge levied against those who betray Commander Brokk, not you."

"I'm already dying," the Jark responded with disdain. "You'll achieve nothing."

The emperor's heart steadied, leaving Tamara uneasy. *Why should he feel comfortable?* Her uneasiness turned to worry. She began examining the chamber and the doors. She couldn't sense anything beyond the walls. The stone was too thick here. "Are you certain these are sealed?" she asked Canis.

He ignored her. "You sold us out," he responded to the emperor. "You didn't have the guts to back us up against the galactic council. We could have expanded your empire across a dozen star systems. You lacked the courage to commit the full array of your forces. You allowed the Mateen to intervene without even a protest. You aren't worthy of the throne."

Tamara became frantic. Had Canis heard what the emperor said? *I'm already dying.* He ignored it completely, choosing to slap the emperor with a past he cared nothing about. *Why was he dying?*

"I'm not about to wage war with the entire galaxy, Canis. Brokk failed. His job was to control Tassi. He couldn't. Now, because of his failure, I'm dying along with the entire Jark species." The emperor started to rise to his feet but was met with a slap in the face from the back of Canis's hand.

The entire Jark species. Tamara mouthed the words again and again. *What had she missed?*

"Sit," Canis growled, "or my priestess will make your body hotter than the volcano that made these rocks."

The emperor grunted again but obeyed. "You failed," he continued, "to isolate the planet. I needed time to keep the council out of our affairs. You dragged the Mateens right into the war. Brokk's pride is what ruined our campaign, not my governing."

Canis stared at him for a moment. His eyes narrowed. Tamara could sense his anger. She watched him relive the battle and his sacrifice to the grootslang. Tamara looked around the chamber at the two green females and young boy lying motionless. Their heartbeat was weak, but they were alive.

"Have you resorted to stealing the blood of slaves to prolong your life?" Canis asked condescendingly.

The large Jark scoffed. "We were experimenting with cures to the plague." He paused to let out a cough. "To save the people."

Canis was perplexed and looked from the emperor to Tamara and back to the emperor.

"Infected," Tamara said slowly, finally putting the pieces together. "You're infected." She swarmed his body, thinking back to the strangeness that was inside of him when he'd entered the room. His body felt hot now, feverish. The same strangeness she felt earlier leaked from his forehead. It was in his sweat, in his cough, in the air. Tamara felt weak. She could sense the panic in Canis as well.

"Who did it?" Canis growled. "What is the source of the plague?"

"Who do you think?" Tamara cut in. "I knew all along, but I was too stupid to realize what I was feeling. I sensed it as I see you in front of me now. The stench on the soldiers that came in on the road. The pyres that billowed remnants of the plague into the air. It was familiar, because it felt like the Tassian general Remmel. It feels like this boy," she said, motioning at the Tassian sacrifice that lay motionless on the black slab.

Canis remained silent.

The hairy Jark at the center of the octagonal room grinned. "You are the dumbest pawn in the galaxy Canis, and now you'll die. Well done," he snarled.

"Can you feel it, Tamara?" Canis asked in a voice that came as close to begging as she had ever heard from a Jark.

Canis's tone had changed so much that it was almost a plea for help. Everything was backward. The emperor had come here to test himself for the lives of their people. Of Canis's people. Tamara felt his scorn, but it was no longer divorced from his concern. The return to Jark weighed heavily on Canis. He loved these people and this land. His hatred for the emperor was in direct contrast with his love for his home, a love that the two of them now clearly shared.

"Yes, Canis," she said quietly. "I can feel it. We're both breathing it in. We have been since we entered the city."

"A bio-weapon." The emperor responded. "Created by the same wicked empire you failed to subdue."

Canis backed up until he was against the wall. His hands trembled, and his heart thumped in his chest. Tamara could feel his fear. This mighty warrior who had steeled himself in battle was broken now. Desperate. Suddenly, his face changed. The Jark inside him returned.

"And in that boy," he asked. "Infected?"

"And healed," responded the emperor. "We only had to tailor it to the Jark immune system until you ruined everything."

Canis growled. "You failed your people" Canis declared flatly. "It's time for you to die."

The emperor rose to his feet and looked at the dead priests that lay across the floor. Canis didn't bother to stop him. They had a mission to accomplish. Canis would have her carry it out, and she would. It was her role after all. *Assassin.*

The emperor looked from his priests to Canis, and then finally to her. "You'll never get out of this palace alive," the Jark taunted. "Even now my soldiers are looking for me. They've surrounded the room."

Tamara ignored him, instead she let her eyes turn from a placid green to a raging fire. She reached out and felt the warmth of his blood.

The old Jark didn't scream. He swallowed once, refusing to break her gaze. *He would die with dignity, then,* she thought to herself as she made him boil.

***

When his heart stopped beating, Tamara felt a strange coolness surround her. She had killed others since joining Brokk and his crew, and she had killed countless more while serving with Red. This one felt different. To kill an emperor was to insert yourself into the ordained order of a planet. It felt holy, sacred. In killing him, Tamara was certain she had just aligned herself with the others in her species and completed something truly momentous.

Assassin. The title that scared her mere moments before now filled her with pride. She had done it. She had killed the leader of a planet and permanently altered the course of its future.

Tamara placed a golden hand on her victim's hairy face. He still felt warm to the touch. She stroked his hair, adjusted the collar of his robe, and examined his eyes. They were a placid red. He was at peace.

Deep inside a voice told her it wasn't true. He had died an agonizing death, one that made her cringe to think about repeating, and yet, she envied him a bit. His struggle for power was over. His striving to manipulate his surroundings would be no more.

"We need the head," came a familiar voice behind her.

Tamara pulled herself back from the emperor and realized she was still in the octagonal room. Soldiers beat ferociously on the outside as they tried to reach their precious emperor. Dragging indicated they were bringing up a battering ram with an explosive charge. Tamara could have rushed out to destroy them but chose not to. *Let them see,* a crude voice inside of her hissed.

"Shall I cut it off or do you want to?" Tamara asked him gently. Her hand still lay against the dead Jark's face, feeling his warmth dissipate and his body stiffen. *Peace,* she thought to herself once more.

Canis coughed and she sensed his weakness. "You better do it."

Tamara nodded, electing not to mention how feverish he felt nor shame his honor in these last moments. *You have it too,* she reminded herself gently, quickly pushing the thought from her mind and focusing instead on the body that lay cold before her. *His head.*

Before it occurred to her to borrow Canis's knife, an explosion rumbled outside of the door to their chamber. Boots scraped along the floor and shouting could be heard as Jark infantry and palace security orchestrated an operation to free their beloved emperor. Tamara sensed the explosion had breached the emergency doors that sealed them inside and now, there was only one barrier between her and the soldiers. They would be upon her soon. She had to move quickly.

Tamara examined the blades that protruded from the gold jewelry adorning her hands. She had only used them once to kill the Tassian general named Remmel and once more against a Jark priest. Now she used them to sever the head of another leader. *Assassin.*

Hammering outside told her they were planting the charge. No time to spare. She would greet them with the emperor's head in her hands. She would make sure enough witnesses saw his body so there would be no doubt he was dead. *Dig,* her mind implored her. And she did. Shoving the claws deep into his neck, she felt warmth pool around her fingers. Like a surgeon making an incision, she dragged her fingers around the skin of his neck, feeling for the spinal cord and severing it with a flick of her hand.

Blood gurgled from his arteries as she pulled the head away. It pooled together on the floor and absorbed into the tips of her coat. Voices called outside as she tugged. They were taking cover. Her hands jerked on his head, trying to separate it from his shoulders while her mind raced to the outside of the door. *Not much time.* An electrical signal from a remote fired, penetrating a blasting cap that provided the spark to an explosive tape that lined the jam and threatened to break the hinges.

Tamara braced her legs against his shoulders as she pulled. Finally, she felt a snap and fell backward as an explosion ripped inward, filling the chamber with dust and smoke. Flashlights and lasers filled gaps where smoke failed to billow, but Tamara had the head and was ready for her finale.

"On the ground!" shouted the lead Jark as a team of ten rushed the room. Canis obeyed. Tamara did not.

As the team surrounded her, she held the head of their leader out as an affront. Blood dripped from the spinal column. Blood trapped in her robe fell with a splat, sending particles of fluid and plague in all directions. The Jarks on the tactical team that surrounded her wore gas masks; it wouldn't help them.

"On the ground, assassin!" shouted another as he approached her. Smoke swirled and parted as he moved through it, clearing his view and giving him a full picture of the room. "What did you do?" he roared when he saw the severed head and its body below it.

Tamara waited. Her eyes simmered a bright green. Flame burned dimly from her palm and cast an eerie shadow on the lifeless face of their eternal emperor. It could become a fireball if she needed it to be, but she had other plans. Months of training in Brokk's battleship had prepared her for a moment like this. Her focus was perfected; rejuvenated by the murder of the emperor and strengthened by the adrenaline that pumped through her body.

Her spirit no longer lingered in her body but, instead, rose above it as if it was an extension of her own arms. She could sense the entire room and control everything that occurred within it. The steady drip of blood in front of her was cooling off quickly as it pooled on the onyx floor. A gloved hand that rubbed against the metal trigger of an assault rifle hummed lightly in her ears. The breathing of ten Jark infantry plus Canis and herself mixed and, within that breath, was the Tassian plague that had gotten the best of them all.

Frozen in time was the expression on the team leader's face when he saw his idol's ghastly green head, severed from its body and drained of its blood.

"Surrender yourself to me," Tamara beckoned as she dimmed the lights within the chamber until it was black. "Place your weapons on the ground and kneel!" she ordered.

She sensed in the Jark a desire to raise his weapon to her, but she prevented it. His muscles constricted, and his shoulder spasmed, but the force she exerted against his body and the others made it impossible for them to move. His muscles strained under her weight. She felt the desire in him to loosen and collapse to his knees. That desire fueled her instincts even farther.

Fear evaporated from his skin, as well as the sweat and energy his body generated to resist her.

"What are you doing?" he struggled to ask. His voice wavered. His lips quivered. His head shook. And finally, he kneeled. They all did.

Tamara knelt too, letting the fire in her eyes dim so the team leader could see her clearly as she spoke. "When you kneel to me," she told him, "you kneel to Brokk. He has accepted your allegiance. The emperor is dead. A new one is rising. Take me to the throne room."

CHAPTER TWENTY-SEVEN

Bright white light drew from stainless steel fixtures in the ceiling above to illuminate Sabik's features and give him a ghastly pale color that made Gemini nauseous. A curtain divided Sabik from the other members in the medical facility aboard Commander Bezek's ship. In all, fifteen bodies were recovered out of the twenty-four that deployed with the Fleet's reconnaissance. Of those fifteen, only Sabik and Mlyma survived the ordeal.

"Why is his chest still open?" Gemini asked the doctor who stood quietly behind him.

"We need to make sure all of his internal bleeding has stopped," he responded.

Gemini didn't want to look at him, but he forced himself to step forward and took the frail gray hand that lay motionless on his mattress. His nausea was more intense now. His own hands and face felt clammy. *Don't pass out,* he ordered himself.

"Can he feel any pain?" he asked, feeling Sabik's hand tighten against his own.

"No," his doctor responded. "We have him pretty hopped up on painkillers."

"The good stuff, I hope," Gemini tried to joke, forcing a smile and feeling the blood slowly return to his face. "Good work, doctor," he added. "We all owe you."

The tall thin Mateen turned away, leaving Gemini alone with what remained of his lead scout. Gemini waited a moment longer until he heard the curtain close behind the doctor and then sat on the chair next to Sabik's bed. Sabik shifted his legs slightly. He was waking up.

Before Gemini could speak, Sabik started murmuring. "Mlyma . . . the fleet?" he asked weakly.

Gemini patted Sabik's hand and looked into his eyes. A docile brown returned his stare. "She's recovering. The fleet is safe. You're a hero."

Sabik mumbled something and then grunted before trying again. "Didn't think we'd make it," he managed to sputter.

"You made it, friend. You did everything you could. Don't blame yourself for what happened. It was my fault. I sent you into an ambush."

His lead scout opened his mouth but nothing came out. Gemini noted the mangled black gums where teeth once sat. He looked down again and patted his hand once more. "Don't say anything, Sabik. You need your rest, but I wanted to visit you and tell you that everything was going to be alright. I've deployed the entire fleet to Radaishar space. We're going to get the ones who tortured you and put an end to this whole rebellion."

Sabik looked at the ceiling and blinked quickly. The harnesses around his neck and torso kept him still. Then, a smile crested his toothless mouth. He forced a painful chuckle. "I can't wait to see their faces," he muttered. "The Collective must have been really angry with all this to have you finish the Radaishar off."

Gemini wasn't sure how to phrase his answer. Giving orders to subordinates who didn't ask questions was one thing, but actually saying your intentions aloud was something else entirely. Verbalizing his intentions would give a level of gravity to his actions he wasn't sure he was ready for.

"The Collective hasn't approved my actions," he announced plainly. "I intend to decimate the Radaishar and their capabilities without providing my course of action to the high command."

Sabik blinked again but said nothing as he processed Gemini's response. Treason was undoubtedly the word that soared through Sabik's mind, but he would never be able to project that thought to Gemini. Not anymore, not ever again. The barbarism of the Radaishar was too much, too brutal, too not Mateen.

Gemini couldn't afford to have his actions caught in the bureaucracy of government while the Radaishar had time to analyze Mateen technology and adapt their tactics. Worse, the Radaishar were using forms of artificial intelligence that had been long banned in the galaxy. They would be able to adapt, and the next fight could be far worse than the first. Gemini could not give them that opportunity.

"I shouldn't have gotten—"

Gemini cut him off. "Stop it. You did exactly what I asked. I will face the consequences when all of this is over. Not you. They will either understand my motives or they will relieve me, but my intentions are just. I need you to rest now, friend. I'll visit you tomorrow."

Sabik loosened his hand, and Gemini allowed his own to return to his side. Sabik had become a shell of the scout Gemini once knew. He was now Mateen in name only. The essence that connected him to the others no longer existed. Gemini could not allow this to go unpunished. Without looking back, he left the curtain-sealed recovery room and moved quickly to his command center. It was time to end this.

***

"Did she have any family that we should notify?"

Cale shook his head. "Just me," he muttered quietly. This was the second time he had been to the mortuary affairs office in the last month. First for his father and now for his fiancé.

"How would you like her body displayed?" the mortician quizzed. He was heavyset with wide, short legs but had a pleasant demeanor about him. His voice was quiet and calm. When Cale wasn't sure how to answer, he waited patiently.

Cale was at a loss for words. Even with the experience of his father behind him, a child usually grows up expecting to bury his father sooner or later. With Casika, the thought had never entered his mind. *How would he like to remember her? What would she have wanted? How much pain was she in when she died?*

"Beautifully," Cale finally responded. "Make her look beautiful. I'll find her a dress. I want this to be an open casket." He paused as he remembered unzipping the bag that contained her body and looking inside. His stomach churned as he remembered seeing her battered face and bruised body, beaten at the hands of the Jark prison guards for her testimony at the council.

The mortician placed his pen down for a moment before writing his request. "Have you seen her?" he asked gently. "I would recommend—"

Cale cut him off. "I know what you would recommend," he barked. "It's time for the people of Tassi to be reminded of the evil that exists out here. Since the war, we have been hunting, pursuing disciplinary action against Jark to no avail. Casika has been the latest victim of their barbarism. You will provide her with an open casket funeral, and the attendees will have to gaze into the eyes of a battered and innocent Tassian."

Sweat formed on his brow as he listened, and then, without a word, the mortician penned Cale's wishes on his form and placed the pen on his desk. His hands shook as he took glasses from his face and laid them on the desk.

"Please," he started, "I want you to accept my deepest condolences. Nobody should have to bury their father and their fiancé. Add that to the war and I know you are struggling to find purpose in all of this. But you have to slow down and think: what are you really trying to do here? Do you intend to get us into another war?"

Cale could feel anger rise inside of him as the older Tassian presumed to lecture him as a father or adviser. He was of the old generation, forever relying on the security of a Galactic Council that didn't care for them. Cale looked into the mortician's brown eyes and frowned. He could see the fear in them. The concern the man felt about abandoning what he knew. The inability for him to adapt and change, even though his very life depended on it. "I intend to wipe the Jark Empire from the fabric of this galaxy," he responded curtly.

Instead of waiting for a response, Cale stood to his feet and turned to leave, moving quickly to the door. As he opened it, he was hit by what should have been the beauty of a white Tassian sun setting beneath the horizon. Rays glistened brightly off rich blue water and sent vibrant greens and radiant oranges across his beloved crystal city. He should have felt awe at the majesty of the Tassian creation. But he couldn't. Not anymore. His home felt dull. Bleak. Futureless. Hatred welled up inside him of. It was a hatred he had spent his whole life condemning. Yet there it was. Raw, bitter, venomous hatred. Cale wanted to want to fight it. But he wouldn't. Not ever again. He hated Brokk. He hated the Jarks. He despised the Galactic Council.

As Cale walked the darkening streets he allowed his eyes to linger on a newly hung election poster. Since the invasion, Tassi hadn't had an official ruler. An election loomed and Cale desperately sought the votes. He thought he would be a shoo-in. Now it seemed he had a legitimate competitor. Ambassador Grubbe's face taunted him from the poster. The words "Choose Peace" insulted Casika's sacrifice.

This would be a battle between generations and ideologies. As Cale stewed he considered his response to the mortician more deeply. *War. That is exactly what I plan for Tassi. War.*

CHAPTER TWENTY-EIGHT

Shined black hallways reflecting elaborate onyx ceilings wound upward through the palace towards the emperor's throne room. Torches embedded in stone pillars burned a bright orange to light their path as Brokk's clearing team opened the final door to the inner sanctum. He had passed hundreds of captured soldiers and administrative staff in the hallways, and, at each passing, they kneeled and watched hopelessly as he strode confidently past them.

As the doors opened, Brokk grinned. The room itself was a rectangle, stretching some hundred meters long and sixty meters wide. White marble floors accented diamond and garnet slabs that made the exterior walls of the room. Stone pillars, each with lit torches on all four sides, held up a vaulted ceiling. At the back of the room sat a solid gold throne large enough for even the biggest Jark. Thorns the length of his arm protruded at various angles from the throne, and the skulls of the Empire's enemies hung above it, a vivid reminder to diplomats how the Jark Empire took no prisoners.

Seated upon the throne was his beautiful Lysop sorceress, a tool that every conqueror yearned to have but only he possessed. Her golden claws sparkled in the torchlight as she stoically ran them across the nearest thorn. On one of the thorns was the severed head of the emperor, his mouth curled eternally in anguish from his final moments.

"The mighty Brokk!" she proclaimed as he stopped at the entrance. "All hail the ruler of the Jark Empire!"

"Leave us," Brokk ordered his security. "Report to me once the entire palace has been cleared."

The chief of his loyal guard saluted and shuffled out. Massive gold and iron doors sealed behind him, echoing boldly off the stone and garnet walls and vibrating the ground on which he stood.

Tamara remained seated. He felt the inextricable pull of her, beckoning him forward, but he would not budge. Could not budge. *Infected.* This was where the two of them would part. Where her usefulness ended.

"Well done," he called to her from the entryway. "What you and Canis did changed the tide of the war."

She smiled at him. In that smile, he knew that she understood. "Won't you come near me?" she asked, this time allowing a rasp in her voice to surface. "I did all of this for you. If you've been vaccinated, then you know there is no risk."

Brokk allowed her call to pull him closer but then forced himself to stop again. *Close enough.* "The vaccine is not 100 percent," he reminded her. "We are distributing it, yes, but there is a margin of error. You know I can't come any closer."

She sighed a sad breath of air followed by a painful cough. Her body looked weak. Brokk noticed now that her forehead was damp, and her face was pale as she battled the infection. *Contagious,* his mind reminded him.

"Canis . . ." she started before he interrupted her.

"I know. He didn't make it. I wish I could have arrived sooner and that you didn't have to wait these three days in solitude. We'll dress and burn his body properly. I know what he meant to you."

Tamara rose from the throne and looked towards a balcony that overlooked the city to her left. "All is set then?" she asked before submitting to another fit of coughs.

He nodded. "The major regions have signed my treaty. Minor clans in the south are vowing to continue the fight, but because I control the vaccine for the Tassian plague, I suspect they will quickly enter negotiations with us." He paused and looked towards the balcony as well. "The battle above has mostly ended. The fifteenth fleet commander has gone into exile. The remainder have sued for peace."

"Will you hunt him?" she quizzed.

Brokk shook his head. "No, I'd rather win him over, so we can use his fleet to accomplish our destiny. There will have to be a time for reconciliation between the tribes too, and a chance to expose Tassi for their actions against this planet."

"And the grootslang?" she asked, moving closer to the sulfuric air that poured in from the balcony. Except for the occasional crack carried by the wind, the capital was silent. Law was being restored.

"Once I came into orbit, we triggered their kill genes. It worked exactly as you suggested," he reassured her.

Brokk watched as Tamara left the room and stood on the balcony. Her black coat fluttered in the constant breeze and her braided brown hair slapped against her shoulders and her face. He saw her hands grip the rails and shivered as her gold nails scraped against the steel support. He sensed her breathing quicken and when she moved a hand to her face, he knew she was crying. *Run to her.* He quickly beat the thought back. *She isn't worth it,* he told himself. *This part of your life is over.*

Turning, Tamara acted as if she hadn't heard his comment about the grootslang. Tears fell from her face to the ground as she beat back another fit of coughs, refusing to take her eyes from him. "Maybe I'll join Red now," she said, forcing a smile. Brokk watched her walk away from the balcony to a small door behind the throne. As it closed, Brokk allowed himself to breathe a sigh of relief.

You are the chosen one, he told himself as he admired the throne. Everything he had planned was accomplished. The empire was his. It all was. Brokk was the ruler of Jark. He finally had his revenge, but this was no time to pause and gloat. With the Jark Empire behind him, Brokk had a new strategy already formed in his mind. He would bring the glory to the Jark Empire that it deserved, and he would start with Tassi.

Brokk slammed his hand on a button on the side of his armrest. Immediately, two servants entered the room. "I plan to address the empire at noon tomorrow. I want my military and the people gathered below the palace." They nodded, but his hand stopped them from leaving. "And have the emperor's head mounted behind my throne before anyone else enters this chamber," he ordered.

Brokk rubbed his hands against the gold chair as they left and smiled. It was all his now.

***

Brokk surveyed the scene from the balcony of his throne room. Just off the nose of the cliffs to the north, his massive battleship could be seen anchored against the skyline. The ship's bronze, dual-pronged nose was unmistakable against its dark gray exterior. Below him, thousands of Jark soldiers, decorated in red and black dress uniforms, stood in formation with rifles at the ready. Behind them were tanks and missiles staged to demonstrate the very best Jark had to offer. Jark citizens waited silently behind his military parade while others sat on the roofs of their homes or leaned from their windows to hear his speech.

In the distance, a volcano spewed molten iron and ash. He closed his eyes, breathing in the fresh sulfur air and thinking back to his childhood in a borough not far from here. He remembered his clan instilling the proud lineage of a distant grandmother who had been exiled from Tassi long ago. He remembered the hatred they had for the Tassians, the injustice they felt, and the hope that they had for him, the son with the golden skin. *The chosen one.*

Opening his eyes, he looked down at his hands and flexed them. Even in the crimson light of Jark, his skin was a dark golden-brown compared to the red of pure blood Jarks. It was time to address his nation and seize the glory that was his.

"My people," he bellowed, "there was a time when we Jarks were a distinct group of tribes, divided in purpose, and ignorant of the evil powers that existed around us. There was a memory that predated our divisions. A memory that, were it not for my ancestors, might have been forgotten entirely."

Brokk paused to check his notes. He hadn't wanted to give a history lesson but found it necessary to establish both cause and rivalry. The crowd waited.

"Tassi was ours," he declared. "The histories of our people clearly declare this fact. You know the story: one illegitimate half-brother betrayed the righteous brother and exiled him here. He stole the throne and our promised land.

"Tassi is our rightful home and yet, it is full of undeserving cowards, who banished a boy and his mother to this lava-filled wasteland. We have made a home here, but it is not home.

"My brothers and sisters, we are united again and despite the attempts by the thieves that inhabit our home, we are stronger than ever. I went there to take Tassi for us," he instructed pointing at himself to the crowd. "But our emperor lacked the courage to finish what he started. "I was banished, forgotten, and forsaken but now I've returned, and I've done it for the glory of Jark!"

He waited for a moment as the crowd below slapped the ground and cheered. His battleship above fired into the sky, and six fighter jets streaked loudly above his palace. The timing was perfect. The theatrics were superb. He had come in power and glory. His fleet was showing it off for the entire planet to see.

"As you now know, I returned just in time. The Tassians, who hold no honor, attacked our home with a plague that threatened to completely destroy our people. I have the vaccine that will inoculate you, and I have enough for everyone. You must merely come and take it from our hands. The Tassians, however, must pay. Their aggression must be checked. Jark will rise from these ashes, and I will be the one to do it for us. Together," he shouted, "we will bring Jark to a new level of prosperity. Together, we will conquer Tassi. Together, we will destroy anyone in the galaxy who does not submit to Jark rule."

The crowd of supporters cheered again, but Brokk's mind was on other things. The capital of Vyekla wouldn't be enough; he had to ensure he'd captivated the entire planet. He had to ensure they believed him and that they believed in him. It worried him to have so little control over this environment, but he knew he needed to trust his military and his gods. They *had* chosen him. His golden skin proved it.

"In the coming days," he continued, "I will be meeting with the tribal leaders on both Jark and Coridon. I am calling for a time of peace and reconciliation. I am requesting calm. The Jark way has always been order and authority. This is no different. You will be pleased to know I intend to not only bring you honor on the galactic stage, but I will bring you prosperity as well. As we transition to this new rule, as has been ordained by the gods, I ask you for patience and support. Thank you and goodnight."

To the sound of applause, Brokk left the balcony and closed his palace doors. There was still much to do. There were many tribes who had not yet pledged their support to Brokk's rule. Some had even begun to fight with each other and pledged to fight against his government. He would have to be heavy handed with them. He would have to end any speak of rebellion with a ferocity that would quench it for good.

As Brokk moved towards his throne, he allowed a smile to form on his face. He breathed in a freshness that he had dreamed about for nearly a year. He was home. His battle was finished. His kingdom was established. Tassi would be next to fall.

BEYOND THE JUMP

Tamara stared at the dingy, dust-covered cavern ceiling above. Like the teeth of some mystical beast, stalactites hung above her, poised to fall and split her in two and, perhaps, swallow her whole and send her even deeper into the belly of Jark than she already was. Pale light glistened off water droplets forming in the cool cave; it was a light that emanated not from some torch or sun but from the mercury lake itself. The silver glow bathed everything in its light. Even Tamara, who had fortified her mind to the magic and mysticism on Jark, was fighting to keep her thoughts from running towards horrifying outcomes.

Air was thicker here below ground. What would have been a sulfur-infused breeze above the surface was a suffocating sulfur mist down in the cave that, until now, seemed to have descended endlessly into the Jark underworld. Despite the months she had spent on Jark, Tamara struggled to breathe. The gravity deep beneath the planet's surface made her chest feel tight and was permanently constricting her heart and lungs. A dull ache in her head reminded her just how close she had come to death.

But she hadn't. Tamara had won. In the silence of the cavern, she was able to dig deep inside herself and defeat the plague. *Had any other Lysops done such a thing?* she allowed herself to wonder. With that thought came a superiority and invincibility she had never felt before. Red and Canis were specters in her mind now, powerless to provide for her anymore. As Tamara considered her latest accomplishment, she was certain she didn't need their shadows either. Tamara had seized the role of her people. The role of assassin and the over-thrower of worlds. Now she gave herself a new title: destroyer of plagues.

Tamara felt a cold dampness soak through her overcoat and press against her skin. The mud on the cavern floor had soaked into her hair and coated her hands, covering the gold jewelry that she received from Brokk so long ago. Its luster was gone, but its utility remained. Using her claws, she scratched at the mud beneath her and let the secrets of the cavern chamber bombard her senses. *Peace.* All was finally at peace.

Rolling to her side to watch the liquid metal lake glisten from its own light, she marveled at how far she had come. She gloried in it. Behind her, she could still sense warmth, life that emanated from bodies recently deceased. Twelve of them to be exact. Twelve priests who acted as guardians to the lake of liquid metal. They were the first and the last of their order, worshiping their gods at the holiest of Jark sites, hiding from Brokk and the cleansing that he was enacting across the planet against their old religion.

To Tamara's amazement, the ones she killed first were not the first to cool. No, it was the ones who sank into the wettest parts of mud and the ones who had the least amount of fat on their bones to hold heat. What should have been common sense felt like wisdom to her now and, despite her hatred for the Jark priesthood, she came to appreciate the company of their unnatural warmth in this cold, dark cave.

Tamara sat to watch what she hoped would be a grand finale on her journey to the oldest holy site of Jark. This was the place Canis had spoken of, the place of the first grootslang and the most important of the passages that linked space and time as if it was one fabric on the bed of the universe.

As if constrained by some unholy force, the blood of the priests drained slowly and pooled together into a crevice before finally being loosed at once into the silver lake. She watched as the stream of blood inched closer to the mercury's edge and wondered if it would accept the corrupt blood of the priests or if it would reject her sacrifice wholeheartedly. Warning against her own thoughts, she hoped she could see something, something that would validate the supernatural forces she had experienced here before she left Jark for good.

Expecting a recoil of the mercury, Tamara watched the stream of blood roll its final inch and mix with the lake. Red swirled with silver and dissipated throughout the surface, changing to a lighter and lighter color until it had disappeared completely. The chamber remained silent. The pale white light remained constant. A breeze that rose from nowhere chilled her to the bone. Expecting hands to appear, she saw none. Searching for the ancient grootslang beneath the silver surface left her wanting. Finally, she let her concentration go elsewhere. There was nothing left to discover.

Rising to her feet, Tamara determined there was no power here. Canis must have lied. The Jark people must have believed in fake myths and deceptive magic. Before stepping to leave, Tamara cast her eyes once more at the Jark priests who gave their lives in defense of this worthless lake. Their bodies, desiccated and drained of their blood, looked strange. Their faces, curled in a state of agony, suddenly no longer possessed the peace she had sensed only moments before. The cave was cold, and the only warmth that remained was what escaped from her own body.

Tamara considered what to do next. So much of the last year was spent serving Brokk. Before that, it was as a slave on Charoth. She could return to Brokk, but she knew that would be impossible. She had been nothing more than a tool to him, an object of his fascination as long as she continued to provide the tricks he needed to accomplish his desires. She was his witch, his priestess of blood, his personal doomsayer. But she was also discarded and thrown out, not even offered a funeral by the family she thought she had. No, if she returned, Brokk would have her killed out of a fear and paranoia that was legitimate.

She had, after all, conquered death. Perhaps, Tamara allowed herself to think, he would have her killed, because, with good reason, she threatened his reign. Did she not deserve to rule? Did not the overthrower of worlds and the defeater of plagues deserve to be worshiped? The simple answer was *yes*.

But not here on Jark. Jark was Brokk's now, and she needed something that was hers, some rebellion that was simmering and just waiting to explode. A rebellion that needed not only leadership but a symbol that brought them hope. *Had any Lysops reigned before?* she wondered before determining, *No, they hadn't, because no Lysop is as powerful as me.*

End of Book Three

ACKNOWLEDGMENTS

A big thank you to Sarah Keller for the beautiful book design. Thank you to Sarah Keller, Drew Holler, Brian Anderson, John Meier, and Peter Doyle for taking time to encourage me and read and critique my work.

Thanks to all of my readers, especially those that that take the time to review my work on Amazon and Goodreads. I read through every review posted and I'm eternally grateful for the opportunity I get to correspond with my fans. Reach out to me on twitter @thanekeller or contact me on www.thanekeller.com where we can talk about science fiction, space travel, genetic engineering, and everything in between.

ABOUT THE AUTHOR

Thane is a graduate of the Virginia Military Institute with a degree in psychology and a minor in English. Following college, Thane married his high school sweetheart Sarah and started his career as a cavalryman in the United States Army. Over the course of his career, he has deployed to both Iraq and Afghanistan where he was personally engaged in ground combat. His service has thus far earned him two Bronze Stars and numerous other awards and decorations.

Relying on his psychology background, military experience, and Christian faith, Thane writes novels that seek to explore human nature under dire circumstances, the reality of pain and suffering, and the resilience of individuals to accomplish superhuman feats. Thane's hopes are that as readers experience his character's journey through the gift of reading, they will be greater equipped to endure the inevitable ups and downs in life itself and dream to accomplish grander things.

In addition to his wife Sarah, Thane is blessed to have four wonderful children that do all they can to keep him from pursuing his love of writing.

PREVIEW THE NOVEL: TRIALS

Available on Amazon and at your local book stores

CHAPTER ONE

When the ground shook, it started off as a slow rumble, simply vibrating the metal springs on his twin-sized bed causing them to rattle back and forth against its steel frame. Ordinarily, he wouldn't have responded. The ground here had tremors frequently, and other than a little dust from the ceiling of their cavern home, there wasn't much excitement to be had.

He didn't get out much. At least, he didn't used to, but he thought back to his years in captivity frequently, and sometimes he even thought beyond that. The earthquake was the single point in time that changed his life for good. Before the earthquake, he wasn't just a nobody; he was worse than a nobody. He was a killer. A killer that was lost and forgotten in the depths of the most mind-numbing prison. But the earthquake. The earthquake changed all of that.

As he sat on his bed that day, he replayed the pivotal moment that led him down a path that would forever torment him; not because of the action he took, but because he feared he would never be able to feel that free again. For years, he was a prisoner in his own mind unable to act out the impulses that made him feel so free. He remembered watching the boy ride his bike back from school. Every day the boy passed his house. Every day he watched him. Finally, after much torment, he stepped outside.

He remembered the boy's shock at first, the fear that drenched his face. The surprise that a human being could be so cold. More importantly, he remembered how free he had felt afterward, how relieved he was that he could finally reveal himself to the world as he truly was. But then it ended, and all that was left was a memory. Until the earthquake.

Now, he was a king. Sitting high above his subjects, he ruled with sovereign power. An eye for an eye, a tooth for a tooth, and all people would give tribute to him. Minions and pawns scurried about around him, grateful that he had allowed them to live after that fateful day. The day that the gods had declared long ago was his for the taking. One cleaned, the other cooked. Others stood guard. He had sought this recognition for years and never found it. But he was an opportunist. And when opportunity struck, he seized power.

He wasn't large or tall, but he was smart. And he was vicious. All those years imprisoned in his own mind gave him time to think. That is what separated him from the others. He murdered because it was who he was, not because of his circumstances, but because of who he was at his very core. While others concerned themselves with revenge, or getting back at the guards, he went straight for the resources; the one thing that had to be controlled to force everyone else into subjection under his feet.

Then, all that was needed was to make an example of someone. To show the rest how absolutely brutal he could be. He didn't like to get his hands dirty when it came to politics, but that first one had to happen. Soon, others joined him. He consolidated resources and had something to offer. Food, shelter, and protection. All in exchange for unwavering loyalty. Eventually, all the people submitted to his rule.

Here, in this dark, chaos-filled place, he brought order. He brought meaning. He brought purpose. They called him Malek. King. And that's what he was to them. He was *their* King.

CHAPTER TWO

The car was half submerged in the murky canal water. Soldiers on one side; frantic citizens on the other. A crowd gathered around the hasty rescue effort in the center. He could still see her in his mind. Not her face, but her back. Her hair gently dangled in the water as men pulled her out by her feet. The car had been submerged for almost 6 hours. Rescuers cheered as they finally pulled her out; she couldn't have been older than six or seven. They laid her down next to her mother. It was just another day in Iraq.

Jonah lay there sweating. He couldn't sleep. His mind jumped from Iraq to Afghanistan to the Sudan to eastern Russia. His thoughts weren't filled with guilt, or shame, or fear but a deeper form of questioning. One he could never put his finger on. He saw the girl again. Hair dipping into the water as she was lifted out. He always went back to the girl. Sometimes he imagined her frantically trying to escape the car. At the moment the water filled her lungs she was at peace, and he imagined that death for her was a better alternative to the life she might be forced to live. Eventually Jonah stopped trying to figure the events out and simply remembered them for what they were - crazy.

The cold damp cell where Jonah found himself could not be compared to the torment that had trapped his thoughts for years. But this was more than a cell and more complex than a standard prison. Jonah was locked away from the light of day and stowed deep underground where he couldn't hope to hear the laughter of his children or feel the touch of his wife ever again. He remained tormented in his mind, not only for the things he had done and saw, but also for things he could never do again.

His current circumstances made it laughable to think of even one blessing of God. And yet, in the cool dampness of night, with only the slightest whimper of other inmates to distract his thoughts, Jonah could easily find them. More often than not, those blessings existed in the form of memories - his three children and a wife that loved him deeply, remaining loyal in these dire circumstances. He also found them in his prison in the present. Jonah sensed them when the sounds of other inmates reminded him he wasn't alone, at the kindness of a guard giving him an extra portion of food, and every once in a while at the faintest ray of light that managed to penetrate a sewage vent at the end of their concrete hallway.

At Jonah's weakest, he cried bitterly. He had done so many times here while he counted the days of a trial that appeared to never be coming. He felt the absolute inadequacy to defend himself against a power that invented guilt and innocence rather than adhering to an absolute definition of righteousness. Tonight, however, his mind had no time to succumb to the self-imposed pity that he and countless others endured while at the mercy of the state. No, tonight he could only think of her. That young girl strung upside down by her feet as she was pulled from the concrete canal. Frail and lifeless, she was the mere shell of a body that was altogether empty of the soul that had once made her human. Sometimes he thought he might shed just one of his tears for her. But he couldn't. He didn't know her and had arrived too late to blame himself. She was just an image. A picture forever engrained in his mind. The first among hundreds he would see. But she was the first, and she was the only one entirely undeserving of the fate that gripped her.

Sometimes when images of the girl appeared in his mind, he would try to think of his family instead. He remembered the times he and his wife would spend on the playground watching their children laugh and giggle. He would fantasize about taking his children sledding, teaching them to hunt and fish, and watching them grow; all the while marveling with his beautiful wife at how large they'd gotten. Jonah imagined, with guilt, the missed opportunities too. How many years had he thrown away to his work and his job? How many months had he thrown away to this cell, imprisoned by the very people he had spent so many years protecting? Despite his attempts, Jonah's mind always came back to the girl. That girl who so many years ago engrained herself into his mind for eternity. Eventually, on that cold, hard mattress in his damp, dark room, sleep overtook him; another blessing he took for granted all too often.

CHAPTER THREE

"Clark, you're looking at it all wrong!" The sharply dressed Unicore executive argued over a cup of steaming coffee. His hair was as dark as the moonless night that hovered outside the windows of the coffee house. Jacob wore a black suit, a white neatly pressed shirt, and a red tie. The tie had a gold clasp that held it tidily against his shirt. Along the center of the clasp were four red triangles that formed the Unicore logo that so often graced their products.

Across the table sat Clark; a scruffy haired graphic designer with a three-day shadow and a cheap, tieless suit. Clark leaned across the table, over his caramel latte, and attempted to peaceably engage Jacob; clarifying what he meant.

Jacob wasn't interested. "You need to change your perspective. We're offering opportunity. This is a chance to gain new skills and hone old ones. This is a privilege – to be one of the first men on the frontier of civilization."

Clark nodded and tried to follow along but was already distracted by the smell of fresh coffee beans and the promise of caffeine and sugar. He leaned back in his chair, enchanted by the ambiance of the diner, the smells of the coffee, and the dark cold night they were escaping. Jacob was reiterating a point he had already made but was now pressing the table forcefully with his index finger to exaggerate his emphasis.

"This is an opportunity for people that don't get opportunities. This is something that they can be proud of. Something future generations will be taught in schools. These are people that are on the frontier of human exploration. These people are heroes Clark, they're heroes. That's the point you need to drive home." Jacob hesitated and then continued. "Listen. We brought you in to give us a fresh look. Don't let us down." He paused a moment longer while Clark sat in silence and then made one final calculated statement. "Earth might not be around much longer, Clark."

Without waiting for a response, the advertising executive threw a ten dollar bill on the table, climbed out of the bench seat, and disappeared through the wooden door. Clark remained seated, milking the rest of his caramel latte as he pondered the challenge ahead of him and the cryptic warning that Jacob had left him with. *How do you convince someone to leave everything they know and take a one way trip to Mars?*

Artists drew creativity in different ways, and as for Clark, his was stimulated by people watching. Clark had long suspected that he could discern the motives and personality of a person simply by watching their actions and expressions when they thought no one was watching, and, in his line of work, he desperately needed to figure out what made people tick.

Looking around the espresso-colored coffee house, inhaling the fumes of various coffees, creamers, and pastries, Clark found himself fixated on a poster for a political rally. He didn't watch the news much, but he read enough to know what was happening to his country; and it wasn't good. In fact, minus an all-out succession, the lines had been essentially drawn in the sand between what some people were calling the red states and the blue states. The red states jumped on this division first and seized on the opportunity to rename themselves. They began to refer to the states in their coalition as 'Free States'. The Blue States, recognizing their disadvantage adopted a similar title – 'States of Opportunity.' This was a battle for hearts and minds, and despite his distance from the political scene, it was not lost on Clark that this was a war of public opinion. Those names reflected a leader's attempt at controlling thoughts, which was exactly why he appreciated it so much. In fact, the rhetoric was so strong that a red state senator was attacked by an angry mob outside of the capitol building in DC. According to some media outlets, the police did nothing and some even incited the mob to greater violence.

If Clark didn't watch the news much, he did even less considering of political issues, and, quite frankly, he wasn't sure he cared what each sides' grievances were. Art was Clark's escape from the world, and so long as he had a steady supply of customers and didn't live on the street, he was content to just not know. Regardless of which side ended up winning, losing, or separating, Clark wasn't sure much would change for him.

Two teenage girls climbed out of a booth to his right and giggled their way to the bathroom. Left behind were two shaggy-haired young men. As engaged as they were when the two girls were with them, they quickly sunk into the booth and pulled out phones. Entirely uninterested in talking to each other, they waited in silence for their dates to return. These were the people he loved to watch because, through his work, these were the people he would try so hard to convince.

CHAPTER FOUR

Moonlight reflected dimly off a picture that Evie had now been staring at thoughtfully for at least half an hour. She had stared at that photo hundreds of times for countless hours, but tonight, perhaps by the pale light of the moon, Evie noticed something she hadn't seen before. It was a picture of their wedding day, a photo of them with their parents. Everyone was staring at the camera except for Jonah. It looked like he was staring at the camera, but upon closer inspection in this particular light, it was clear he wasn't. His eyes weren't watching the camera at all. He was watching her. *How many times had she looked at this very picture and not noticed?* All of a sudden the joy of their wedding and the years they spent together came rushing back. Even if just for a moment, it was enough to make everything they had suffered together worth it. She refused to accept his guilt, and staring at this photo of so many years ago strengthened her resolve. She *would* see him again.

It would be another sleepless night full of uncertainty, sorrow, and fear. The knocks on their door six months ago initiated by two officers of the state had forever turned her world upside down. The slamming of the iron knocker resonated in her mind until she could no longer take it. Some nights were better than others. Tonight was not one of those nights. While the children slept, Evie snuck out of bed and went downstairs to turn on the TV.

Expecting typical late night programming, Evie was grateful to find an interesting documentary on the Mars colonization effort. Jillian Jaspers' determined and chunky little face was plastered on posters in every mall across America. She was the face of the Mars exploration and had inspired state and federal lotteries of willing (and desperate) families to get off Earth and travel to Mars.

In just ten short years, Jillian and her crew of early explorers had built a massive colony with the purpose of pursuing unique scientific research, all backed by companies exporting rare Earth minerals that were found in droves on the Red Planet. Gold, platinum, lithium, and copper were in abundance and instigated a colonization effort similar to the gold rush in California in the 1800s. The invention of quantum propulsion engines made the trip millions of dollars cheaper and thirty days shorter from the previous average of two hundred and ten days.

The documentary showed a lavish paradise of interconnected structures built under the Martian soil. Massive buildings were lined with the most expensive metals and decorated with the finest materials that could be mined. Hotels with vacation packages erupted overnight and commercials tugged at wealthy families who could afford the trip.

Like any colony, it wasn't without its troubles. Merely a few years after colonization, a contingent of marines was dispatched to the planet to restore order after a dispute broke out between two mining companies. They established a prison system, and under a United Nations mandate, imposed martial law. The United States government decided to capitalize on the establishment, of course, and saw it as a perfect chance to drain out the worst criminals in the U.S. Other countries followed suit, and not before long, Earth's worst convicts were sent to the first extraterrestrial penal colony. Although the documentary didn't say it, to Evie, Mars became the perfect juxtaposition: families seeking a permanent future and the pursuit of riches on the Red Planet occupied one side; while the world's worst convicts with no future occupied the world's harshest prison on the other.

Evie couldn't imagine leaving Earth willingly and permanently; in fact, it seemed like a death sentence regardless of which side you found yourself. Even with the early explorers of America, Evie found it hard to picture leaving a place as comfortable as this to get her name in the history books. Even if her town wasn't quaint and comfortable, it was still her town; and more importantly, it had oxygen and water — something that she determined was as good a reason as any to never go to another planet. As the documentary ended, Evie found the soft glow of the TV relaxing. Finally, sleep won; but it never lasted long.

***

The pitter patter of tiny feet down the hallway ripped Evie out of her late night rest and pulled her back to the present. Evie stared down at the skillet of half cooked scrambled eggs. With one hand on the handle and the other wielding a spatula, she didn't even care that her haphazard stirring was going to result in an unevenly cooked meal. She just wanted to get through one more lackluster breakfast and get the kids off to the store, where she would complete another week's worth of shopping while struggling to maintain order as she pushed the cart down the aisle.

More often than not, she found herself desperately trying to focus on finishing just one more thing, anything, without interruption; which meant striving with every ounce of her patience to ignore the tantrum unfolding at her feet. It started with Nathan, whose request to be held immediately turned into shrieks and screams when he did not get his way. She was used to this. "Hold on just a second, Nathan", she murmured tiredly into the eggs. But his shrieks didn't subside and soon they were joined by Eden who suddenly fell out of her chair at the kitchen table, knocking a fresh glass of milk to the floor in the process. Refusing to be ignored, their eldest, Titus, chimed in "Mom! Mom! Mom! Eden spilled her milk again! Look mom! Look!"

Evie broke.

Dropping the spatula into the hot skillet, she stormed out of the room and up the stairs, knocking Nathan to the floor not caring as she went. Slamming the bedroom door behind her, she rushed to the far side of the bed to get as far away as she could, fighting back the sobs of a desperate woman; desperate for a break, desperate for answers, desperate for the husband who was ripped from her without warning and who left a gaping hole in the heart of their home that couldn't be filled with time or pleas to God or anything within Evie's control. Then she heard Eden and Nathan, still crying, banging on the closed door with all of their might, needing her, demanding her, and ultimately sending her into the tears that she'd tried to fight back.

It wasn't their fault. They were her children, and she loved them. But it was happening more and more. The pressures of single parenthood on top of the grief and weight of unanswered questions surrounding Jonah's incarceration were wreaking havoc on her sanity. She sat down on the corner of her bed and placed her head in her hands as the sobs rolled out of her.

Eventually she stopped. The kids had quieted down and she heard the muffled sound of their giggles, happy again and playing together on the other side of the kitchen door. If only it were that simple for her. Tantrums and spilled milk were so easily fixed and forgotten compared to the weight she carried daily on her shoulders.

After staring blankly at a fray in the rug under her feet for what might have been a minute or an hour, her gaze was drawn to a large oil painting hanging on the wall on the opposite side of the room. It was her painting. For just a moment, her mind went back to its setting; the ornate, ivy covered red brick chapel that she and Jonah were married in. Painting hadn't been something she'd had time for in years, but she couldn't help but forget the world around her in this fleeting moment and admire her work. She looked at the clock on the face of the chapel's steeple, which read 6pm; the time of their wedding ceremony. She'd painted it in painstaking detail, wanting to honor that sacred day and time. But as her eyes moved outward from that clock, the landscape around the chapel became hazier. Farther from the clock, the less defined her brushstrokes became. Soon, they only hinted at the lush greenery surrounding the church on that warm June evening. Then her eyes drifted down to a large black shadow she'd painted in the foreground. She'd added a faint outline of two figures in the center of that shadow; her and Jonah walking together, hand in hand, just as they had after the ceremony was finished.

Suddenly, she snapped out of her brief trance as reality came rushing back. How ironic that their shadowy outlines hidden in the midst of a dark hole on an otherwise bright and cheerful painting would be all that was left of their marriage. Maybe everyone was right. Maybe it was better for her to move on. Forget Jonah ever existed. Relegate him to a hazy shadow of her past and start over. There could be freedom in that.

But even that small, soothing hope of release was taken from her just as soon as it was given. The relative silence was broken by Titus as he called to her from the kitchen, "Mom! Something smells weird in here!"

Turning her head back to the direction of her children, she

remembered two things. One, the eggs were still cooking along with the spatula she'd hastily thrown into the skillet. She could smell the burnt eggs and melting rubber from where she sat. Second, those were Jonah's children in there. No matter how hard she might try to forget him, as if there was any chance she could truly bring herself to move on, his children would never let her forget. Their children. No, she could never stop fighting for Jonah.

With renewed resolve, she stood up, wiped her eyes, and walked back toward the kitchen, toward the charred mess on the stove and toward her beloved children who reminded her who she was, who Jonah was, and what she had to do next.

I hope you've enjoyed this preview. You can buy Trials on Amazon or at your local bookstore today!